Craving Darkness

R Sullins

AF490741

CRAVING DARKNESS

DEMONS WITHIN

BOOK TWO

R SULLINS

Copyright © 2024 by R Sullins
All rights reserved.
No part of this book may be reproduced or transmitted in any form or by any means,
electronic or mechanical, including photocopying, recording, or by any information
storage and retrieval system, without explicit permission granted in writing from the
author.
No portion of this material may be used for training artificial intelligence without
prior written consent by the author. For permission requests, please contact the
author.
This book is a work of fiction intended for adult audiences only. Names, characters,
places and incidents are the product of the author's imagination or are used
fictitiously. Any resemblance to actual events, locales, or persons, living or dead, is
coincidental.

www.rsullins.com

rsullinsauthor@gmail.com

Character cover by - getcovers.com

Foreword

In this world there are realms that haven't even been discovered yet.

But on the Earth realm, there are creatures who have made themselves at home, creatures who humans have made entire stories and lore about in order to explain away the strange things they may have seen or heard.

Many of those creatures are demons who either chose to leave the Underworld, or were banned to the Earth realm. Humans would be amazed to know that there are more breeds of demons than there are races of humans by far.

Every single demon has a fated mate. Their mate is either waiting somewhere in time, or in another realm, but there is a mate that the Fates has chosen especially for them. They will know, because they will be branded with a mating mark upon their mate's birth, or entry into their realm. That mark will change once they come into contact with each other. And that mark will change once again when the mating has been completed.

But there is one indisputable truth—the Fates are *never* wrong.

Prologue

Kallista age 5

"Hey, little Kallie-bean. Why are you lying like that?"

Daddy's big figure standing in the doorway to my bedroom sent a long shadow over the floor. I froze as I tore my gaze away from the closet interior to glance down at the shadow he cast across the floor, before ignoring it to get one last look into my closet.

"Come on, little girl. You know your mother doesn't like it when you lay like that. Your head should be up at your pillows." His tone was soft, but I could still hear the slightest hint of irritation in his words. He didn't like it when Mother got angry, even if it was at me. Maybe because it was at me. I grumbled a little but scooted my way straight on the bed so I was lying the proper way. "That's a good girl."

Daddy walked over to the side of my bed and glanced at the open closet door before shaking his head. "There's nothing in there that should hold your attention so much." He grinned as he pulled the covers up higher to tuck in around my neck until I felt like I was a burrito. He tickled my sides lightly, making me giggle.

The sounds of high heels clicking on the wooden floor of the hallway made the sound die in my throat. Mother didn't like giggling or any type of silliness. She said that I needed to learn how to be a proper daughter. I wasn't too sure what that meant, but I guessed it wasn't fun. Daddy stopped tickling as soon as he heard Mother approaching. Instead, he bent down to give me a swift kiss on the forehead. He straightened back up and stuffed his hands into his pockets just as the light from the hallway dimmed in my big bedroom as Mother stood there. I couldn't see her expression, but I knew there would be a frown on her face.

"Why isn't she asleep yet?" Her tone wasn't like daddy's. Mother's voice was always short and angry. I wished I could make her smile just once. I wanted to be the proper little girl she said I needed to be to make her happy, but sometimes I couldn't help laughing. I liked it when things were funny.

Daddy sighed as he turned to face Mother. "She just laid down a few minutes ago, Vanessa. Give her time."

Mother let out an exasperated sound, making me frown. I always disappointed her no matter how hard I tried. "Well, leave her alone so she can get some sleep. Little kids can be such monsters when they don't get at least ten hours of rest." She turned from the doorway, and the room lit up again without her body keeping the light back. "Even with sleep, they are annoying." Her words were low, but I could still hear them in the quiet of the room. I tugged the blanket closer and did my best to hold back a sniffle.

Daddy cleared his throat. "Get to sleep, Kallie-bean."

"Yes, Daddy," I said and tightly squeezed my eyes closed, showing him I could be a good girl.

He chuckled and turned away. I cracked one eye open when I heard him start to walk away. Instead of going to my open bedroom door, though, he headed toward the open door of my closet, reaching for the handle.

I sat up. "Please leave it open, daddy!"

He turned back to me with his hand on the doorknob. He frowned down at me before looking back at the dark closet. He shook his head but removed his hand and walked to the bedroom door. I let out a sigh of relief and lay back down with my eyes on the open closet. I couldn't see inside it with the way my bed was sitting. I once tried to move my bed myself so I wouldn't get into trouble for lying the wrong way. I thought that if I could just put it where I still see the closet while lying in bed the way Mother wanted me to, it would make her happy, but it was so heavy I could barely move it an inch. When I asked Daddy to move it for me, he reminded me how Mother likes everything to have a place, and the place for my bed was right where it was.

"Kallista," he sighed. "Just get some sleep, okay?"

"Yes, Daddy," I promised as he closed the door until there was nothing but a small crack letting in the hallway light. I didn't know why he insisted I have light at night. It confused me. Night was time for the dark. At least the little bit of light let in more shadows. It was better than the plug-in night light that used to be in my room until I begged him to take it out.

As soon as Daddy's footsteps disappeared down the hall, I shifted on the soft bed until I was lying across it diagonally again. I sighed with relief as I stared into the closet. There were shadows in there— the deepest and darkest shadows. I smiled, wishing that they would come out and play with me.

KALLISTA AGE 12

My legs were cramping, and my butt had gone numb from sitting on the hard floor for so long. I didn't know how long I'd been in the closet this time. I think it had only been a day, though, since my stomach was empty, but it wasn't cramping too painfully yet. Plus, I hadn't given in to the urge to pee on myself.

I should have known better than to get emotional with my mother. When I had gotten home from school, I was already upset because some of the girls had been bullying me again for being anti-social. I didn't know why they always accused me of acting like I was better than everyone else. That wasn't the case at all. I just didn't know how to be friendly. It was easier to read than to try to talk to other kids my age who were talking about boys and wanting to experience their first make-out sessions. Boys didn't interest me at all, and I would rather stay inside reading. But boys were another thing on the long list that I hadn't been allowed, anyway.

I was constantly being reminded of my responsibility to my father's career. He had goals that he wanted to accomplish, and our family needed to be above reproach in the public eye. That meant I was always to be on my best behavior and get perfect grades.

When I came home, my mother had started lecturing me about the B I had received on my geography test the day before. It was too much for me, so I yelled back that I had tried! As it was happening, I had felt something change inside of me, almost like something else was controlling my emotions. It wasn't until my mother had stepped away from me with wide eyes in a way that she had never done before, that I realized that something had happened.

She immediately sent me into my punishment closet and locked the door without a word. Her reaction scared me more than the fear of being locked away in the darkness. That was until the door closed and the lock snicked into place. That was when the fear had made me break into tears as I sat there and trembled.

I used to love the dark. It was my favorite place to be for as long as I could remember. When my mother decided that my obsession was unhealthy and it needed to be changed, I had sat in the closet and begged the shadows to help me. After nothing had come to save me, the fear had started taking over. At least my mother had gotten her wish and I was now afraid of the dark as she felt I should be.

My head was resting on my knees when the door knob began to turn. I was a mix of surprised that it was so soon, grateful to be getting out of the closet early, but also scared of what awaited me the moment the door opened. Sometimes, the punishment after was almost as bad as the isolation in the dark. I was often punished for wetting myself and had to scrub the floor with a bucket of soapy water and a washcloth until she was satisfied that I had done a good enough job getting the smell out before I would be allowed to wash myself and get something to eat.

I also had to write a lot of sentences. The amount of times I would have to write 'I am not evil' could fill up an entire book.

I hid my eyes from the harsh light when the door swung open and couldn't look up, even knowing that my mother would think it was disrespectful. She never hit me, but grabbing my arm and yanking me around was something she did often. I was expecting it as the hand wrapped around my wrist and pulled me to my feet.

I swayed where I stood, light-headed from sitting too long and weak from hunger. She began to tug me away from the closet, and I stumbled along after her while holding my breath, not wanting to anger her any more than she already was. I did my best to hurry to keep up with her long strides since her legs were so much longer than mine. When we reached my bedroom, I was a little surprised. She still hadn't said anything to me, and my mind was spinning, trying to make sense of what was happening.

Once we reached my bedroom, the door was already standing open. I blinked in confusion as I saw all the lit candles standing on my desk and my dresser.

"What-" I began to ask before being immediately cut off.

"Quiet," Mother snapped and pushed me toward the bed. "Lie down and do what you're told before I leave you to your punishment for another two days."

My lower lip quivered as I did what she said, slowly kneeling on the edge of the mattress and crawling to the center of the bed. I sat there in confusion, looking up at her for some kind of explanation or another command that would indicate why she was sending me to my bed in what seemed to be the middle of the day.

She walked to the edge of the bed and leaned over, grasping my wrist and pulling it toward the headboard. "I said, lay down." Her tone was angry but calm, the way she usually spoke to me, as if she were doing her best to stay composed as a lady should be at all times. I swallowed hard but did as she said while keeping my eyes on where she held my arm. As soon as I was on my back, she slipped something over my wrist and pulled.

I gasped when I realized that she had tied a rope around my wrist. I tried to tug on it as panic began to make my heart race, and I felt another hand touching me from the other side of the bed. I jerked my head in the direction to see a face I recognized but never expected to see in my home, let alone inside my bedroom.

The priest from our church smiled down at me as he pulled my arm above my head and secured it the same way my mother had my other arm. "Shh, sweet child. Everything is going to be okay. I promise."

It didn't feel like anything was okay. I was being restrained to my bed by the local priest. I was hungry, and I had to pee so bad I was scared I was going to wet myself at any moment. I turned my head to look back at my mother. "Please, Mother. I have to use the restroom," I whispered, putting as much pleading into my voice as I could so she'd understand how desperate I was. If I wet the bed, I could just imagine what she would make me do as a punishment.

She glared down at me without a word and moved to my feet. At the last minute I attempted to pull them away, trying to bend my knees, but it was too late. My ankles were grasped tightly from both sides, and the ropes were firmly attached to my ankles, securing them to the bed tightly. I attempted to test the ropes, but there was very little slack and I couldn't do much but bend my knees enough to place the heel of my foot against the mattress.

The fear began to kick in as my eyes moved around the room wildly, taking in the candles and the priest who had stepped back. He was wearing robes similar to the ones he wore at church every Sunday, but somehow, they seemed so sinister on him now. He picked up a book and opened it while doing the sign of the cross with his hand held up in front of him.

My mother stepped back toward the door and held her hands together in front of her waist the same way she always did when we were on TV standing behind my father as he spoke to the crowds about his policies and promises for the city. It was the way she had taught me to stand, too.

The priest began to speak, but it wasn't a language I understood, though I was almost certain it was Latin. I was pretty sure that was what priests spoke when they did the prayers at church. When he picked up a small bottle and popped the lid off with his thumb, my breaths started coming faster and faster. He was terrifying me with what he was doing. The whole situation was scary. I thought about calling out for my dad, but it had been so long since he'd spent any time with me. He used to tuck me in and kiss me goodnight, but then he got too busy with his work, and I barely saw him anymore. He never smiled at me the way he used to. No, I couldn't call for my father. He probably wasn't even home anyway.

I turned desperate eyes on my mother, hoping she would see that I needed help, that I needed to be free. I was scared and needed the comfort of my mother. When I remembered that she'd never been the type to comfort me, was when the tears started falling. Once I started crying, I couldn't stop. All my pain, desperation, and terror just poured out of me. I wanted to be loved. I wanted to be paid attention to. I wanted my mother to tell me I had done a good job or to brush my hair.

I was trying to ignore the way my snot had gathered in the corner of my nose and was about to slide embarrassingly down my face when a splash of water made me flinch. The priest was splashing me from the little bottle in the same motions as when he did the sign of the cross. After he was finished, he turned and set the bottle down on the dresser, and then he picked up a piece of rope. I could see enough through my tears that it was red, and I briefly wondered what it was for when he stepped to the side of the bed.

I watched as he pulled his arm back and then brought the rope down across my legs, which were exposed by my school uniform skirt. It didn't really hurt, but the shock of being struck had me gasping out loud. His chanting got louder as he pulled his arm back and struck me again repeatedly. Over and over, he brought the short piece of rope across my legs and belly until it began to sting.

I turned my head to look at my mother. "Please!" I begged. "Please make him stop. Why are you doing this? What did I do?"

"You have the devil in you," she hissed as her fingers tightened on each other until her knuckles turned white. "You need to be cleansed."

"Don't speak to the girl." The priest admonished her in a severe tone. "The demon will try to trick you. You must not engage."

"I'm not a demon!" I cried out at the rope sliced across my upper thigh in a spot that it had already struck several times, making me hiss in pain. "Please! I'm not a demon, I swear!"

My whole body was shaking uncontrollably as the fear grew. I heard my mother gasp and turned to look at her as she stared at me with her eyes wide with horror. I had no idea why she was looking at me that way, but it made my fear unbearable. Suddenly, she threw her hand up to brace herself against the wall. It wasn't until I heard the priest grunt that I looked at him and saw a piece of the ceiling fall and hit his shoulder.

The whole room was shaking. I looked up at the ceiling to see there were small cracks across it leading from the center of the room over my bed and spreading outward. The cracks grew larger as I stared, transfixed. I watched as small bits of plaster fell, and dust rained down, covering the bed and my body.

"Be gone, demon!" The priest bellowed at me when I turned to look at him, but it was my mother's scream of pain that had my heart freezing in my chest. When I turned to look at her, she had her hand on her forehead, and there was a small stream of dark red blood dripping from between her fingers. The sight had me squeezing my eyes shut and begging everything to stop.

The room stopped shaking abruptly just as my bedroom door flew open.

"What the hell is going on in here?" my father bellowed as he glared around the room. His gaze landed on my mother as she sniffled before squaring her shoulders back.

"She needs help."

He sighed as he looked over at me, trembling, covered in welts from the rope and dust from the ceiling. I was also wet from my bladder, losing control some time since it had all started. I couldn't even remember when I had peed, but I could feel it as it soaked through my clothes and bedding.

"Of course she does, Vanessa. But in our home? It's going to take some quick talking to explain away these kinds of repairs."

At his words, the last bit of hope I had in me faded. I wasn't going to get my old dad back. I was truly alone now.

Chapter 1

Valen

There were only two eras I had lived through so far that I truly enjoyed. The first was at the beginning of the new millennia when the Roman Empire was still the ruling government. Not because I had any love for the Romans. No, it was because they knew how to have a good time. My favorite part of the era was the Colosseum. There, I could just be another faceless, nameless fighter. The crowd didn't give a fuck about me or the destruction I caused. If anything, they craved it.

I hadn't made many friends over the long years of my existence, but fighting alongside someone for survival and the cheers of drunk, rich assholes, had a way of bringing you close in a type of brotherhood. Of course, many of the fuckers couldn't be trusted to watch my back in or out of the battleground we called a sand pit. But there had been one who I could trust, and I did so after a ridiculously short amount of time.

My memories of those days were fuzzy at best. Very few of my memories remained clear in my mind. Only the lingering feelings remained, reminding me that I had enjoyed that time of my life. Honestly, I was glad for it. If I had to remember every fucking thing that I had ever seen or done, I'd be a whole lot crazier than I already was. A person wasn't meant to live forever, and I wished I knew what the fuck I'd done to warrant that type of punishment from the universe.

As I watched the miles pass in a blur, I had the thought that the current era I was living in might be able to top even the feeling of holding a sword in my hand, while my muscles ached from the exertion of fighting for my life. I no longer used a sword to lop off the heads of my enemies, a loss I sometimes regretted since those days were so much easier. But it couldn't be denied that the invention of the handgun was more convenient than the necessity for close-range combat that the sword required. Though, I had to admit, it wasn't as sporting or fun.

But this current time period was fucking fantastic. There was only a need to hunt for my food if I chose to. The food available to eat was full of all kinds of shit that was probably killing everyone except me, of course, but most of it tasted incredible. It was nothing like the bland food that had been the most common throughout the ages with the lack of spices available. Clothing that was comfortable and fit my large frame without straining the seams was readily available at any big box store in just about any city without the need to pay someone to make what I needed and have to wait days to receive them. And there was much to be said for the perfect leather jacket. It had taken me years to find one that fit my long arms properly without my wrists hanging out all the time.

Transportation was the best part, though. Since the beginning, as long as my memories allowed, the only option I remembered having was a horse or your own two feet. Along with that came the responsibility of feeding it, grooming it, and generally trying to keep it alive. Those days were long gone. Now, I enjoy riding a beast of a different nature. One that was black and chrome and roared like thunder.

The Harley-Davidson motorcycle rumbled loudly beneath me as I sped down the highway. It had been a long time since I'd last been through this part of the country. Due to my dangerous nature, I didn't stay in one place for long. I traveled nearly continuously, only stopping for a couple of months out of each year, waiting out the winter weather until I could safely ride the highways again.

I hadn't planned on heading through this way, at least not for another couple of decades or so. The last time I had been through here, there had been way too much of the type of activity I learned to avoid. But yet, here I was, willingly, albeit reluctantly.

I had heard of the demon king who had taken up residence in the city. Anyone would probably think that I'd want to be a part of that type of community, to join in with the beings who were like me. But they weren't like me. No one was. In my long existence, I have learned it is best to stay far away from everyone.

The only reason I was driving down this dark highway heading toward what was probably my next regret was because one of the only friends I had in this never-ending cycle of breathing and disaster had called me. When Syn asked me to come, it was on the tip of my tongue to say no. I had no idea what she could possibly want from me now. I hadn't seen her in probably thirty years, maybe fifty. I knew it was during a time when her last club had a shining mirror ball hanging from the ceiling, and the clothing was so horrendous I had wanted to find a cave somewhere to wait for the inevitable change. It wouldn't be the first time. Likely, it wouldn't be the last.

So, I had no idea what caused me to give in and agree to make the trip from the West Coast mountains. But I felt a strong pull, unlike anything I could remember feeling before. It had been impossible to ignore. So I put down the axe that I had been content using to chop wood for my own fireplace and put away my tools for carving shit like bears and deer that I would anonymously drop off at the local tourist shop, just for something to occupy my time.

So much for being a feared and deadly gladiator.

Even though I knew next to nothing about what exactly I was, I guessed Syn was some type of Succubus. Hell, maybe she was a hybrid if that were possible. Since the day back when the West was wild and untamed, and I had heard the screaming coming from a brothel I was passing by, Syn had always been involved in sex work of some kind. It seemed to be a reasonable guess that she was a Succubus. I'd foolishly chosen to stop and help toss out the trash who thought they could abuse women that day, and it seemed that, though the years passed, nothing much had changed when it came to Syn.

I saw the lights of the strip club shining like a beacon for lost souls in the darkness ahead, just the way Syn had told me I would. As I watched the neon sign grow larger, I wanted nothing more than to come to a stop on the deserted highway, turn my motorcycle around, and just drive away. I had no true desire to go back to my cabin in the mountains, but I could go to one of my other homes. I had property all over the place, from the United States to Europe. I could choose any one of them to head to.

But even as I considered it, I shook my head. Something was drawing me in. I had no words for the pull, only that there was something that was important, vital even. It was the feeling that had me agreeing to the trip when I had gotten the call days ago, and it only grew stronger the closer I came to those lights up ahead. I had no explanation for it, but I was starting to get pissed off. If something or someone was fucking with my head, they were going to find out why I spent my life in solitude. Nobody wanted to be around me when I was angry.

Instead of turning my bike around, I hit the accelerator and let the lights of the club pull me in.

Chapter 2

Kallista

I stood against the hallway outside of the main entertainment room and let the heavy bass vibrating through the walls soothe my aching back. I wanted to swipe my hand across my forehead to remove the sweat I could feel there. It was itching underneath the heavy makeup that Candy, one of the dancers, had painted me with. But I knew it would just make a huge mess of what she'd managed to do for my face.

My shift was nearly over, and I had already been on my feet while wearing stilettos for the better part of eight hours. Since I was an unpaid employee, Syn, the owner, didn't let me work the night shift when the money was better. I was grateful that she allowed me to work at all. I didn't have to share my tips with anyone, which was a huge plus, but the lunch and early afternoon crowds were pretty thin, and I was sure I didn't get tipped nearly as well as the night shift did. I really should be out on the floor for my last few minutes as the day and night shifts crossed over instead of waving my serving tray over myself like a giant fan.

I watched as more people entered the main room. Men and women alike strolled into the strip club with expressions ranging from excitement to guilt. It was those who had the look of someone waiting to be smitten by some fierce god that had me grinning and shaking my head. I hoped they managed to relax and enjoy themselves. I couldn't see how a couple of hours of watching live nudity swinging around on poles would damn a soul, but then, I also understood how one's upbringing could make one believe it. My own parents would be appalled, and the punishment for even being seen in this place would be severe.

I shook away the dark thoughts and stepped forward, placing my hand on the swinging door that separated the rest of the club from the entertainment room. The hallway I was in led in either direction. On my left would lead to the kitchens where food for the patrons could be prepared. The club served pretty decent meals, including steaks and burgers, which seemed a popular dinner choice. The path to the right led to the changing room and the owner's office.

Before I pushed the door open, movement caught my eye through the small glass window. A tall man wearing a thick black leather jacket strolled forward, stopped by the bar, and began glancing around as if he were looking for someone. There was something about him that made the breath stall in my chest. Good looking men came into the club all the time, but there was something different about this one I couldn't quite put my finger on.

Often, the most attractive seemed to be looking specifically for Syn. I didn't know what it was about her that seemed to draw men and women alike like bees to a flower. I understood that she had a beauty that seemed to radiate from her in a way that even the gorgeous, naked dancers couldn't achieve, but I just couldn't understand it. Syn didn't dance, but the way she walked around the place in her flowy skirts that did little to hide her amazing assets drew the eye of everyone, no matter the gender. I suspected that she did a little entertaining of her own back in her office if the number of patrons who followed behind her as she led them through this very door were any indication.

As I stared at the man, a part of me was screaming inside at the injustice. If he was looking for Syn, there was a good possibility that I would be going home to my tiny apartment and crying into a pint of my favorite ice cream before curling up into a ball on my futon and rocking myself to sleep.

He was broad, and even though I couldn't see his body under the bulky jacket he wore, the breadth of his shoulders alone hinted at the physique of someone who took care of himself. His shoulder-length black hair was almost as mesmerizing as his face. There was a strangeness about the color. It didn't shine under the dim lights of the room. Instead, the darkness of his hair seemed to be absorbing the dark shadows, or even appeared to be a part of them.

I felt a shudder run through me at the sight as I absently rubbed my right wrist against the skimpy lace skirt that did nothing to cover my panties. As I continued to stare, his face finally turned toward the door I was hiding behind, and I let out an inaudible gasp, nearly choking on my own saliva. It was impossible to tell the color of his eyes through the dim lighting, but there was no mistaking the beauty of his face. But his drool-worthy features weren't what had me shivering in both fear and delight. It was the aura that he had wrapped around him like a cloak.

There was something about the man that screamed danger. There had been all manner of men walking through the doors of this club. Men in business suits who were probably as rich as Midas, and powerful politicians. Bikers came in looking like they would as soon stick a knife through your gut as to shake your hand. But none had ever made me feel the need to lower my eyes and drop to my knees in submission before.

"Kallie, what are you doing?" Syn's sultry voice startled me, and I jumped back from the door. I swallowed nervously and glanced down at the serving tray that I had dropped at some point during my surveillance of the man. "I don't pay you to stand around." Syn's smirk had me laughing hollowly.

I bent down to pick up the tray, tucking it under my left arm and rubbing my wrist against my skirt again. I looked back at her as she stared down at me from her tall height, the heels she wore making her tower over me even more than she already would. I gave her the same answer I always did when she made that comment, "You don't pay me at all."

She winked. "Then I guess you should get out there and earn a few more dollars in tips before the end of your shift." I nodded and watched her turn and push open the door. The music grew louder for the brief moment it was open before quickly becoming muffled again. Her hips swayed with her innate sexuality, catching the gaze of everyone within eyesight of her. I kept my own eyes on her and watched as she strolled forward, the chanting plea in my mind that she head anywhere else ending abruptly in a whine as she walked straight for the tall stranger.

As I watched with dismay, a corner of his lips tipped up when his eyes landed on her. I blinked as Syn quickened her pace until she reached him. I had never seen Syn hurry for anyone before. When she stopped in front of him, she practically threw herself into his arms. I never thought I would see my boss throw herself at anyone, man or woman. Definitely not with the way she had them, all of them, practically crawling to her.

With an ache in my chest I didn't understand, I sighed. I felt a profound loss I couldn't comprehend. I didn't know the man, but somewhere deep inside me, it felt as though I did. It felt like he was mine. With a shake of my head, I pushed the door open and stepped into the main room, the atmosphere of sex and debauchery immediately surrounding me.

As I took the first step deeper into the room, heading toward the closest table, a fiery pain engulfed my wrist, making me want to scream in agony. Before I could open my mouth to let it out, the pain ended as abruptly as it began. I stood there, shaken to my core, and breathed heavily as my heartbeat pounded in my chest at the unexpectedness of the strange event.

I looked around to see if anyone else had noticed and froze when I saw Syn grab the man's hand with a frown and begin to pull him straight to the door where I still stood. I quickly backed away, blinking rapidly at the sight. She was leading him to her office; I just knew it. They both seemed to be in a hurry as she led him past me. My gaze met the tall stranger's for the briefest of seconds, and my knees nearly buckled at the intensity. All too soon, Syn had him through the swinging door, and the two of them were gone.

Abandoning my plan to hit up a few last tables, I turned toward the bar, ready to call it a night. I knew I wouldn't be able to function properly, not with the deep green eyes of the man scorched into my mind. They were eyes I wouldn't forget, not even when I was ninety and on my deathbed. I will always remember the man, and I will always remember the utter feeling of loss that filled every atom of my being as he walked away with my boss.

I dropped my tray down on the bartop with a heavy thud that blended in with the thumping bass of the song playing on the speakers all around us.

"You okay, Kallie?" The bartender, Brad, stopped in front of me with a frown. "You look, I don't know. Did someone die?"

I let out a dry laugh and shook my head. "Only my hopes and dreams."

Brad leaned forward and tugged a strand of my hair. "If I need to kick someone's ass, let me know so I can get Tiny to do it."

That had my lips tipping up into a genuine smile. "I appreciate your sacrifice for my honor."

"Any time, doll. Hey!" As he made to move back down the bar to help a waiting patron waving a twenty-dollar bill in the air, he stopped abruptly. "You finally got some ink to decorate your virgin skin?"

"What?" I asked in confusion. I had nothing against tattoos, but I had yet to find the perfect something to forever mark my skin. I glanced down at where his eyes seemed to be zeroed in. When I caught sight of the blood-red mark on my inner right wrist, I gasped and held it up to get a better look. It was only about two inches long and two inches wide, but it was intricately designed. It looked more like a brand than a tattoo, to be honest. I lightly ran my fingertips over it to feel how it was slightly raised. It looked like a symbol of some kind, and instinct told me that whatever the symbol was, it was very ancient.

My mind pinwheeled as I thought back to the searing pain I had felt just moments ago. "What the fuck?" I mumbled as I continued to stare down at the mark.

"It's badass, Kallie. I like it," I heard Brad say before he moved back down the bar to get whatever drink the woman with the twenty wanted.

As I continued to stand there in shock, taking in a mark that shouldn't be there and wasn't rubbing off, a conversation from the closest table filtered in over the loud music. My hearing had always seemed to be unusually good and now proved no different. It was a conversation strange enough to pull my attention from the impossible.

"The newest King ain't shit."

From my lowered eyelashes, I glanced at the three men standing around a tall table, ignoring the bar stools. They looked like the typical biker club members we got on a regular basis. Their vests were typical black leather, and their appearances had that usual messy vibe going on as if they'd rather be out causing mayhem than bother with hygiene.

One of the other guys scoffed. "You wouldn't be saying that if the old King was still here."

The first guy grunted. "Fuck off. None of us would even be here if the old King was still here."

The third one, the one that seemed meaner than the other two, even if he were the most attractive of the three, smiled menacingly. "The old King has a dhampir kid. Get the dhampir and control the Council member. In the meantime, take out the current King."

"Even if you killed him, you wouldn't be able to take his place. The Master would take your head for trying."

Their conversation was confusing. I had no idea what they meant by Kings or Council members, but there was something about that word, *dhampir*, that had my brain working overtime. I knew I had heard it before, but it wasn't clicking for me yet. But what was most concerning was the direction of the whole conversation. They were talking openly about killing people. It had a shiver of trepidation running down my spine.

KALLISTA

A bottle slamming down on the tabletop had me jolting in shock. My head swung to face the trio fully without thought, only to see the blond leader sneering at me.

"You working here or not, slut?" He picked his bottle up from where he'd slammed it down a second ago and waved it in the air mockingly. "My boys and me want a refill."

I winced at the grammar and looked around. No other servers were near, and I had a feeling that this guy was a full-on asshole that would throw a fit if he weren't served right away. As much as I wanted to leave him hanging, I wanted to cause a scene even less. My job was at the mercy of the boss. She wouldn't be inclined to keep me on, letting me work for tips, if she got a complaint about me not wanting to help someone.

With hesitant steps, I walked toward the table of rough-looking bikers. When a strobe light passed over the features of the blond, I jolted. I could have sworn his eyes glowed an eerie yellow for a second before going back to the blue. I mentally shook my head, figuring it was either an effect of the light or my imagination was running away with me.

"Three more beers?" I asked quietly, not bothering to put on a smile or even attempt to flirt. I wasn't going to get a tip from these guys. There was no doubt in my mind they were nothing but trouble and didn't give a shit about tipping the help.

As I reached for the empty bottles, the blond nudged his roughly, making it wobble, and then tip over. Before I could reach out and stop it, the bottle rolled right off the edge of the small round table and crashed to the floor.

"Oops."

I wanted nothing more than to wipe the smirk right off his pretty boy face. Instead, I gave a small, tight smile before squatting down with my knees together, carefully doing my best not to flash everything I had to the room. "No problem," I muttered. "It happens."

I gingerly picked up the jagged pieces of the beer bottle and piled them carefully into my left palm, wishing I had brought my tray with me and hoping I didn't end the night with a trip to the ER.

"You'd look good on your knees. Maybe you should put your mouth to good use while you're down there." His hand reached for me, making me jerk back with a quiet shriek. The no-touching rule went for more than just the dancers. I had always felt safe working at the club, knowing that it was against the rules and that Syn didn't put up with any type of manhandling of her staff. The bouncers always did a good job keeping a close watch on everything. It had lulled me into a false sense of security.

As I jerked away from the man's touch, I lost my precarious balance, the high-heeled shoes not helping the situation any, and threw my hands back to catch myself before I fell on my ass in an undignified heap. As soon as my left hand hit the floor, I knew I had made a grave mistake. Pain lanced through my palm, this time making my shriek much louder. I ended up on my ass anyway as I rolled to the right, trying to take pressure off my aching palm.

As the men sniggered loudly above me, I scooted back far enough away from the table to avoid more of the broken bottle and carefully maneuvered to my knees. I had to use the table to brace myself as I climbed back to my feet. My eyesight was blurry with tears as the pain radiated through my hand and up my arm. *Fuck.* I couldn't go to the hospital. I didn't need any records of my whereabouts to enter the system. I blinked down at the floor that already had a small puddle of blood on it and grimaced at the thought of all the germs that were probably making their way through my system as I stood there bleeding all over a strip club bar table.

A hand reached out so fast it was nearly a blur. I gasped as my wrist was grabbed roughly and yanked toward the blond. With wide eyes, I watched in terror as he brought my hand to his face. There was no mistaking the yellow glow this time as he stared down at my bloody hand with an expression I could only describe as hungry.

With mounting horror, I watched as he gripped the large sliver of beer bottle glass that was still embedded in my skin and yanked, dropping it to the floor without a second thought. Then he lowered his nose and sniffed, inhaling deeply.

"What the fuck?" I screamed as he opened his mouth, sharp white teeth much longer than ordinary human teeth flashing in the light. "Stop! Let me go!"

I glanced around frantically, searching for any of the bouncers, relief immediately filling me as Tiny stormed closer, murder in his eyes. I was glad to see he had noticed, since nobody at the neighboring tables seemed to realize there was anything wrong. I looked back at the man holding me firm, knowing I was about to be rescued. These psychos were going to be thrown out of the club and banned for the rest of their lives. My struggles were utterly useless as he held me steady in his grasp. Revulsion filled me as I watched him stick out his tongue and lap at the pool of blood that filled the open palm of my hand.

Growls seemed to rumble from the other two as they pushed

closer. I whimpered as the two men I had almost forgotten about in the struggle leaned in, crowding my space as if they were about to take a lick—or a bite of my body. I whimpered, wanting to close my eyes but unable to as my gaze trained on the sharp teeth that the two other men sported as well. Their teeth were exactly like the blond's, who licked up my blood and was now sliding his disgusting tongue across the cut as if he were trying to get every single drop.

The blond lifted his head long enough to growl a warning at the other two men, his eyes flashing yellow at them. They didn't back away, but they stopped coming closer. I watched as their nostrils flared wide as they inhaled.

"I want a fucking taste," one of them growled, his voice deeper, as if he were on the verge of becoming an animal. My mind was screaming at me, and I was frantically denying it even as I watched it play out right in front of me.

Finally, Tiny arrived, a thunderous expression on his huge, round face. "What the fuck?" he yelled at the blond. "No fucking touching. Ever! You're out of here, asshole!" Before he could say or do anything else, the blond struck out with the hand not holding my wrist and rammed his fist into Tiny's chest.

Screams erupted from around us as people finally noticed the havoc happening. The closest scrambled away from where we were while staring with wide-eyed shock. Some people ran straight for the door while the dancer on stage stood under her spotlight, her hands covering her mouth as Tiny stumbled backward. He came to a stop and raised his hands as if he were going to go after the blond guy again, but then they dropped heavily to his sides as if his strength had left him entirely. Tiny looked down at his chest before falling to his knees, the impact hard enough to make the floor tremble under my feet.

It wasn't until I followed his line of sight that I noticed the glistening wetness on Tiny's black STAFF T-shirt. It took me several heartbeats to comprehend what I was seeing. Then, as Tiny fell face-first to the floor, I looked up with dazed eyes to see the blond holding something dripping and red in his fist.

"Oh, my god," I whispered as I watched the man toss the heart over to his friends. One of them snatched it out of the air and immediately brought it to his mouth.

"Take her to the house," the blond snarled, shoving me to the other guy as a second bouncer came up to our group. "But don't fucking drink from her. She's mine."

"What about the Master?" one of them asked as he snatched my arm.

He snapped his teeth seconds before he grabbed the hand of the second bouncer and bent it backward so fast the bones breaking were audible. Blood immediately began to pour from the open wound in his arm as he screamed in pain.

"The Master owes me. Just do it," he snarled.

Tears were running down my cheeks as I struggled to catch my breath. These guys were monsters. They shouldn't exist, but they did. And they wanted me. Seeing what the blond guy was doing to the bouncers I had always trusted to keep me safe, I had no hope of surviving whatever they had planned for me. For the first time in a year, I actually wished I hadn't run away from home.

CHAPTER 4

VALEN

"What the fuck?" I growled as we came to a stop in a posh office that was reminiscent of Victorian era boudoir.

I tugged on my hand and frowned as Syn's grip tightened for the briefest of seconds before she allowed my hand to leave hers. She clenched her now empty one into a fist and gave out a low hiss of frustration before spinning away from me and heading toward a small bar set up in the corner.

I took the time to glance around, listening as crystal clinked against crystal. It was obviously Syn's domain. There were rich red curtains that matched the throw pillows on a settee that I would have bet my life was an antique and was likely one that she'd owned when it was still new.

In the corner of the room sat a small high-backed chair, also antique, with a filmy black lace robe draped over it. I turned back to Syn with one eyebrow raised, eyeing her as she lifted a delicate looking glass of clear liquid to her lips. If I didn't know her, I might not have spotted the slight trembling of her fingers as they tightened on the glass.

She gave me a grim smile, then picked up the second tumbler with her free hand and walked it over to me.

"The finest vodka, a gift from Alexander Romanov after, well…" She cleared her throat while holding the crystal filled with what was likely one of the most expensive vodkas in existence. I folded my arms over my chest and waited.

Syn sighed in disappointment. "It's rude to reject an offer from a lady, you know." She turned to the small couch and sat reclining in the seat, draping her arms across the back after setting both glasses on the low, gleaming mahogany table in front of her. I eyed her, still waiting for an explanation for why she had so suddenly appeared panicked. She'd hurried me away from the main room and into her admittedly lush office. However, I wouldn't have expected anything less from a room that belonged to Syn. She had always had a taste for the finer things in life.

Syn pouted at me, her perfectly lush lips turning downward just enough to show her displeasure. Any actress getting paid millions to act the part of a simpering seductress could learn a thing or two from Syn. But then, she was the very epitome of seductress. It was who she was, and she couldn't be anything else. Her life depended on it. I sighed but didn't move toward the tiny couch. I would likely break the thing in two if I even considered it. Instead, I leaned my hip against the solid wood desk across from her.

"Syn, for the sake of our friendship, I rode over two thousand miles to come see you when you told me you needed me. I'm here, but you are acting strange. What was that back there?" I threw out my arm, gesturing back the way we had come. "You looked almost terrified when I grabbed my arm."

I looked down at the arm in question, remembering the way it had burned as if someone had poured acid over my skin for the briefest of moments. It was more Syn's reaction to the whole thing that had taken my attention than the burning sensation I'd felt. Looking down now, I froze.

I had been too distracted to see it then, but now that I was focused on my arm, I could only wonder how I hadn't seen it immediately.

"What the fuck is this?" My tone was strange even to my own ears. I made a strangled sound in the back of my throat as I traced the intricate lines across my wrist. The symbol looked ancient, almost Celtic in design, though that wasn't quite the right description. I had no words to describe the blood-red symbol that was now burned into my flesh.

I glanced up at Syn, hoping she held the answer to the question, insistently screaming through every part of me. When I saw the expression of fear filling her delicate features, I straightened to my full height and dropped my arm to my side.

"What is it?"

Syn cleared her throat and closed her eyes, pain making her look older than the perpetual twenty-five she had always appeared. In a flash, the pain was gone as she opened her eyes, replaced by a steely determination.

"I'm guessing that in all your time roaming this realm, you have never heard about fated mates?" Her tone was sarcastic, punctuated by a raised eyebrow.

"Fated mates? That's just a myth." I thought back, trying to sort through my memories, but it was like trying to swim through cold molasses. Nothing was coming to me, nothing solid I could grasp.

"Why didn't you tell me you had been branded?" Syn rose from her reclined position and strode over to me, taking my hand in hers and holding my arm up to see the symbol for herself.

"You saw what happened at the same time I did." I shook my head.

She sighed, dropped my arm, spun around to pick up her forgotten drink, and tossed it back in one swallow.

I snorted. "If that vodka really is one hundred and fifty years old, I'm surprised you would be so careless with it."

Syn grimaced and picked up the second glass that I hadn't wanted before taking a healthy swallow of that one as well. She shrugged one thin shoulder. "Desperate times and all that."

As much as I wanted to hurry her along with her explanation I knew that would get me nowhere. Syn was nothing if not stubborn. She also enjoyed the control she gained by making others wait on her. I crossed my arms again and resumed my leaning pose against the desk as Syn paced a few steps. I got the impression she was trying to find her words, maybe she was even trying to find the courage to say what she felt she needed to.

I glanced back at the door toward the main room where all the entertainment was happening. Something was drawing my attention back out there, like an itch under my skin. I glanced down at the symbol on my wrist, the curiosity beginning to prick at me. I traced the lines, a little bit awed at the intricacy of something that just randomly appeared as if by magic.

"The fates are a bitch." Syn's words brought my attention back to her even though my fingers didn't leave the new mark. "Somewhere, somehow, some*one* decides who all demons' fated mates should be without a single bit of care about the lives they are messing with."

That caught my full attention, making me stand up straight, dropping my arms to my sides with my fists clenched. "Fated mates really exist?" My tone was harsh, the words coming out in an almost incoherent grumble. I wasn't sure about what she was saying, but somehow, it felt right. My chest felt tight as my mind spun with the implications.

Syn huffed out a laugh and ran her pointed red fingernails through her perfectly styled hair. "Yeah, Val, fated mates." She turned back to face me, a wry smile on her plump lips. "Congratulations, you have a mate out there who you have never met before. Someone who the fates think you should be with for the rest of eternity. Whether you even like her or not." She shook her head and gave a humorless chuckle. "You didn't know that you have no say over who you want to be tied to?"

She stepped back over to the couch and dropped into it, crossing her legs and looking up at me with a sad expression. She tilted her head and studied me while tapping her fingers on one exposed knee. "Did you not feel the same type of burning feeling sometime in the past? Maybe twenty or thirty years ago?"

I thought back, running through my memories of the last few decades. One moment in time stood out to me. I had been riding my motorcycle down a scenic highway in North Dakota. I had felt a pain in my wrist, and the burning sensation had made me swerve before I managed to gain control again, all while cursing violently. It had ended as quickly as it began. By the time I could safely stop, there was no sign of anything there. Though, if I really thought about it, there were times I could have sworn I'd seen just a hint of *something* on the skin if I looked at it just right.

"Perhaps." It was all I was willing to give without more information. Her reaction to the entire situation was making me question why. What was it that made her so upset? She wasn't acting like her usual flirty self. Syn and I had never been anything but friends. I had helped her and her group of girls out all those years ago. Since then, we have been close acquaintances. I allowed very few people close to me over the years, and she was one mostly because she wouldn't let me push her away for long. I narrowed my eyes.

"Why is this upsetting you, Syn?"

She narrowed her eyes back at me before barking out a husky laugh. "You have no idea, do you? Wow. Just so you know, handsome, just because you were assigned a fated mate, it doesn't mean that you have to accept it." Her smile was blinding as she looked me over.

I frowned. "What does that mean?"

Before she could answer, sounds coming from the main room of the strip club startled both of us. Without thought, I rushed to the closed door, gripping the handle and twisting it. I threw it open so hard it crashed into the wall, where the handle became immediately embedded into the plaster.

"Damn it, Val. you're going to pay for that damage."

I ignored Syn as I rushed from the office and down the hallway, where the sounds of screaming were louder. I glanced through the small window in the door a second before that too, was thrown open. That one brief look was all I needed to have me seeing red.

Vampires were in the club, and they were causing mayhem. I looked back at Syn with an accusing glare. She knew better. Vampires were nothing but troublemakers who wreaked havoc everywhere they went. I would be demanding answers as to why she would put her club and all the people in it at risk so recklessly.

I stalked over to the blond vamp who had just torn the heart out of the guy who'd been standing by the front door when I'd arrived. I grabbed him by the back of the neck with one hand and shot my fist into his ugly face. The moment I had entered the room, I felt a pull unlike anything I could have imagined. That draw was keeping me from concentrating fully on the vampire in my grasp, allowing him to turn and bite the shit out of my arm.

With a curse, I pulled him closer, ready to rip his head off his scrawny shoulders. I had my hands wrapped around his neck and prepared to tear it off when I was suddenly stopped by a scream from Syn. She placed her hand on my arm and tugged it as she yelled into my ear.

"Valen! You can't!"

I turned to glance down at her with an incredulous look. "Why the fuck not? Did you see what he did?"

She gave me a pleading look. "I know, Valen, but you don't understand. You just can't, okay?"

With disgust, I reared back my fist and punched the asshole in the face hard enough to knock out one of his fangs and dropped him to the floor. I turned to see the other two vamps backing away with wary expressions, one holding a struggling brunette dressed provocatively in what looked like a serving outfit that Syn would require her girls to wear. The girl was crying and covered in blood.

In two strides, I was in front of the greasy-looking vampire holding her to his chest. He hissed at me like a fucking cat, as if that were any deterrent. I reached out and grasped the terrified girl by the arm and pulled her toward me, somehow finding myself in a strange tug-of-war with the guy, the girl in the middle. He didn't appear to be ready to let go any time soon.

"Valen, stop! Just let them go!"

I ignored Syn's pleas, knowing that if this girl went with them, she would never walk away alive.

"Val, if they want her, there's nothing we can do. They will hunt her down until they get her. It's okay. Just let her go."

I couldn't believe what I was hearing. There was nothing inside of me that could have let the girl go with those monsters. With a snarl, I did what I hadn't allowed myself to do in over two hundred years, and I let my power out.

In seconds, the man holding tight to the woman I was trying to save began to visibly show signs of what could only be described as melting. His face turned a sickly yellow as the flesh began to sag around his eyes. He didn't seem to notice right away that he was dying until his grip loosened enough that I was finally able to pull the woman into my chest. With a sob, she leaned her weight into me, and I had to wrap an arm around her to keep her from falling to the floor.

I continued to glare at the vampire and watched as the flesh pulled downward, hanging around his chin and exposing the wet, pink flesh around the bottom of his eyeballs. I would have kept going until he was nothing but wet flesh puddled on the floor, but Syn punched me in the arm, jarring me.

"Stop it! You're going to get us all killed!"

I turned my glare to her, but before I could say anything, she shoved my shoulder. "You need to get out of here. Now! Before he finds out."

I shook my head, not wanting to leave her to face the vampires alone, but at a second command for me to go, I gave a stiff nod and began striding quickly toward the entrance, the young woman still held firmly to my chest. If Syn was right, and these guys would hunt her down, I was going to keep her with me. I'd be damned if I allowed an innocent to be taken by fucking vampires.

CHAPTER 5

KALLISTA

My mind was spinning, and it felt as though I were wading through a hazy fog as the man who had been with Syn in her office practically carried me through the now empty strip club. The only people who hadn't run away screaming were the six of us. Well, I suppose I had been screaming. I certainly would have been running if that guy, that *vampire*, hadn't been holding me so tight it felt as if my bones were bruised.

I wasn't screaming anymore, though. Instead, I was silent, with only the occasional hiccup escaping from my chest as my breathing slowly came back under control. I was still in the same disbelieving daze as I had been as I watched Tiny's blood spread across the wooden floor.

The door slammed shut behind us as we moved quickly through the cool evening air, making my body jerk at the sudden noise. The man who was ushering me further away from the gruesome scene murmured softly as if to reassure me. I barely heard a word of it, though.

We stopped in front of a huge Harley-Davidson motorcycle. At any other time, in any other place, I probably would have been awed by the sheer masculine beauty of the metallic beast. I couldn't help but admire its matte black paint and shiny chrome appearance.

I must have been standing there staring down at the motorcycle for too long because the next thing I knew, I was being lifted and sat astride the narrow back seat—not that there was much of one. The main seat was leather, wide for comfort, and long. Leather saddlebags framed the back part where I was sitting, which I assumed carried his belongings. A helmet much too big for me was plunked down over my head, and his hand tilted my chin up with two long fingers.

For a brief second, our eyes met, startling me from my horrified stupor, but the moment he looked down at the clasp he held in his hand, breaking eye contact, I went right back to the vision of all that blood. A shiver wracked my whole body at the memory. He probably took it as revulsion because he yanked his hands away as soon as the clasp clicked together. Without a word spoken between us, he swung his leg over the motorcycle and revved the engine.

As soon as the bike began to move, my hands flew around the man to grip tightly to his leather jacket. We quickly rolled out of the parking lot and out onto the highway, gaining speed. My shivers increased with the night air rushing past us. His body was giving off so much heat that I couldn't help but snuggle closer, using his large body to block as much of the wind as possible.

The helmet slipped down over my eyes somewhere between leaving the parking lot and the miles it took to reach our destination. I was at a loss as to where we were going. Somewhere in the back of my mind, I was screaming at myself at the stupidity of being on the back of a stranger's motorcycle. He was taking me to an unknown destination, and no one would know where to look for me. Perhaps my boss knew; she seemed to be very friendly with the stranger, though that offered little comfort.

Another part of me, though, knew I was safer than I had ever been in my entire life. A small part of me that was trying to push through was telling me I was where I was meant to be. I did my best to shut the door on that voice. Just because the man invoked feelings of calm and rightness didn't mean anything. My life taught me that nothing was ever what it seemed, so I kept a firm grasp on my trust.

While fighting memories of what happened at the bar, I also battled the demons inside of me. I needed to find a way to get far away from this man. I didn't know why I was here, with him on his bike. I didn't know if he was protecting me or if he was taking me somewhere in order to harm me. I couldn't trust anything.

The bike slowed as we turned a corner. The air had gotten noticeably colder, and my shivers had turned violent. Every part of me was freezing, and no wonder. I was still wearing the outfit all the servers were expected to wear, which was practically nothing, though obviously much more than the dancers did. I shifted my feet and groaned audibly at the pain that movement induced. My bare foot turned on the peg under me, and I realized for the first time that I lost one of my stiletto heels. It was part of my minuscule uniform, and it was going to come out of my tips, an expense I couldn't afford. But then, did I even still have a job after tonight?

We slowed to a stop, and I heard a mechanical whirring, indicating that a garage door was opening. At the sound, my heart sped up even faster than it already had been. I lifted my head, feeling as if it weighed a hundred pounds, and tried to look around, but all I was able to see in the brief space of my vision that wasn't covered by the helmet was asphalt.

Before I could make a decision to jump off the back of the motorcycle and try to make a run for it, the engine revved again, and we rolled forward into an enclosed space. The rumbling of the engine was loud enough to make any speaking impossible. Before the outside door closed completely, the engine turned off, though engine fumes still managed to choke me enough to keep from being able to talk.

I loosened my death grip on the man's jacket and almost cried out in pain as my fingers cramped at the cold that had frozen them in place. He must have sensed my discomfort because he covered my hands before I could straighten them out, the heat from his touch soothing the worst of the pain.

With a jolt, the floor beneath us began to move, making me realize that we were sitting in a huge elevator or lift. I still couldn't see much of anything except the metal floor. It was only a few seconds before we came to a slow stop with another jerk. The big biker removed his hand from mine, giving my fingers a pat as if to let me know it was safe to move. I hesitantly pulled my hands back, flexing my fingers, trying to regain mobility back into the aching joints.

As the man dismounted, I raised my fingers to the strap under my chin, attempting to unclick the latch, but I wasn't able to accomplish anything except shiver from the coldness seeping into my neck at the touch of my fingers there. My hands were brushed aside, and once again, the man lifted my chin, though this time, I couldn't see his eyes.

With a hard shiver, the helmet lifted from my head, and I blinked several times, taking in the dim lighting and not much else. After I sat there numbly for a few more seconds, the big biker sighed and wrapped his hands around my waist, lifting me off the bike, much like the way he had deposited me there in the first place.

I wobbled, off balance, until I remembered I was missing a shoe. Placing my hand on the warm leather seat, I leaned over to grasp the remaining stiletto and slipped it off before letting it drop to the metal floor with a dull clatter. Once I was finally able to stand on my own two feet, I wrapped my arms around my torso as much for warmth as for comfort and got my first real look around. I had been right; I was standing in a huge metal lift, probably for cargo. At the sound of heavy footsteps, I turned to look at the back of the man as he walked away from me and into what I assumed was a large open warehouse.

However, the space seemed to be converted into a very minimalistic living area.

I took a tentative step forward, swaying slightly from the ride on the motorcycle I was unaccustomed to riding, as well as the cold and the shock from the events of the night. I took another step and had to brace my shoulder against the opening of the lift to keep from stumbling.

"You can have a seat. I'll find you something warm to change into."

The deep rumble of his voice had my head jerking from my examination of the small two-seater sofa, the large bed in the far corner, and the kitchen across from the lift. I couldn't see a bathroom, but I imagined there had to be one somewhere.

"Why," I stopped to clear my throat before I could try again. "Why am I here?" My voice was raspy, as if I had been screaming. It took me a moment to remember that I actually had been screaming. I closed my eyes as the memory of Tiny getting his heart ripped out in front of me played out in my mind again. A scalding hot tear slid down my frozen cheek. As I glanced down at my fingers, I gasped at the sight of the blood smeared on them.

Frantically, I swiped at my face, at once realizing that I was covered in blood spray. Of course I was; I had been right fucking there as a man was murdered by a monster. Bile rose quickly in my throat. I slapped a hand over my mouth and knew I needed to find a trash can or a toilet immediately.

The man must have been watching me because he lifted a small black trash can off the floor behind the kitchen island where he'd been standing. I rushed forward without thought, grabbing the can and emptying the contents of my stomach until everything ached, and I just wanted to curl up into a ball and cry for a week straight.

Once I was sure I didn't have anything left inside of me to vomit up, I sagged against the concrete kitchen island. I still held the trash can, embarrassed and unsure what to do with it. I was certain it smelled terrible. I didn't know the stranger, but as ridiculous as the idea was, I cared if he thought I was disgusting. But when I brought my teary eyes up to meet his, all I saw was a quiet understanding.

"Here," he rumbled out in that deep voice of his, his hand extended. I hesitantly handed the can over. I watched with flaming cheeks as he pulled the sides of the trash bag up and tied it swiftly in a tight knot. He walked over to the lift and sat it in the corner next to his motorcycle. When he turned back to see me watching, he just said, "I'll take it out while you're in the shower."

I glanced around again, this time with my view from a different vantage point. This time, I could see there was an open door next to the lift with a toilet inside. On the other side of the freight elevator, there was a metal door that looked more like a normal-sized elevator, maybe a little smaller than one I would have seen in an office building. Two entrances?

The biker opened one of the saddlebags on the back of the motorcycle and withdrew a handful of clothing items before walking over to the bathroom. He flipped on the light and set the clothes on the counter. I heard the water running as he stepped back out again.

"Take a hot shower and get changed. We'll talk when you're done."

With those words, he turned his back on me, going to his bike and rifling through his belongings again. With my arms wrapped tightly around myself, I decided to do what he said. I needed to get warm. I needed to get the blood off of me. And I needed answers. It seemed that I would be relying on this stranger for all of those things.

Chapter 6

Valen

I roughly yanked my fingers through my hair as I paced the length of my warehouse apartment. It was similar to my other places around the United States and Europe. Warehouses were cheap, but they also seldom held enough attention for anyone to wander too close out of curiosity. It left my places safe from prying eyes, and the security systems helped keep squatters from taking over. I hadn't been to this one in particular in more years than I cared to remember. The faceless property manager I'd hired years ago kept it prepared for me, just as he had all the others, thanks to the very generous salary I paid him.

I turned my head again to look back at the closed bathroom door, hearing the sound of the shower I couldn't escape from if I wanted to. But the fuck of it all was, I didn't want to. I had allowed myself to be ruled by instinct to protect this girl from the danger I didn't even fully understand. I just knew that the fear on Syn's face told me I needed to leave before whoever those fucking vampires worked for found out who I was. There was no way I could have left without the girl.

The instinct to protect was so strong that it was impossible to fight, so I brought her with me. It wasn't until we had pulled into the warehouse lift that I noticed the mark on her frozen wrist—one that matched mine perfectly.

I grunted and ran my hands over my face, feeling the stubble that was shadowed along my jawline and cheeks. A fucking mate. One I didn't know existed or could ever exist. This is exactly what I got for choosing to live so far removed from the world that I should have been a part of but carefully held myself away from for hundreds of years. The little I did know was only from the short interactions I'd had over the centuries with others who were like me. Well, not like me, exactly. No one was like me. I was a true monster in every sense of the word.

Syn was the one and only I had let in far enough to get to know me. Even then, it was such a small piece, and only because she pushed like a mother fucking demon for that tiny sliver. I should have been more concerned for her welfare, leaving her behind the way I had, but she hadn't lived as long as she had without being able to defend herself.

I glanced back at the bathroom door again as the sound of the shower ended. That girl in there, though? She was human. She was defenseless against demonkind. She was helpless against me. A part of me was turned the fuck on at the thought, the larger part of me wanted to kick my own ass and was determined to get her somewhere safe, and the only place that could be was away from me. But I had yet to work out how I was going to accomplish that and still protect her. Because the overriding need, above all, was to ensure she was safe.

I growled low in my chest, the sound of a dangerous hum not unlike that of a rattlesnake poised to strike. "Fuck!" I had a mate, and I couldn't do a goddamn thing about it.

I imagined again for the thousandth time what she must look like in that bathroom. I had grabbed her while she was wearing little more than what someone would consider lingerie, so I had a good idea of how her body was formed—pure perfection. If I could design my ideal woman, she would check every mark.

Her hair was like a sheet of rich mahogany, and her eyes seemed brown at first glance, but the closer you looked, the more easily you could catch the myriad of colors hidden in their depths—greens, and golds, with slight hints of blue. They were mesmerizing, and it was all I could do to pull myself away from her when we first arrived. If I had to guess, I would say she had more than a little bit of Native American ancestry.

It didn't matter that she was the first woman I found myself attracted to and was tempted to actually take for myself; I would find her a safe place and leave her there. Perhaps she had a family I could take her to.

As soon as the door opened and she walked out hesitantly in her bare feet and wearing nothing but my shirt riding low on her thighs, nearly every thought left my brain. I blurted out the first words that came to my lips.

"Tomorrow, I will take you to your family."

The color immediately leached from her face, and the nervous smile she had been wearing instantly slipped from her plush lips. She broke eye contact and dropped her gaze to the floor while I clenched my jaw tight to keep myself from demanding that she give me her eyes again.

She twisted the sweatpants I hadn't noticed she was holding in her hands and cleared her throat. "I, uh, couldn't keep the pants on. They were too big, even by rolling them up. I'm sorry." She darted a look back up at me before turning away, heading to the small sofa sitting in the middle of the otherwise bare room. "Don't worry about taking me to my family. I have a safe place to go. I'll be fine. I doubt there will be any issue with those guys anyway once Syn clears it up."

I tilted my head as I watched her jerky movements while she made herself comfortable on the seat, appearing as if she were preparing to lay down for the night there.

"Those guys? You do realize what they were, right?"

Her whole body gave a violent shiver as she held up her hand as if inspecting it for something. "Vampires," she whispered so low I could barely hear her from my place across the room. I watched as she turned her hand over, inspecting it.

"What's wrong with your hand?" I asked as I walked closer, needing to be near her but also curious about her actions.

She shrugged her shoulder before tucking her arms together, her hands under her thighs. "Nothing, it seems. I think I just imagined something that didn't happen, I guess." She shook her head as if trying to erase a bad memory.

I stopped next to the couch. "What do you think you remember that didn't happen?"

She glanced up at me, startled to see I was so close, and for a long second, stayed silent as we stared into each other's eyes. When she broke away, I held in the growl that wanted to erupt from my chest again.

"I thought I cut my hand open. I remember the pain and everything. But," she held up her palm for me to see it in the low light. "There's not even a scratch."

I reached out and took her hand in mine and ran a calloused fingertip across her smooth palm. It was flawless. "Did one of the vampires lick you or drink your blood?" Her whole body jerked in shock at my words, and I let her hand go when she gave it a slight tug.

"The blond one, the leader of the group... he, uh, he seemed fascinated by the smell and started licking it." She turned pale with her words, and I wanted to smash something.

"That mother fucker," I rumbled low and viciously.

She jumped up from her seat to face me. "What? What's wrong?" The scared expression had me wanting to find the vampire and finish ripping his head off his shoulders. Syn and her command to stop be damned. I forced my breathing to slow as I took in the girl.

"Vampire saliva can heal wounds; it's how they drink from humans without leaving a trace. When he licked up your blood, he healed you." I took in a calming breath before looking her in the eye. I had figured the guy was obsessed with the way they were determined to take her with them, but now I was sure it went so much deeper. "Sometimes they become fixated on certain people based on the way their blood smells or tastes."

She gaped at me in disbelief. "You think he wants me?"

"I think he will stop at nothing to get to you."

She dropped back down onto the seat and hugged her torso, slightly rocking as she shook her head. "That's... I don't know what that is. Why me? I am nobody. Why would a vampire be fixated on me?"

"There's no reason I can explain to you. To be honest, my understanding of vampires and other supernatural creatures is limited," I said with a grimace.

She looked up at me with fear in her eyes. "There's more than just vampires? Are there werewolves, too?"

At that, I shook my head. "Uh, no. Shifters are actually vampires with a gift for shifting. The only other shifters I am aware of are demons who can change their form. Usually to fit in with humans more easily."

I watched her shake her head in disbelief as she took in my words. "Demons and vampires can shift. But, hey!" Her tone grew more high-pitched, edging into hysteria. "Werewolves don't actually exist. So that's a win, right?"

I glanced around, wondering what the fuck I should do. This conversation was going to take some time, and I didn't think she would be comfortable with me sitting smashed up next to her on the cramped couch. With a sigh, I walked back to the kitchen and opened the small refrigerator. I grabbed two bottles of beer and took them back to the girl. Fuck, I needed to find out what her name was. I handed her one of the chilled bottles after removing the top and watched as she brought it to her lips, taking a tiny sip. She wrinkled her nose up in distaste, and I hid my smirk behind my own bottle. I made myself comfortable on the floor with my back against the wall.

"I'm going to try to make this as condensed as possible since the full explanation could last a year or more of non-stop talking, and I don't know about you, but I could use some sleep." I paused, waiting for her to agree after taking a larger sip. Her grimace wasn't as strong as before. It seemed my little mate was a bit of a lightweight.

"Demons have been around since time began. There are different realms of existence. Much of what humans are taught is based on truth but pretty far from reality. There is the Underworld, as it is universally known, where Demonkind are from. Then, of course, the Earth realm. Others exist, but as far as I know, I have never come into contact with a being from one. For all I know, they could be invisible, like ghosts."

"That's not disturbing at all," she muttered into her bottle, her eyes looking a bit glassy.

"But, since we are talking about demons, the important thing to know is that there are more breeds of demons than there are races of humans. Basically, every mythical monster you've ever read about has a basis of truth in it."

"They are all demons."

There was the slightest slur to her words, making me chuckle. Unfortunately, the sound was foreign to me and came out more like a snarl. I was grateful she was too busy draining the last of her beer bottle to have noticed.

"They are *almost* all demons. Some either don't exist, or vampires are responsible for the stories."

She squinted at me and slumped over in her seat, tucking one hand under her head and the other between her thighs, showing off the mating brand. The shirt she was wearing had ridden up so high it was barely covering her ass anymore, and it was taking all my self-restraint not to give in and take a long look. "And what are you?"

At her question, I decided I was done explaining for the night. I stood up quickly, downing my own beer in one large swallow. I picked up her bottle from where it rested against the floor. Before I walked away, I stopped and looked down at her. She looked sleepy, and as much as I hated to leave her on the small couch to sleep all night, she was small enough to fit somewhat comfortably, even if her feet would hang off a little. She was far safer there than in the bed.

"No one knows what I am, babe."

She blinked slowly up at me. "But you are a demon. I know you are."

"Yeah? How do you know that?"

"Because I've been waiting for you to come to me from the shadows since I was a little girl."

I jerked, my spine going stiff at her soft, barely coherent words. But as I stared down at her, she let out a quiet snore, sound asleep. I backed away slowly, then turned and headed toward the kitchen, quietly setting the bottles down on the counter.

Before I got ready for bed, I went to the chest at the foot of the bed, opened it, and pulled out a folded blanket. There were always extra supplies in my homes, just in case I ever decided I wanted to stay longer than just a few days.

I carried the blanket over to the woman who fate had apparently decided should be my mate, and carefully laid the blanket over her, cautious not to touch her body in any way.

When I was finally lying in bed after a long, cold shower, I reflected on everything I had done wrong in my life, and wondered how I had been offered someone so perfect. I lay staring at the industrial ceiling tiles and wondered how I could make myself walk away.

Chapter 7

Kallista

The inside of my mouth tasted like a dirty gym sock, and I felt like I hadn't had a drop of water in a year. With a groan, I rolled over in the small bed that barely fit inside my studio apartment. With a muffled oof, I found myself on the floor and staring up at a ceiling I didn't recognize. Luckily, it only took me about three seconds for my brain cells to start firing and remember the events of last night.

Instead of untangling myself from the blanket that had somehow wrapped around me like an anaconda, I continued to lay there as I replayed the conversation we'd been having before I must have passed out. Parts of it were a bit foggy, but the majority came clear enough. Humans didn't rule the universe the way we liked to pretend. Honestly, that was probably a good thing since we were well on our way to destroying it with our antics.

I thought about all the mythological monsters I had learned about throughout my life. I wasn't sure if the swirling in my belly meant I was giddy with excitement or if I was feeling trepidation that I might have been in contact with a Banshee or a Cthulhu.

"Are there demons who are Wendigos?" I called out, wondering if they really needed to eat human flesh because... eww. A chuckle, sounding like rocks being ground together, came from the other side of the converted warehouse.

"Perhaps."

I let out a huff. I needed to know, damn it. What was I supposed to do if I came across one? I wasn't going to offer up a finger or a slice of thigh to get it to go away.

I continued to stare up at the drop ceiling tiles until something else occurred to me. "What's your name?"

Rustling of bed sheets sounded before feet hit the cold concrete floor and started walking in the general direction of the kitchen area. I was beginning to think he wasn't going to answer me as I started to smell the rich aroma of coffee brewing. My stomach gave an unhappy gurgling sound as I hoped his hospitality would extend to offering me a cup.

His heavy footsteps began to walk in my direction until he was standing over me, wearing nothing but the pair of gray sweatpants I hadn't been able to wear last night since the legs would have reached my armpits if it wasn't for the crotch. Then there was the waist. I wasn't even going to attempt to roll it enough to make them stay up. He held out a black ceramic mug and I gratefully scrambled to a sitting position, leaning my back against the sofa I had slept on.

"Thanks," I muttered, my nose buried in the heavenly aroma wafting from the coffee. He sat down on the seat with a heavy sigh, and I tried not to think about how his thigh brushed against my shoulder.

"My name is Valen. And we need to have a talk."

"Another one, huh? I'm Kallista, by the way. Please don't call me Kallie." I inwardly shivered at the memories that surfaced as I thought of the nickname my adoptive father had always called me. I once thought it was because he loved me. What a joke. I hated that nickname, and for some reason, every person I met wanted to call me that.

Before he could say anything further to start the new, ominous conversation, though, the sound of a motor came from the direction of the elevator. Valen was on his feet, and seconds later, the door next to the lift was being banged on harshly.

"Open up, Val! I know you're in there!"

Valen let out a growl that was actually kind of adorable and held out his cup for me to hold without looking at me. As soon as I had a tight grasp on it, he stormed over to the door. I could tell it was my boss. The fact that she knew where he lived had jealousy swirling in my gut. I didn't know how I could have forgotten she had taken him into her office last night. It was where she always took her conquests.

Valen swung open the door but didn't back up; he just stood there glaring down at the curvy redhead bombshell with a thunderous expression. "How the fuck did you know where to find me?"

She let out a scoff. Even her scoffs sounded sexy. Damn. "I know you, Val, and I know this city. It doesn't take much to find out information."

"Bullshit, no one knows about my places. Who told you? If it was my assistant, I'll kill him."

I inhaled sharply at the conviction in his tone, at how casually he spoke of ending someone's life.

"Don't be so dramatic. I knew he was here for you. I followed him yesterday, knowing he was going to get your place ready." There was a quiet shuffling of feet before Syn sounded irritated. "You're not going to let me in? We need to finish our conversation from last night."

I peeked over the side of the couch to see Valen standing in front of the door with his arms crossed. "I don't think there's anything more to say on the matter. You already told me everything there is to know." His tone was dismissive, but she either missed it or had chosen to ignore his unspoken words.

"But I didn't have the chance to tell you how to get out of the mate bond."

There was a beat of silence as Valen hesitated. Grudgingly, he took her bait. "How?"

There was a sexy chuckle from Syn. "You have to kill her."

"I'm not going to kill my mate," Valen all but growled the words.

Syn sighed. "It's the only way to break the bond. Until you do, you won't want to be with anyone else. You can choose to, of course, but your mate will always be there, in the back of your mind, like a shadow. The only way to allow yourself to love another is to get rid of her. Permanently."

I watched from my position on the floor as Valen ran his fingers through his long black hair. "Thanks for letting me know. Now, tell me what was going on with those vamps last night, and why you wouldn't let me kill them?"

"Valen, your mate..."

"Leave it, Syn. Tell me about the vamps."

She let out a frustrated sound. "Fine, but this isn't over. Their Master is Powerful. He told me a few months ago that he would protect my club in exchange for allowing them to feed from my girls."

"And if you don't let them?"

The silence was heavy between them as I stared in horror. She was letting those monsters take blood from her employees? Did anyone even know? Did they agree to it?

"Look, Valen, it's a good deal. He's not someone I wish to get into a battle with, and it's not hurting anybody."

"If that's true, then why did you call me, telling me you needed my help? I rode across the country for no reason?"

There was the briefest of hesitations before she spoke. I immediately sensed that whatever she was going to say was going to be a lie or half-truth. "He has been pushing for more, and I panicked. But it's really not that big of a deal. Now that you're here, though, we can spend more time together. Like old times." I couldn't see her face, but I could imagine the seductive smile she must have been wearing based on the tone she was using. She was trying to seduce him.

I started putting the pieces together as I turned to look into Valen's coffee cup, then gave in to temptation and took a big swallow. Syn was in love with Valen, and he only thought of them as friends. It would have been tragic if she weren't encouraging him to kill some woman who was apparently standing in her way. A woman whom Valen wasn't convinced he wanted to keep or not. Poor girl.

"Sure, we can have lunch sometime." It sounded like a brush-off to me, but Syn clapped her hands in excitement.

"Wonderful! Let's make it tomorrow. I can see you're not in the mood for company right now, so I guess I'll go..." Her voice trailed off as if waiting for Valen to change his mind and welcome her inside. When he didn't, she let out a low hum. "Oh! Before I go, I need to know what you did with the girl last night. I went by her shitty little apartment this morning, but she wasn't there. I need to turn her over to the Master."

Valen let out a menacing sound that even had me cowering back, and I wasn't even in front of him. "Why the fuck would you do that, Syn?"

"Because I had to make amends for what you did to his second in command, Valen," she snapped back. "You don't fuck around with this guy. He wants the girl, so he's going to get the girl."

As quietly as possible, I set the coffee down on the floor, then I scouted around to the end of the couch furthest from the doorway, hoping that Syn wouldn't look in and see me lurking in his home. I wrapped my arms around my knees and buried my face against my legs. No matter what I did or how far I ran, I could never get away from people trying to hurt me or give me away to someone I didn't want. I sat quietly, with tears burning hotly behind my eyelids as I waited for Valen to give me up.

"This isn't you, Syn. The woman I knew would never sacrifice a young woman to protect herself. I don't know where the Syn I knew went, but she sure as fuck isn't here. Go back to the vamp Master and tell him to fuck right the hell off. He's getting no one." With those parting words, Valen slammed and locked the door. Syn banged on the door once, pleading with Valen to open back up and listen to her before I could hear the elevator motor start to run as the lift lowered back down to the ground level.

I didn't move from my spot as I heard the heavy footsteps come towards me and stop right in front of where I had curled into myself. I took several deep breaths until I was sure the tears that threatened to fall had dried up. My face was probably a blotchy red from being so upset, but at least I wasn't crying.

I brought my head up to face Valen, surprised to see that he was hunched in front of me. "Hi," I said weakly, attempting to smile but failing miserably.

"Hey," Valen rumbled, studying me as if attempting to figure out a complex puzzle. "I'm guessing you heard all that?"

I could only nod, still a part of me expecting him to walk me to the door and send me on my way with Syn to an unknown future where I became vampire chow, or worse. It was the second time in twenty-four hours I was beginning to think that perhaps I should have stayed with my parents instead of running away.

"I'm not going to let the vamps get you, okay? I'll protect you from everyone, even Syn. I swear it."

I blinked up at him, my eyes suddenly watering all over again. "Why?" I swallowed through the lump in my throat. "Why would you protect me?"

I watched as he carefully withdrew my arm from the tight grip I had on my legs and straightened it. With confusion, I stared down as he held his own next to mine. With the two wrists held side by side, there was no mistaking that the symbol branding both of us was identical.

"Because you are my fated mate, Kallista."

CHAPTER 8

At Valen's words, I jerked my arm from his hold and scooted sideways in an effort to get as far away from him as I could. I kept going until I no longer felt the couch at my back and scrambled to my hands and knees. I knew I was likely flashing him my bare ass since I hadn't wanted to put my worn panties back on after my shower last night, but all I cared about at the moment were the words that replayed over in my mind. *"You have to kill her."*

Valen hadn't said he would, but he had also wanted to know how to stop the mating process, or whatever the hell it was. He didn't want me. Or he didn't want any mate at all, but the end was the same. Valen didn't want a mate, and the only way to get rid of one was to kill her. To kill *me*.

"Stay away from me!" I held up my hands after I made it unsteadily to my feet. I backed away quickly, heading toward the only place in the whole nearly empty loft that might hold a weapon. I edged around the counter, keeping my eyes on him the entire time as my chest heaved. He stood silently, his arms crossed over his chest and his face carefully blank. Damn him. How could my potential murderer stand there looking so damn sexy in a pair of low-slung sweatpants, his hair hanging around his face? He made me think of a street fighter with those muscles on full display. If this were a few hundred years ago, he would look like a knight.

I chanced breaking eye contact to look into the first drawer I reached, yanking it open, only to see that it was empty inside. Fuck. I darted my eyes back up to see he hadn't moved a muscle, and his breathing was still slow and steady. I could have sworn, though, that his eyes held a glint of amusement.

The next drawer held a plastic spatula and spoon, the next a few eating utensils, and finally, in the fourth drawer, I found a set of wickedly sharp-looking kitchen knives. I took out the largest carving knife and held it in front of me, pointing the tip in his direction.

"I won't be murdered easily," I promised, lifting my chin in a false show of confidence. There was no way I would be able to win a fight against this man. I tightened my grip on the knife, hoping to still the visible trembling.

He dropped his arms and took a step toward me, any traces of amusement long gone. At his sudden move, my fear spiked. Deep inside me, my insides twisted with terror while my heart raced out of control. I squeezed my eyes shut and tried to steady my breathing, but it didn't help. I soon felt the trembling of the floor under my bare feet. As hard as I tried to control my fear, to stop what I knew would happen if I couldn't, the tremors grew stronger. I found myself in a loop of being afraid for my life and sheer fright of what I was capable of, each emotion amping my ability for destruction.

I let out a whimper, fear for what I was causing overriding my fear of Valen at the moment. Suddenly, strong arms wrapped around me, tugging me into the broad chest I had been admiring just a few short minutes ago. The warmth and comfort of his embrace began to calm my racing heartbeat. As he soothed my frayed nerves, the tremors of the building slowed to a stop.

Valen was speaking in low tones I could barely make out through the rushing of blood in my head. It wasn't until my breaths were slow and steady that I noticed I had subconsciously matched my breathing to his. Still, he just continued to patiently murmur in my ear with his deep, gravelly voice.

"You're okay, Kallista. I've got you. No one is going to hurt you. I swear it on my life. You're okay."

The low rumbling soothed me more than anything else ever had. "I'm sorry," I muttered against the warm, bronzed skin of his chest.

"Don't be sorry. I get it. You were frightened, and you had every right to be after what you heard. But, Kallista?" He paused, waiting, and I gave him what I knew he wanted. I pulled my face away from his chest and blinked my tears away so I could look up at him. "I will never hurt you. I won't let anyone else hurt you, either. Okay? I swear it."

I studied his expression, looking into his emerald eyes, and could only detect sincerity there. "But you don't want a mate."

He stayed silent for a long moment as he took me in. Finally, he spoke. "I never wanted to be close to anyone, Kallista. I have spent my entire existence trying to stay as far away from humans as I could. I'm dangerous. I destroy lives, sometimes without even meaning to. Hearing that I have a fated mate I never even knew was possible to have..." He stepped away from me, and I immediately felt the loss of his warmth and strength. I watched him warily as he ran his hands through his long hair and looked down at the gray cement countertop.

Finally, he looked back at me, skimming his gaze over every inch of my body. His perusal left me with the sensation of having his hands touching me, gliding over my skin, grazing all my intimate areas, and making me feel heated flutters low in my belly I had never felt before.

"I'm scared, Kallista. I could hurt you, and that would finally destroy the last shred of humanity I have left inside of me."

I wanted to reach out and touch him. There was something about seeing his raw honesty as he left himself vulnerable that made me want to wrap my arms around him and show him he was wrong. I looked down at the knife in my hand. He had comforted me even after I held a weapon and threatened him. I didn't need anyone to tell me he was a good man; his actions had shown me since the beginning. I didn't know his story, but he was full of honor and kindness.

"I can hurt people, too," I whispered as I stared at my reflection in the carving knife. "I've scared my parents badly enough that they thought I was a danger to myself and everyone around me. I can destroy, too." I set the knife gently down on the counter and turned to face him. "I'm scared of what I am."

He looked at me, tilting his head to the side as he studied me. "What are you?"

I shrugged my shoulders and held my hands out at my sides before letting them drop again. "I don't know. I was adopted as a baby. I just know there's something inside of me. Something... dark."

I shivered at the thought I hadn't spoken out loud before. My parents had done an excellent job of breaking my love of darkness. For so long, I had believed the darkness, the shadows, to be comforting. The darkness was my friend. When I started showing signs of being dangerous, of evil living inside of me, my mother had done everything she could to 'fix' me. I came to fear the dark instead.

"Hey," Valen's fingers came to my chin and pushed gently, lifting my face up to meet his gaze. "There's no way you are dark. I have seen some of the worst beings on Earth, and you are not one of them." He grinned, but it quickly faded as his lips turned down. He studied me with a frown. "When you became scared, and the floor started shaking, you squeezed your eyes shut. But I could have sworn your eyes had changed."

With shame, I closed my eyes and turned my head away as far as I could without him actually letting me go.

"Kallista." At his unspoken demand, I glanced back at him. "Tell me."

I waited a beat as I tried to figure out how to say the words. "My eyes..." I swallowed hard, then let the truth spill from me. "When I get upset, my eyes change to black. If I can't get control of my emotions, the room will shake," I whispered. "One time, I made the ceiling break into pieces. It almost killed my mom." *And the priest they brought in to perform the exorcism*, but I couldn't bring myself to admit that part. "My parents believe I am possessed by a demon," I admitted, shame and agony filling every part of me.

Instead of being repulsed by me or even scared the way I would have expected, Valen started chuckling. Then he started laughing so hard he had to grip the edge of the counter to keep himself from falling over. I was shocked into numb silence, my jaw hanging open as I watched him lose his mind.

As he continued to laugh, I began to frown, and then I crossed my arms with a huff. "I don't see what's so funny," I muttered.

Valen finally straightened up with one arm wrapped around his ribs as if he'd given himself a stitch in his side from laughing so hard. He swiped his thumb under one eye and gave me a grin. "No, I don't suppose you would."

Without saying another word, Valen suddenly began to change.

Before my eyes, his bronze skin tone grew slightly darker, a little grayer. Horns suddenly grew from his head through the dark hair, wisps of shadows swirling around them. Giant wings that resembled those of a bat appeared behind him, a little taller than he was and touching the floor at his bare feet. Those, too, had shadows swirling around every inch of them. They were solid; I could see that, but at the same time, it was as if they *were* the shadows. Insubstantial, yet... not.

"Valen?" I breathed his name in wonder at the sight. Perhaps I should have been screaming and running away in terror. But after the way he cared for me and the gentle way he'd held me, I had no room in me to be scared of him. Instead, I was fascinated as I itched to reach out and touch the shadows. He was my every girlish fantasy, every thought I'd had as I stared into the darkened closet when I was five years old. I had a fleeting sense of sadness that he was only now coming to me and hadn't been there to save me from my childhood the way I had prayed for.

It wasn't until my wondering gaze finally made it back to his face that I gasped and took a step back. It wasn't from fear, just shock. "Your eyes..."

"Do I scare you, Kallista?" He growled low, a menacing tone that made shivers run down my spine, but not from fear.

"No." I shook my head slowly without losing eye contact. "Your eyes, they look just like mine do when I..." I swallowed hard and tilted my head. I was suddenly scared to know the answer because I had spent my entire life being told I was one thing, and now the truth was finally in front of me. And from what I was looking at, my mother had been right all along. "What are you, Valen?"

"What do you think I am?" He took a step toward me. Movement from the corner of my eye had me looking down to see a thin, whip-like tail move back and forth. It had a small, pointed end, almost like a spade. Just like the horns and wings, it was made of those same shadows. I had a feeling that all he would have to do was will them away, and every part of him would just go back to normal.

"You're a demon, aren't you?"

"Very good, little girl," he said in an almost mocking tone. "You know that you are, too. Right?"

I shook my head, then nodded. Then I shook it again before shrugging helplessly. "I don't know."

In an instant, the same Valen I had met the night before was back. All the proof that he was something other than just a man was gone from sight. I blinked as my mind tried to process all the new information over the last few minutes. I was tempted to ask him to bring back the shadows but squeezed my hands into fists instead.

"I think that you are, at the very least, part demon. Either your birth mother or biological father was a full demon. It makes sense."

I shook my head, denying it even if I could feel in my heart that he was right. "Why is that what makes sense?"

"You can make the Earth tremble. Your eyes change when your demon is close to the surface." He stepped closer. "We are mates."

"I'm a mate you don't even want," I shot back, still hurt over his earlier words.

He grunted, not denying it. A white-hot pain bloomed in my chest, and I had to work hard not to show any outward signs. I fought not to bring my hand up to rub there. Instead, I turned away from him and walked back over to the couch. I picked up the blanket from the floor and began to fold it. Despite everything I had learned so far that morning, nothing had changed.

"I need to get back to my apartment."

Valen's low words, gritted between clenched teeth, had goose-bumps rising on my arms. "You aren't going anywhere."

Chapter 9

Kallista

"Excuse me?" I dropped the blanket and looked up to take in the angry expression of the man across the room. No, the *demon*. Surprisingly, he didn't frighten me, but a small, tiny part of me wondered if he would pull out the wings and horns if he got angry enough. Idly, I shook off the thought and crossed my arms. "Why do you get a say in what I do?" The words, *You don't even want me as your mate*, hung silent and heavy between us

He was across the room and within touching distance with just a few of his ridiculously long strides. "I saved you from three very pissed off vampires last night. Do you think I want you to walk out that door just to end up with them again?" he snarled down at me.

I scoffed, even though I knew he was right. "Way to make it all about you, big guy. I thought this was my life we were discussing, not yours?"

He ran a frustrated hand through his hair. I noticed he did that a lot when he was upset and tried not to think about how sexy he looked doing it. "That's not what I meant," he glowered down at me. He dropped his hand and took another step closer. "You're in danger, and you fucking well know it. The safest place for you is here, with me, so that I can keep an eye on you."

My mouth dropped open. "I'm not a helpless baby! You don't have to watch me. Besides, I highly doubt it's so safe here with you, considering everyone seems to know where you live."

"Syn won't tell the Master," he snarled, but I got the impression his snarl wasn't directed at me. I had a feeling it was at the thought of Syn betraying him that had that look on his face. I cocked an eyebrow, not caring if I poked the bear.

"You sure about that? She seemed pretty determined to get rid of me. I wonder why that is?" I was taunting him, but I didn't care. I wanted to push him to see how far he would go to defend her. A petty jealousy was simmering inside my gut. Ever since I saw them greet each other the night before and watched them disappear together into her office, knowing what kind of shenanigans she got up to in there, I had been positively green.

A look of confusion flashed across his features before waving my words away as inconsequential. It made me deliriously happy that he didn't seem to notice her crush on him, while at the same time, I wanted to call him an obtuse dumbass. "She would never give anyone my location."

"But she would give me away in a heartbeat," I insisted. I could tell he wanted to argue that point, but she had already gone looking for me at my apartment for that very reason. Which meant he was right, damn it. I couldn't go home.

"Your apartment isn't safe. Every vampire in the city will be on the lookout for you."

"Perhaps. That's why I should get my things and leave the state before anyone is the wiser. I can just go somewhere and start over new. I've done it before, and I could do it again."

"I won't allow you to put yourself in danger!" His words were practically roared in my face, and that was when I realized that we were toe to toe and nearly nose to nose. Both of us were breathing hard, our chests rising and falling in almost perfect sync.

"Aw, pookie bear, we're having our first fight!" I smirked up at him and then turned to walk away. I needed to gather what few belongings I had and make a plan for my escape out of the city. Before I could take a full step, my arm was grabbed, and he tugged me around, my hands landing against his broad chest. His wide, warm, *bare* chest. Damn, what I wouldn't give for a chance to be able to explore all the dips and valleys his muscles provided.

"I said I would keep you safe and always keep a promise, *mate*." With those words hanging between us, his face descended, coming closer until his lips hovered over mine in an almost caress. "And, babe?"

My voice was nothing but a breathy ghost of a whisper as I stared into his brilliant green eyes, nearly eclipsed by his widened pupils. "Yes?"

"Don't ever call me pookie bear again."

In a heartbeat, he was gone, just the warmth of his breath still hovering over my lips. With wide eyes, I stared at his retreating back as he entered the bathroom, firmly shutting the door behind him. A moment later, I heard the shower turn on. With a huff, I dropped onto the small couch, my fingers drifting over my mouth as the memory of him so close to actually kissing me replayed on repeat in my mind. Did I want him to? I closed my eyes and dropped my head back against the cushion with a groan. Of course, I wanted him to. I had been drawn to him at first sight before I even knew who or what he was. Even knowing that he didn't want me in his life didn't stop the need from coursing through me.

I had already fixed myself another cup of coffee before Valen finally emerged from the bathroom, a cloud of steam wafting out with him. I sipped the cup of hot coffee as my eyes followed him to the corner where his bed was. He had obviously forgotten to take a change of clothes with him when he'd decided to leave me hanging on the cusp of receiving my first real kiss—the jerk. I couldn't regret the sight of him wrapped in nothing but a low slung towel, though.

He glanced back at me as he rustled through his bag. I watched as he withdrew a pair of black jeans and a black T-shirt. Typical. It was the same thing he wore the night before. If I had to guess, it was all he ever wore. I glanced up from admiring the way his muscles bunched and flexed as he moved to see him looking at me with one eyebrow raised. My face flamed hot at being caught ogling his body. Before I could apologize, his hands went to the knot of the towel at his waist, and with a single flick of his wrist, the towel dropped to the floor, baring every glorious inch of him.

With an embarrassing squeak, I jerked my head away until I was facing the wall. At the sound of his deep chuckle, my face grew hotter, and it took all my control not to lob my hot cup of coffee at his arrogant head. I might have if I didn't want to waste a second cup.

Holy shit, I wished I had gotten a better look. The brief view I did have wasn't enough to satisfy my curiosity, but it would live rent free in my brain for the rest of my life.

The heavy tread of his motorcycle boots was loud as he walked toward me, but I refused to look up. Instead, I kept my eyes glued to my rapidly cooling coffee.

"Is there anything in particular you want me to get from your apartment?"

His question had me jerking my head up so fast I felt a twinge of pain. "You're going to my apartment?" I asked, the shock I felt clear in my tone.

"Well, if you're okay with wearing nothing but my T-shirts and flashing me your pussy while crawling on the floor, I won't bother."

My mouth gaped open at his audacity. Then my eyes narrowed into slits. "I did *not* flash my vagina."

He simply stared at me with an exasperated, *are you kidding me?* expression. "Babe," he drawled.

I spluttered. "I did *not*."

"Okay, you didn't. Now, is there anything in particular you want me to grab?"

"I didn't," I insisted stubbornly, even though I specifically remember crawling away from him when I got freaked out. I totally flashed my, err, pussy at him. *Damn.* I sighed. "Can you just bring everything?"

He snorted and then pointed in the direction of the lift. "You do know I ride a Harley-Davidson, not a U-Haul, right?"

I just smiled ruefully. "Don't worry. Everything will fit." He looked doubtful but seemed done with the conversation.

"I'll bring food back. If I can fit it on my bike somewhere," he muttered. He turned and started walking toward the big freight elevator as I sat staring into my cold coffee and rolling my eyes. "Don't leave this loft, Kallista. I mean it. No one can get in without the code, even if they find out where you are. You're safe as long as you are inside this building. Got it?"

"Don't worry, I have no desire to become vampire chow."

"Good girl." Why did those two words make me feel all squirmy inside? I would have to take it out and examine it later. Much later. "Be back soon, babe. Keep being good while I'm gone."

With those parting words, the lift slowly began to lower while my temperature grew hotter. I've read one too many romance novels to not be asking myself what my reward would be. Or even, *what would be my punishment?* I stood up and headed straight for the shower as I reminded myself over and over that he didn't want me. I wasn't sure that the reminder was going to help stop my growing infatuation with the man.

Chapter 10

Valen

I wasn't expecting much as I approached the small apartment Kallista had been calling home. Between the comment made by Syn and Kallista herself telling me she didn't have many belongings, I figured there would be maybe a couple of drawers full of clothing. Maybe a few of the momentos that humans liked to collect. What I hadn't been prepared for at all was seeing her door practically hanging off the hinges.

I shoved the door open wider to gain access. The broken door creaked ominously, and I waited for it to fall to the ground as I stepped around it. Surprisingly, the flimsy wood held on. Inside was a mess of broken furniture and ripped fabric. It was difficult to tell what was what from the way it was all tangled together in scraps of colors.

"Hey, bitch! You need to pay for this damage!"

The sound of someone stomping down the hallway outside the second floor apartment had me reaching for the gun in the holster at my back. I stood to the side of the doorway out of sight, waiting for him to walk through.

"Hey! Did you hear me, cu-"

My hand was wrapped around his meaty throat before he could get another insult out. "Who the fuck are you?" I growled into his round, shiny face. He smelled of sweat and beer, and the stains on his Hawaiin shirt told of his penchant for Cheetos and lack of hygiene.

"I'm Bob, I-I own the place," he garbled out from the pressure I was putting on his windpipe.

"Did you see who did this?"

He tried to shake his head, his sagging jowls wobbling back and forth with his jerky movements. "No. Someone called down a complaint of noise. When I saw the broken door, I waited until she got home," he wheezed out. I let him go and wiped my hand on my jeans, needing to get the sticky feel of sweat off me.

"Someone has to pay for the damages," he whined as he coughed while leaning his heavy weight against the wall. He eyed me warily as he rubbed at his reddened neck.

I pulled the wallet out of my back pocket and opened it. His greedy eyes lit up at the sight of cold, hard cash in front of him. I peeled two one hundred dollar bills off the stack and held them out toward him with the bills between two fingers. As he reached for the money, I pulled my hand back.

"No one saw who it was?"

He swallowed hard, his eyes not leaving the bills as I slowly waved the cash in front of his face. "I might have looked outside and seen two guys dressed a lot like you. It was still dark, but I'm pretty sure one was blond. The other had short dark hair. Neither one was as big as you, though. You're pretty fuckin' big, ya know?"

His description matched that of the vamps from the night before. I held my hand out and let him snatch the money before quickly tucking it away in his pocket.

"I don't want any trouble around here." He squared back his

shoulders, suddenly full of bravado again now that he'd made some cash. "Tell the girl she ain't welcome back here." His sudden bravery almost made me smile. Guys like this were so predictable. He owned the place, so he liked to throw his weight around, making demands and trying to make his tenants feel inferior.

"She won't be back." I turned my back to him, taking another look around at the tiny, trashed apartment. There was a small kitchenette, a bed in the corner, and an open door next to the kitchen, which was likely the bathroom. From what I could see, nothing was salvageable.

"She still owes rent for this month." I turned back to see the short, paunchy man with double chins staring around the apartment. I could almost see him sizing up everything inside that he might be able to sell for even the smallest profit.

"How much does she owe?" I asked, not giving a shit but not wanting this greedy asshole to have a single extra penny he didn't deserve. He obviously provided the bare minimum to his renters. The flimsy door that was hardly more than cardboard was proof of that. At any time, someone could have easily kicked it in and robbed Kallista blind. If she had been at home, she would have been virtually defenseless against a home invasion.

"Three hundred." He paused. "If you don't clean this up, it's going to cost a cleaning fee, too."

I pulled my wallet back out of my pocket and picked off another five crisp one hundred dollar bills. "You can have this and one more if you can tell me anything else about the guys who trashed her place."

His wide eyes darted toward the door, and his gulp was audible. When he looked back at the money, it seemed he had made up his mind. "I hear they are a gang that lives on the other side of town. A whole bunch of them live in a big fancy house. Kinda like a big frat house or something. I've never seen their leader. I hear he's a real ugly son of a bitch, though." His laugh was obnoxious, nervous, and high-pitched.

"Where, exactly, is this frat house?"

I allowed him to snatch the money and stuff it into his drooping trousers, which were hanging dangerously low on his non-existent hips. I averted my eyes, not wanting to see what would be exposed if they managed to slide down his flat ass.

"I hear it's over on Buchanon, about a block from the high school."

I nodded once and peeled off two more bills before tucking them into the pocket of his stained floral shirt. I patted his chest roughly. "No one knows I was here, and no one knows anything about the girl." I patted him harder, hard enough to make him wince. "Do we have an understanding, Bob?" He nodded emphatically. "Good. You can come back in ten minutes to start cleaning."

With that settled, I turned back once again, internally sighing. I had no idea where to even begin trying to figure out if there was anything salvageable in the mess. As soon as I heard his footsteps retreating, I stepped forward and began picking up different scraps of material before tossing them to the side. It seemed the vampires did a good job destroying everything they touched. If their goal was to send a message, they succeeded. I wouldn't allow this to serve the other intended purpose, though. She wouldn't be frightened because I would make sure she knew she was safe. With me.

It took me less than the allotted ten minutes to figure out that pretty much nothing was left intact. Instead of gathering the cut-up clothing, I looked at the tags of the destroyed garments, committing the sizes to memory. I was down the metal stairs and straddling my bike before the owner stuck his head out of his office.

The ride across the city was short and I took notice of the different boutiques as I passed the more upscale shopping district. As I got closer to the side of town where the vampire nest was, I noticed it continued to grow more dilapidated. The buildings showed more neglect and offices closed completely with boarded up windows. Entire strips of store fronts were empty.

Once I hit the street where the nest was said to be, I slowed down, looking for the fancy house that Bob, the scum-lord, had described. It didn't take long. If the house was indeed the one he said they lived in, it was the only decent house on the entire street. The Master obviously had money, but that wasn't unusual. Supernaturals with longevity tended to have plenty of expendable money. Throughout the years we saved, invested, or the less scrutable ones stole their way into a hefty portfolio. Not that we kept our money in banks. At least, not much of it, even if we managed to get our hands on fake identity papers that would allow us to do such a thing. We also learned how to hide our funds from any government entities.

The house itself was nice enough to be considered a mansion, but the Master didn't seem to care much about the land around it. Weeds were growing untended. The grass, what there was of it, was scraggly, even for the season. I snorted in disgust. If you didn't give a shit to take care of what you owned, you didn't deserve it. The man who was the vampire Master of this shitty nest wasn't someone I would ever be able to respect.

I revved my engine and sped down the street, leaving the mansion behind with the row of shiny cars and motorcycles sitting at the curb. It seemed physical objects were the only things that mattered to these assholes.

With the sizes I had gathered from Kallista's apartment in the back of my mind, I headed back to the boutiques I had passed earlier. I had to swallow back the dread of having to walk inside those stores, knowing that I would stand out like a three-legged mutt at a dog show.

The experience was just as bad as I had feared. When I was done, I tucked the multiple shopping bags away on my bike, thankful as fuck that the whole ordeal was over. I had gained just as much attention as I thought I would. The first store I had stepped into nearly landed me in a squad car when the employee's eyes went wide with terror. I was sure I heard a whimper as the young brunette stepped closer to the phone the moment she saw me.

I had tried to give her a smile and nod, attempting to act casual, but she hadn't been reassured in the least. Before I even had a chance to do more than look around at the shiny, smooth materials covering the anorexic looking mannequins, I turned around and walked back out the door. I offered her a departing greeting, but at the sound of my deep, gravely tone, she looked like she was on the verge of peeing herself.

I walked to the next shop, pleased to see the display in the big window at the storefront looked more realistic with mannequins that had curves. I paused in front of a pretty white sundress with big yellow sunflowers across the skirt. I could easily envision Kallista wearing it while walking along the lakeshore, her hair flowing in the breeze. I had to shake my head to clear it of the scene and pushed the door open.

An older woman with dark hair wrapped in some type of updo on her head walked toward me with one eyebrow raised. She had a small smile on her lips and a glint of amusement in her eyes.

"Can I help you find something, sir?"

It was the first time I could ever remember being called sir. I couldn't help the chuckle that escaped. I cleared my throat to cover the sound. "I want to get that dress in the front window, the one with the yellow flowers. I'll want more clothes, too." I finally looked around the small shop and nodded.

"Your wife will be thrilled. We don't get many men coming in here looking to do the shopping for their ladies."

I opened my mouth to deny our connection, but snapped it shut. Something kept me from correcting her. A part of me warmed at the thought of having a woman to call my own. I had always been alone, never trusting myself around others for longer than a few minutes. That didn't mean I never felt lonely, or even wistful at times. There had been moments when I saw young families together looking happy and wondered what it was like.

"Yes, I want her to have a little of everything." I couldn't deny the truth of those simple words.

I would always be grateful to that woman for her helpfulness and for not throwing me out of the shop at first glance. I would make sure I paid her back for the kindness she didn't have to show. In my very long existence, I had learned how rare it was.

KALLISTA

After cleaning the already fairly tidy kitchen and then making sure the bathroom was as spotless as humanly possible, I turned to the bed Valen had slept in. I took a deep breath and then walked slowly over to the sleeping space. I resisted every urge to lift his sheets to my nose and take in a deep inhale of his scent. That would make me a creeper.

No matter how long I tried to drag it out, it still didn't take me long to straighten up the bed. I left his belongings alone since that would have been an invasion of privacy. Instead, I backed away and then marched over to the couch before dropping down with a huff.

I was bored.

A loud, insistent banging jarred me hard enough to almost have me falling over the edge of the couch. Again. I swiped the hair out of my eyes and ran the back of my hand over my mouth, wiping away the small bit of moisture from the corners. I must have drifted off as I stared up at the ugly tiles on the ceiling that reminded me of an office building.

The sound of the knocking repeated, making my head swivel toward the direction of the smaller door next to the now closed cargo lift. I frowned as my heart sped up a little. No one should have been here, right? Valen promised that nobody knew where he lived. Or, I suppose, he didn't actually live here. He made it sound as if he traveled a lot and didn't stay in one place for long.

I sat up slowly, swinging my bare feet to the ground. On shaky legs, I took slow steps toward the door, trying to stay as quiet as possible. I had no idea who would have been banging on Valen's door. I glanced over at the stove, seeing the time there on the small digital clock. He'd been gone a little over an hour. I must have only been asleep for a few minutes.

"Kallista, I know you're in there." A low, husky chuckle sounded from behind the metal door. "I can hear you."

I frowned harder. I wasn't sure if I should be more disturbed that Syn could hear me through a heavy steel door or that she had come back after Valen had told her to go away. I chose to stay silent.

"You probably heard the conversation earlier, right? I promise, I only have good intentions." There was a long pause as if she were waiting for me to respond or perhaps open the door for her. A heavy sigh sounded before she began again. "Look, the vampires aren't that bad, okay? They will treat you well, I promise. You caught their attention. After the havoc you caused last night, they want reparations. They want you, Kallie."

I grimaced at the nickname I hated. Did she really think I was going to fall for that shit? And how the hell could she even begin to blame me for what had happened? Tiny died last night because one of those guys was a psychotic murderer. That was after he went insane at the smell and taste of my blood. None of that would have happened if those guys hadn't acted like assholes. And she wanted to hand me over to them?

Her tone switched from cajoling as she tried to convince me to fall in line, offering myself up to the vampires. Suddenly, she was irritated.

"Valen's a nice guy, right? He's always been a real sweetheart under all that gruff exterior. It's why I love him so much. I've been the closest person to him for almost three hundred years. I know that's probably hard to imagine, but it's true. He's lived a very long life. We have that in common." There was a brief pause. "What do you have in common with him?"

I looked down at my wrist, at the dark red brand there that matched his perfectly. I wanted to tell her that we were mates, that it was so much more than what she could ever hope to have with him, but instead of saying any of those things, I bit my lip hard enough to sting. She was goading me, trying to make me think there was more between her and Valen than just friendship. But maybe there was. He had never explicitly said they hadn't been intimate together. He had just said they were friends.

I frowned as I went back over our conversations. What had he said about Syn, exactly? I shook my head. I didn't believe for a minute he thought of her in the way she was implying. Nice try to get me to back away from him, though. That was the oldest trick in the book. She was trying to paint a picture that would make me doubt him. If I didn't trust Valen enough to keep me safe, it would be the opportunity Syn needed for me to open the door. Syn would give me to the vampires without hesitation. However, I was sure her goal was more personal when it came to the sexy demon.

"What is the human lifespan, Kallie? Eighty years? Valen has been alive for longer than even I know. Thousands of years, girl. He sees you as nothing more than a small blip in his life. Of course, he's trying to help you; it's what he's always done. It's how we met all those years ago."

There was the muffled sound of her heels clacking as she paced back and forth on the metal floor of the elevator outside the door.

Suddenly, she hit the door one more time, making me jump with the force of it.

"Damn it, Kallista! I promised the vampires they could have you. If you don't go to them, they are going to destroy my business. Do you want more deaths on your hands? All the girls working for me? You already caused Tiny to lose his life. What was it like to see him die right in front of you, knowing you could have prevented it?"

Tears pricked my eyes at her words. I hated the memory flashing through my mind of watching Tiny die. Of course, I didn't want anyone else to die. But did that mean that I was responsible for their lives? I covered my ears with my hands and walked away, no longer caring if she heard my footsteps. I needed to think.

I walked to the bathroom and slammed the door behind me in a fit of anger. I leaned against the small counter, my hands against the edge, bracing me. As I stared into the mirror, I could see through my blurry vision that my eyes were switching from hazel to black, back and forth rapidly. I squeezed them shut and took several deep breaths as I tried to calm myself before I got out of control.

Without looking at myself again, I went straight to the small shower and turned on the spray. I stripped off the T-shirt quickly, dropping it unseeing to the floor, and stepped in without waiting to test the temperature. My heart was still hammering in my chest, but the beating of the water against my back was already starting to soothe my frayed nerves.

Last night, when I showered, it was merely to rinse away the blood and sweat from the attack. There hadn't been any toiletries, so I wasn't able to do much to actually cleanse myself. Now, as I glanced around the stall, I could see it was no longer empty. I picked up the black bottle resting on a shelf and grimaced at the label. I didn't understand how men could use the stuff. An all-in-one shampoo, conditioner, and body wash seemed like a crime against nature. I didn't have much of a choice, though.

I was already dreading the mess my hair was going to be later when I tried to finger comb it out. I thought of Valen's gorgeous black hair and shook my head. Maybe if this stuff could keep his long hair looking so good, it wouldn't destroy mine.

I sniffed the bottle, inhaling the fresh, manly scent, and decided it wasn't all that bad. It wasn't my usual fruity scent, but it smelled good. It smelled like Valen. I poured a generous amount into my palm and began to lather my hair before moving onto my body. It wasn't until I was rinsed off and ready to get out that I realized I walked into the bathroom with no towel.

I turned off the tap and stood there for a long minute as I dripped, debating on what to do. I shivered as I looked down at the discarded tee and let out a long sigh. Without any other options, I picked the shirt up and patted my damp skin. It did little good as my dripping hair just proceeded to saturate me as quickly as I could pat myself down until the tee was as wet as I was.

"What a mess," I muttered to myself as I cracked open the door. I held the tee tight to my breasts as I poked my head out. The large open space was as silent as a tomb, and no sound could be heard from the elevator door, so it seemed Syn had finally taken the hint and left. Remembering her instantly caused her caustic words to flood back in. I had to shake off the hurt and shame they caused me. It wasn't my fault. None of this was my fault.

I walked on tiptoes over toward the bed in the corner, remembering how Valen had dropped his towel to the ground earlier, causing goosebumps of delight to replace the ones from the cold water, making my skin prickle. I spied the towel where I had folded it neatly, laying it on the end of the bed. I really should have hung it back up earlier.

I dropped the sodden T-shirt to the floor and reached out for the towel just as the cargo lift started a mechanical rumbling, lightly vibrating the floor under my feet. I stared with wide eyes at the door, frozen in shock. As the big metal door began to slide open, I squeaked in panic and snatched at the towel.

In seconds, the door was wide open, and Valen sat there straddling the big leather seat of his Harley-Davidson. He hadn't looked up yet as I fumbled with the folded towel, but before I could get it straightened out and wrapped around me, he lifted his head. He sat staring for a long second as I held the crumpled terrycloth to my chest, doing very little to cover my nakedness. A sudden heat flared in his green eyes, making them grow darker as I swallowed convulsively.

He swung one leg over the side of his bike and stood to his full height. He reached into one of his saddlebags, retrieving something, and then slowly, one step at a time, he walked toward me. The distance between the lift and the corner of the loft where the bed was located seemed like a huge chasm, but he crossed to me in what felt like a blink of an eye as I stood frozen.

I felt the icy water dripping down my back, and in the silence between us, I could have sworn I heard it as the water plopped onto the concrete floor beneath my bare feet. The goosebumps that had been on my arms earlier spread to every inch of my body as I kept eye contact with Valen as he stalked closer. My chin lifted, accounting for our height difference, until my neck was bent back at an awkward angle.

He stood towering over me, staring down into my eyes without letting his gaze wander over my naked body. But there was no denying the desire that had flared to life when he first saw me and only grew with every step he had taken closer. I just knew that if he allowed himself, he would have touched me with his large hands and wouldn't have stopped there. At that moment, every part of me wished he would. I could almost feel the brand on my wrist throbbing at his nearness and at the tension that was beating between us like a drum.

Then, without a word spoken between us, Valen dropped what he had been holding in his hand onto the bed and turned around. He began to walk away but paused. Without looking back at me, he snatched the towel from my trembling fingers, leaving me bare to the room, and moved toward the bathroom. His footsteps were much quicker, taking him across the room in a flash, and then the bathroom door was slammed shut.

I let out a frustrated groan as I heard the shower turn on. We were going to be taking a lot of showers if whatever was between us didn't break. I glanced down at the bed to see what he dropped there and saw a bag with the name of a boutique I'd heard of but had never been inside. I'd known I could never afford anything from the upscale store, so I hadn't bothered stepping inside.

I peeked inside the bag, and a smile spread over my face.

CHAPTER 12

VALEN

When I finally left the shower, the water had long since gone cold, yet my body felt as if it were still hot enough to make the water evaporate and fog the room. I had a brief glimpse of her pussy this morning when she had her freak out, but there hadn't been even a second to appreciate the sight when all I had wanted to do was help her. Seeing her standing in front of my bed, dripping water all over the floor, while holding nothing but a wadded up towel that barely covered the front of her gorgeous body? It took all my willpower to walk away instead of throwing her down on that mattress and taking her rough and raw.

After patting myself down, I shoved my damp legs through my pants and tugged until I could get the shit back on. I was starting to get pissed off. I wasn't sure if what I was feeling was directly because of the woman or if the fucking mating bond was screwing with my head. I had gone hundreds, thousands of years without giving in to the need for a woman. My need to be alone far outweighed any compulsion I would have had to have sex with a random female. But now, after taking one look at this little half-human female, I could barely control myself.

"Fuck!" I growled into the mirror, resisting the urge to put my fist through it. I turned to the door and grabbed the knob, flinging the door open hard enough to hear it splinter near the hinges. I could control myself. This was the work of some mystical or mythical force, and I wouldn't allow it to string me along by my dick.

I stomped into the room carrying my heavy boots, ready to toss them by the bed when I stopped dead in my tracks. Kallista was looking at me, startled, from her perch on the couch. She had her hands clasped together in her lap and was wringing them together in a show of nerves. I wasn't sure if it was due to what I had walked in on or if she could sense the turmoil I was experiencing.

As I stood there and stared at her, she gave me a small smile, just the corners of her mouth tipping up ever so slightly as if she were afraid of my reaction, and stood up. It was then I noticed that she was wearing the dress with the big yellow flowers on it. She smoothed her hands over the skirt and tilted her head as she looked back up at me.

"It's beautiful. Thank you so much." Her voice was soft and her smile was shy, hesitant. I wanted to go to her, to take her in my arms and crush her lips with my own. Instead, I grunted in acknowledgment and turned away, but not before I saw her face fall in disappointment.

When I got to the bed, I dropped my boots to the floor with a heavy thud and closed my eyes as a shot of pain punched me in the chest. I had hurt her with my rejection just now, and the thought of it nearly sent me to my knees.

I glanced down, expecting to see the mess I had made earlier. Instead, it was neat and orderly. My bed was made, and my bag was set on the floor beside it. Fuck, she had done that. I looked over to the kitchen, where the few items that had been used earlier were gone, and the sink was empty. Kallista was in a dangerous situation, with vampires out for her, ready to use her for likely more than just her blood, but she cared enough to clean this pathetic place I rarely visited.

I closed my eyes and breathed through my nose as I took in everything I knew about her. It wasn't much, but I was learning that beyond the fright of her own demon living inside her, she was a caring woman. I thought about the years I'd spent in solitude, about how lonely it could be, even if I were trying to protect the world around me. Kallista thought she was a danger to others, but she had no idea what danger truly was.

I strode back over to my motorcycle and reached into the storage compartments to locate the rest of the bags full of clothing I was sure she could use. I had allowed the saleswoman to talk me into buying garments I had no idea women would need. After hauling out the last of the bags, I pulled out the food that had been tucked away, glad to see that it was still somewhat warm.

With my arms full, I stalked back over to the couch and stood there awkwardly.

"I got food. I'm sure you're hungry." At my words, Kallista's stomach let out an angry rumble, and I wanted to kick my own ass again for forgetting to feed her earlier.

"It smells good," she offered quietly, not looking up at me. I wanted to demand she give me her eyes so I could see the colors that I had grown fascinated with. Instead, I dropped the bag of food onto the couch beside her without a word. I turned and placed the packages of clothing on the ground by the wall before taking a seat where I had the last time.

"It's just tacos," I rumbled as she picked up the bag and peered inside. "I didn't know what kind you would like so I bought several different ones. There are salsas, too. Different heat levels." I clamped my teeth shut to stop my rambling as Kallista rummaged through the bag.

"I love anything. I think," she sniffed at a couple of the foil-wrapped tacos. "Except raw onions. For some reason, I love them cooked, but I just can't stand the taste of them raw."

She handed over several of the small foil packages, and I took them, careful not to touch her soft skin. I wasn't sure if she noticed, but her small smile dropped, and she cleared her throat.

"You should probably know that Syn came back a little bit after you left."

That got my attention, and I stopped peeling back the wrapper on the taco I was holding to stare up at the woman fate had decided was mine. The muscles in my jaw tightened as anger flared inside me.

"Did you let her in?" I demanded. She shook her head as she bit delicately into the side of her food. Her soft moan had the rest of my body tightening.

"No. I didn't make a sound, but she knew I was here." She frowned down at her taco, and I hated the sight. "She said she could hear me anyway."

I finished the taco I was holding in three bites as I waited for her to continue. I watched as her tongue darted out to lick a small bit of sauce from the corner of her mouth and fought the urge to be the one to lick her clean.

"She said that she promised me to the vampires and that they swore they would treat me well." She hesitated, and I knew I wouldn't like what she had to say next. "They threatened the rest of the girls from the club if I didn't show up. Syn made it clear that I would be responsible for whatever happens to them if I don't comply."

I slammed my fist into the floor, my entire body vibrating with rage. I was certain there had to be more that Kallista wasn't telling me, but what I had already heard was enough for me to want to destroy Syn. It didn't matter how long I had known her. It was evident that she wasn't the person I thought I knew. A wave of disappointment swept through me at her behavior. She had already been putting her girls at risk by agreeing to let the vamps feed from them.

She hadn't said if anyone had been hurt, but it didn't matter. If they hadn't given consent to be fed from, it was as bad as rape.

"You will not sacrifice yourself," I growled as I stood to my feet, abandoning my uneaten food.

Kallista scrambled to her feet as I strode quickly to my bike. "Where are you going?" Her voice was full of worry, but I couldn't take the time to reassure her. "Valen! Please don't go."

I stopped before hitting the button to lower the lift. I was already straddling the motorcycle and was ready to ride back to the strip club. "Step back, Kallista," I demanded. "Go back and eat your food. There are more bags of clothing for you. Go through them. By the time you're done sorting them, I'll be back. If there is anything you don't like, we can exchange them for something else."

With her hands clutched together in front of her, Kallista did as I said. Her face was full of worry, and she opened and closed her mouth a few times as if she had something she wanted to say before she finally gave a jerky nod and stepped back another foot. I paused once more before pushing the remote button.

"Do not leave this room. I mean it. Don't. Go. Anywhere. And don't let anyone in."

She mouthed the word "okay", but it was too soft to hear. The worry in her expression only increased as she watched the doors close in front of me, sealing me inside the lift before the motor began to whir and the floor began to lower.

As soon as the doors to the outside opened, I started the bike and quickly sped down the street, heading back toward the highway where the remote strip club was located. Syn and I needed to have a long, overdue conversation. Our friendship wasn't going to save her from the mess she had made for herself.

The sun was already beginning to set on the horizon, the air taking on a chill as the shadows lengthened. Thick tree growth took place of warehouses and other buildings. The drive didn't take long before I was pulling into the gravel parking lot that was already beginning to fill up with cars. The bright neon from the sign provided plenty of light over the gravel in flashing reds and pinks.

I pulled right up to the doors, the bouncer giving me a grim nod, obviously remembering me from the night before. I gave a chin lift back in acknowledgment and walked into the dimly lit club. Music was already pounding while a mostly naked girl gyrated against a shiny pole up on the center stage. I stopped and swiveled my head from side to side, looking for Syn. I took in a few steadying breaths to get my anger under control. I would never purposely hurt Syn or any other woman, but I couldn't be sure that my power wouldn't leach out of me without my consent. I had told Kallista I was dangerous. That was why. I couldn't always stop the destruction I was capable of.

"Val, darling!"

Syn's voice was the same sultry purr it always had been, but now I could hear the sickeningly sweet undertones, the ones that beckoned a man to follow. I finally understood what she was. She wasn't a Succubus. The demoness was a Siren. Working in the sex trade was likely the easiest way she had discovered to lure in her prey. I thought it was so she'd have a steady supply of food. In a way, that was still correct. It's just that her food wasn't through sexual energy. She was literally in the business of sucking the life out of men.

Before she could reach me, I turned and stalked toward the door she had led me through the night before. I didn't wait to see if she'd follow; I knew she would. As soon as I pushed through the swinging doors, I turned to the right, heading toward her office. The lights were still dim down the hallway, but the music was, thankfully, a lot quieter.

I shoved the heavy wooden door open and strode in, stopping next to her desk. I ignored the rest of the room as I watched Syn walk in with a smile tipping up the corners of her brightly painted lips. Even though she was smiling I could see the irritation she was trying to hide.

"Eager to be alone, darling?" she asked in a mocking tone as she sauntered over to her drink cabinet and began to pour herself a shot of something clear. I idly wondered if she ever finished the glass of expensive vodka last night after I left.

"Cut the shit, Syn. What the fuck is wrong with you?" It took all my control not to walk over to the woman and knock the small glass out of her hand as she ignored me to fill it a second time.

After downing the second shot, Syn finally turned to face me, her shoulders squared back as if preparing for a fight. Instead of shouting or demanding I leave, she surprised me by simply waving a hand dismissively.

"Always so dramatic with you, Val. You really should let me take some of that tension from your shoulders. I'm rather good at massages, you know."

I strode forward until I was a foot away, making her tip her head back to look at me. "You threatened Kallista."

She scoffed and folded her arms over her chest. "Is that what the little human told you? I did no such thing. I simply told her the truth."

"You told her that if she didn't turn herself over to bloodsucking sociopaths, she would be responsible for the deaths of everyone else."

"Well, yes. It's the truth, is it not?" She cocked her head with a smirk. "No one else has to get hurt, Val."

"No one except Kallista."

"Correct."

"That will happen over my dead body," I growled as I clenched my fists next to my sides. I was ready to ride back over to the mansion I had driven by earlier and slaughter every bloodsucking vampire in the place. I hadn't intended on doing anything to them if they left Syn and the other women alone. But that was before I learned what they had planned. Now that I was aware and knew precisely where they lived, I was more than willing to destroy them all.

"Why are you so determined to protect the human, Valen?"

From her tone, I knew she was baiting me. She knew Kallista was my mate, and she just wanted me to spell it out for her. I wasn't going to play her little game, though. "She has done nothing wrong, Syn. She doesn't deserve this. I promised to protect her, and I will."

"You stupid, stupid man!" She threw up her hands and spun around to pace across the room before coming back to stand toe to toe with me. "You don't need her. I swear to you, you won't even remember her after she's gone."

"I need to know she's alive and safe." My anger was making my tone harsh, while hers was making her sound brittle and desperate.

"Valen," she pleaded, placing her hands on my chest, making my whole body feel cold with revulsion. "Why won't you see? I just need you to give me a chance."

I stepped back out of reach and watched as her jaw ticked with the fury she was unable to mask completely. "It will never happen, Syn. You have always been a friend. But if you continue to push this, if you continue to put your employees at risk, whatever friendship we had will be over."

"You don't want to make an enemy out of me, Val. Not when I had hoped we could one day be so much more," she warned.

I stepped back and turned to move toward the door. I placed my hand on the knob and paused before leaving. "Tell the vampires to back off and leave Kallista alone. She is under my protection, and that will never change."

Without a backward glance, I pushed through the door and headed toward the entrance and my warehouse loft where my mate waited. It didn't escape my notice that there were several vampires standing around the parking lot. Nor did I fail to see the ones situated along the route back.

Chapter 13

Kallista

I wasn't sure how long I stood there staring at the closed door to the lift. My heart felt wrecked. I knew he left because of how angry he was that Syn had shown up unexpectedly to confront me after he told her to back off. But it was the way he left that hurt. I shook my head, knowing that I had no choice. I needed to leave this place. Not just the loft that he had me stashed away in, but the strip club and the city.

I glanced toward the elevator door, knowing that was the way I needed to exit. I was about to turn back toward the couch where the bags that held the clothes he bought me were, when something caught my eye. With tentative steps, I inched closer, trying to determine what it was. Once I was standing over the piece of paper wedged just under the metal door, I realized that Syn must have pushed a note under the door. She just wouldn't give up.

Frustrated at everything, I bent down to retrieve the note, ripping it a little in the process since it was really stuck under the low bottom edge of the door. The note was simple, just her saying she thought I would like my things. I let out a huff because she wasn't wrong. I just hated that she would do anything nice for me at all. I didn't want to be grateful to her.

I looked up at the panel next to the door and bit my lip, contemplating if I wanted to push that button. I doubted it would be a trap, not after all the time that had passed. But nothing could make me trust her after the threats she had already thrown my way. Not to mention her very obvious jealousy when it came to me being in Valen's warehouse apartment, a place she wasn't welcome.

I pushed the button to call the elevator and open the door. I stepped back, holding my breath, then let it out with a relieved sigh once the open space revealed nothing but my backpack. It was the one I had used the last year of high school and one of the only things I took with me when I ran away from home.

I quickly snatched it up and then pushed the button to close the door panel, not wanting the elevator to remain open. The thought of it had a shiver running down my spine. I didn't care for the idea of an open space that I couldn't see into from the sitting area.

Once I had the door closed and my bag in hand, I hurried back over to the couch and placed it down. "Everything better still be inside," I grumbled to myself as I spread the fabric open to reveal what seemed to be a completely untouched bag with my belongings inside. My street clothes were folded neatly on top, exactly the way I had left them.

I dug around underneath to locate my wallet and the keys to my small apartment, not that I planned on going back to that place, ever. At the very bottom were my shoes, a simple pair of flats that I wore daily. They were beginning to look a little worse for wear, but they were my favorite pair, and I was super happy to see them. I didn't know if Valen had included any shoes during his shopping spree, but it wasn't as if I were planning on keeping any of the stuff anyway.

I set my backpack to the side and finally took a long look at all the shopping bags he'd tossed on the floor. I squeezed my fingers together in indecision. I shouldn't look. I wasn't going to keep anything. Then curiosity won out, and my hand darted for the first bag, hauling it into my lap. My fingers met silky fabric, and I gasped at the blouse I pulled out. It was so soft and pretty, exactly what I would have chosen for myself if I'd been able to.

I had a very limited wardrobe back home. From the time I could remember, all my clothing had been chosen for me. Our family had an image to uphold. Literally, everything we did was based on the image we meant to project. I was the good daughter with perfect grades. I was never allowed to get into any kind of trouble, which meant my friends were chosen for me as well. High school was a particularly difficult time in my life.

I hated the friends that I had. Not that they were actually friends. They were just other children with similar families who had similar interests in keeping up appearances for the public. I never spoke to them outside of scheduled outings or family dinners at restaurants. They didn't speak to me at school, which meant I was alone. Anyone else who tried to be my friend was discouraged quickly and quietly. I learned early on to keep my head down and do what was expected of me. When I wasn't studying for my perfect report card, I buried myself in books. Unfortunately, most of those were chosen for me as well. It wasn't that I didn't enjoy the classic stories that appeared on my bookshelf; I just loved getting lost in romance books, relishing in the happily ever afters. I had to be stealthy, but I had learned how to hide one long enough to read it before I had to return the book to the library.

By the time I was done emptying out all the shopping bags, I was surrounded by beautiful colors and fabrics. There were also jeans and regular shirts included as well, which made me sigh in relief. As much as I would love to wear pretty skirts and floral dresses every day, traveling would require clothing that was a bit more sturdy.

My fingers trembled as I folded the jeans to take up the smallest amount of space in my backpack. It hadn't escaped my notice that everything appeared to be perfectly sized. Either the man had an impeccable ability to eyeball a woman's size, or he took notice when he went to my apartment. Either way, I was touched and grateful for his thoughtfulness.

As I chose a few items that would work best to travel in, my mind ran over the words I should say in a thank you note. I hadn't planned to leave one at all, as much of an ungrateful brat that would make me seem. But after seeing what he had done for me, I knew I couldn't do that. I thought of, and discarded, several versions of "thank you, and goodbye" but still hadn't come up with anything that didn't make me cringe.

Finally, I stood up, sliding the straps of my bag over my shoulders, and slipped my feet into my shoes. Walking over to the kitchen, I began to hunt around for a pen and paper. After searching through the few drawers in the small kitchen, I came up empty. I was frustrated as I looked at the time on the stove. I didn't know how long he would be gone, but I knew I needed to start moving if I wanted to get away before he returned.

At the sound of the lift moving, I realized it was already too late. I threw a nervous glance at the smaller elevator next to the lift and contemplated making a run for it. Sure, it was cowardly, but it was probably better to avoid the awkwardness of a goodbye. Unfortunately, my choice was taken from me when the doors slid open.

Valen was already stepping away from his motorcycle, his expression just as angry as it had been before he left. I wondered if he had been able to confront her after all. His steps faltered, then froze as he noticed me. His eyes quickly took in my appearance with the full backpack and the shoes on my feet, then his expression closed off as if he were shutting down all his emotions.

I felt my lower lip tremble but quickly jutted my chin out and squared back my shoulders. Before I could say a word, he began to move forward. My jaw dropped in surprise when he turned his back to me. I had been ready for a fight. The thought that he had already dismissed me from his life hurt more than I could stand. That quickly, he had written me off as a lost cause or someone he had once crossed paths with for a brief time.

It was the beeping of the security control panel next to the door that made me understand what he was doing.

"You can't lock me in!" I protested when the light blinked red twice, and the lift door closed swiftly.

Valen turned back to take me in again, then began to prowl closer. His expression was still shuttered, but his eyes were almost scary, with the intensity shining from deep within their depths.

"Going somewhere?" His tone was raspy, making butterflies dance around wildly in my gut.

I tightened my resolve before replying in a firm voice. "I told you, it's best that I leave."

He cocked his head, ignoring my words, and jerked his chin in the direction of my back. "Where did the bag come from?"

I glanced down at my shoulder, somehow forgetting for a moment that I was even wearing it. I looked back up at him with narrowed eyes. "Apparently, your girlfriend dropped it off earlier when she was threatening me." I grimaced as soon as the words left my mouth. His eyes narrowed a fraction as he took me in. "Sorry, that was uncalled for. I found a note stuck under the door. She must have left it when I went into the bathroom to get away from her."

"That woman is not, and never has been, my girlfriend. She was a friend, one of the only I've had in my life, and now she's not even that anymore."

I dropped my chin, shame for my awful words making me lose some of my stiffness. "I'm sorry I caused you to lose your friend."

His steps ate up the remaining distance between us in a heartbeat. His large, calloused fingers tipped my chin up until I was staring into his deep green eyes. "You are not responsible for any of this, Kallista. You are innocent, stuck in the middle of a war that you shouldn't be a part of but was dragged into by evil men." He studied my face as I blinked up at him with unshed tears swimming in my eyes. "Now, tell me why you were leaving."

Those last words were ominous, and I swallowed hard at the anger brewing in his tone. "It's too dangerous for me to stay."

"You don't think I can take care of you?"

"It's not that! You shouldn't have to keep a woman you barely know safe." I was pleading with him to understand. "I appreciate what you've done for me, the clothes, the warehouse. But it's okay. I'm letting you off the hook now. Thank you for everything," I trailed off in a whisper.

I sniffed as I stared at his chin, unable to bring myself to look into his eyes and see the disappointment there. Or worse, relief. What I wasn't expecting was for him to bend his knees until he was closer to my level and bring his face nearer to mine.

"No."

I gasped. "No?"

"No."

"B-but, I don't understand. You can't tell me no!"

"I can demand to keep my mate safe, and the safest place for my mate is by my side."

His words made my own anger start to rage inside of me. I tried to jerk my chin away from his tight grip, but he held me steady. "You don't want a mate, Valen. You already made it clear that you are a loner, and that's fine. I'd prefer to be alone too, than to be around someone who doesn't want me. I'm letting you off the hook. You're free. Move on with your life, and I'll move on with mine."

His sudden growl had goosebumps rising on my arms.

"Off the hook?"

I nodded as well as I could in his firm grasp.

"You're moving on with your life?"

"Y-yes?" I hadn't intended the word to come out as a question.

"Do I have any say in what I want, or do I just have to take your assumptions for fact?"

I swallowed hard and blinked rapidly, trying to hold back the tears that threatened to fall. An emotion was tightening my chest so hard I was finding it difficult to take in a full breath. It took me a long moment to realize the emotion I was feeling was hope. "You have a say," I whispered brokenly through my clogged throat.

He stood there for a long moment, just taking me in before he finally straightened back up. His posture was rigid, and I got the impression that he was readying himself for rejection.

"I never wanted to be close to anyone because of my past and my fear that I could hurt them unintentionally. I didn't even know that fated mates were a thing because of it. Maybe if I had known more about my own kind, I would have realized what the burning sensation I'd had a little over twenty years ago meant." He paused and studied me for a long beat. "I would have looked for you, Kallista. Because I am learning that even though I wasn't expecting it, and it was a shock to find out, the Fates weren't wrong. You're perfect. For me."

I let out a strangled sob at his words.

"What I want, Mate, is a chance to prove that I am perfect for you, too."

His words sent the small bit of hope I'd felt a moment ago surge through me like a flood. "What changed your mind?" I couldn't help but ask because it was such a change from that morning.

He backed away and ran his fingers through his hair. "There is the pull. I tried to ignore it." I nodded because I felt the pull, too. "But every second I'm around you and get to know you a little bit more, I realize the Fates know what the fuck they are doing. If I were to build the perfect woman for me, she would have your face, your mind, your body, and your heart. But seeing you ready to walk out of my life forever? That felt like a sledgehammer to my soul."

I blinked and wiped a tear that had escaped down my cheek. His expression softened as he took me in.

"Will you give me a chance?"

What else could I do? I nodded.

Chapter 14

I reached for her face, cupping her cheeks. I gently swiped away the tears with my thumbs as I stared down at her with a sense of wonder filling my chest. This was my mate. I could continue to fight it, or I could accept the gift that had been given to me.

"Valen?" She blinked up at me, her bottom lip trembling, making me want to wipe away the insecurities I could read in her eyes. "Will you kiss me?"

I froze and then groaned. Of course I would kiss her. A part of me felt as if I had been waiting my entire existence for this moment. Slowly, I bent my head down until our mouths were a breath apart. I could feel the heat radiating off her lips, and suddenly, I needed to taste her more than I needed my next heartbeat.

I brushed my lips gently across hers, just a soft pressing of flesh against flesh. I felt the plushness of her, the warmth, and needed more. Shifting to get closer, I tilted the angle of my head, allowing our mouths to slide together like two pieces of a puzzle slotting into place. Her hands went to my chest and gripped the cotton of my shirt tightly in her fists.

"More," she breathed.

With a slowness I didn't know I could possess, I pressed closer, sliding first one way and then another, still just a press of lips, but Kallista slid her hands up over my shoulders and onto the back of my neck, tangling her fingers in my hair.

"Kiss me like you mean it, Valen." Her softly spoken demand was enough to finally break me. With a groan, I slid a hand under her ass and the other across the center of her back and lifted her off the floor. Her thighs went around my waist, and her feet hooked together behind my back.

With our height difference erased, I slid my tongue across her bottom lip, tasting her skin for the first time. Every part of me tightened as all I could do was give her the more she had demanded. With a gasp, she parted her lips for me, and like the beast I was, I took full advantage.

I swept my tongue inside, meeting hers and stroking over it with mine. Her whimpers fueled my desire, turning the burning want into a flaming need. If she wanted more, I would provide her with everything I was capable of giving.

We broke apart, gasping for breath, and stared at each other. Her whole body was trembling as we held onto each other tightly. I suddenly realized how hard I was holding her to me and loosened my grip.

"No! Don't stop. I'm not ready to stop yet." Her whimper of denial had me swooping down for another soul shattering kiss. When I pulled away a second time, it was to press kisses to her cheek and neck.

"I will never stop, Mate. I want to kiss every inch of you. I want to taste you everywhere." Now that I had accepted the inevitable, I was ready to fulfill every desire we both had. "I want you. My body is screaming at me to take you and claim you." I nudged the strap of her dress to the side so I could taste her skin there with my tongue. "But my instincts tell me if I do, we will complete the bond. We will be mates forever. Are you ready for that?"

Her entire body tightened up, and her breath caught in her throat. I pressed another kiss to her collarbone, wishing that there was no clothing between us until I realized she had yet to answer. At her silence, I loosened my grip on her again, taking her lack of response as her not being ready for that kind of commitment. I couldn't blame her. As she had pointed out earlier, we barely knew each other. There would be plenty of time for bonding later. I could wait. I'd wait forever.

When I started to slide her down my body, ignoring the throbbing ache in my cock, she suddenly became unfrozen and clawed at my shoulders to get a tighter grip on me and pulled herself back into the position she had just been in. She tightened her legs around me once more, and I groaned at the feel of her heated center pressing firmly against my cock that was being strangled inside my jeans.

"I want that, Valen." Her breathy whisper was filled with longing and promise. I pulled back as far as she would allow me in order to take in her expression.

"Are you sure, baby? There will never be any going back. Once we are bonded..."

"I know." She smiled sadly. "I do want that, more than you can know. I just never thought I would find someone who would want me that way."

My fingers clenched tighter before I caught myself and loosened my grip so I wouldn't hurt her. "We are going to talk about our pasts very soon. For now, though, I just need to own every inch of you as I give you every inch of me." I ground my thick erection into her and watched her eyes grow wider as she took in the unfamiliar sensations. I would bet my immortality that she had never been this close to another man before.

I strode over to the bed, and with our gazes locked on each other, I laid her down on the mattress while climbing over her body, caging her in. Our size difference meant there wasn't a single part of her that I didn't cover with my body. The thought was so erotic, I groaned at the image I knew we portrayed of dominance and submission.

"I'm going to worship every inch of your gorgeous little body." Even I could hear the desperate need barely concealed under the rough growl of my voice. "And then I am going to fuck you, claim you, mate you, until neither one of us can move tomorrow." I punctuated my words with kisses down her neck and to the gentle swell of her chest until I was stopped by the neckline of her dress.

I looked back up at her to see her face flushed with a dazed expression on her face as she took me in.

"Baby, if you want to keep this dress, I need you to help me take it off you. Otherwise, I'm going to leave it in rags on the floor."

Her swallow was audible as she released the tight grip she had on my shoulders. I could see the slight trembling in her fingers as she pointed behind her neck.

"The zipper is back here."

In an attempt to soothe her nerves, I ran my nose over the column of her throat, inhaling her deeply into my lungs. I couldn't resist adding her flavor to the mix, licking a stripe up her neck and up to the sensitive skin behind her ear, where I nipped gently, causing her to shiver and goosebumps to dance across her flesh. All the while, I found the small tab to the zipper, lowering it until the mattress prevented me from lowering it any further.

I sat up abruptly, taking in the sight of a flushed and trembling Kallista. It was a vision I would carry with me forever. My memories of everything else may fade over time, but I knew this one would last. I'd commission the most talented artist to paint it for me and hang it in every home I owned, just to keep the memory as fresh as this moment.

Her surprised gasp made me grin as I flipped her onto her stomach. I needed that zipper down so I could relieve her of the dress she was wearing. With her on her belly, I quickly found the zipper and tugged it the rest of the way down. The material parted, revealing the bare expanse of her smooth back. I didn't know why the thought of my woman walking around my place without undergarments was so arousing, but it certainly had my cock jerking in my pants.

Kallista lay with her face partially buried in the blanket as her breaths came fast and shallow. As I ran my large palm up the center of her bare back, I could feel her entire body shudder and could see the pulse in her neck flutter wildly. I leaned forward, kissing the same path my hand had just taken. I ended back at the spot that was quickly becoming my favorite. I nipped the spot behind her ear again, my lips tipping at the corners at her breathy little moan.

"Do you want me to continue, Mate?"

Kallista twisted her head enough to look me in the eye with a look that was part glare, part pleading when she responded. "Valen, if you don't stop teasing me, I'm going to die, and then I'm going to kill you."

The chuckle that escaped at her words felt rusty and unfamiliar. "Baby, if you think I can't see how nervous you are," I shook my head. "I have a secret for you." My lips brushed over the rim of her ear as I rasped low and deep.

"What's that?" she asked on a shiver.

"It's my first time, too. I'm just as nervous as you are."

With a shocked gasp, she struggled to flip back over until I leaned up on one elbow to allow her space. "Don't mess with me, Valen." Her chest was heaving, the loosened dress pooling halfway around her ribcage and twisting from her struggles. She looked glorious and pissed. I ran a fingertip from her sternum down to where the dress covered her belly. Once I reached the fabric, I hooked my finger and started pulling, my eyes unable to move away from each new inch of pale skin that was revealed.

"Baby, I would never lie to you," I murmured distractedly as I continued to tug the dress until the top of her bare mound was exposed. "I told you how dangerous I am. I have hurt too many people with my anger." I frowned and glanced up at her face to see her look of sympathy. "I've hurt innocents, too."

"But, you'd never hurt me."

The words were said with confidence, not a question, and it made my once dead heart thump wildly inside my chest. "No, Mate. I could never hurt you. Of that, I am more sure than I would ever have thought possible."

With those words coming from the depths of my being, I tugged the dress down her hips. I paused only briefly to take in the sight of her bared to me, from the tops of her shapely thighs up to her delectable breasts. With an almost feral need, I pulled the fabric down her legs and off completely before dropping it to the floor.

Unable to wait another second, I wrenched her legs apart to see the glistening wetness smeared along her inner thighs. She whimpered and shifted restlessly, begging for more without words. With a snarl on my lips, I dove in, lapping up every drop of her arousal. Once there was no more to be found on her skin, I parted her soft lips with my thumbs and licked a path up from her entrance to the top of her clit, tasting what was now only mine for all of eternity.

With a single-minded focus, I licked, nipped, and sucked every part of her cunt until I was drunk on her flavor and fully obsessed with her reactions to my ministrations. With her every whimper and cry for more, I grew harder until I ached with so much pain and need that I was worried that I would release inside my jeans.

I reached down to tug the button on my fly. My straining cock nearly broke the zipper as it fought to be freed. I fisted my naked cock, glad that I hadn't stopped to put on my boxer briefs that morning. I squeezed painfully hard until my vision swam in an effort to stop myself from coming as Kallista's entire body tightened, on the verge of release.

I watched in wonder as my beautiful, unexpected mate writhed and screamed uncontrollably as her pleasure seemed to steal every ounce of her sanity. I licked her gently through her orgasm, waiting until she collapsed back in a boneless heap, panting heavily and staring sightlessly at the ceiling.

I sat up, then slid off the mattress, hurriedly shedding my clothes. Finally, it was time for me to make Kallista mine in all ways.

Chapter 15

Kallista

I lay there as aftershocks wracked my body. I felt electrified as if bolts of lightning lit me up from the inside. Every inch of me felt boneless and yet tense at the same time. I knew the pleasure that had made me delirious with ecstasy was only the beginning.

Valen shifted off the bed while I continued to lie, panting and breathless, as my heart pounded inside of my chest with anticipation. I wanted to look at him, to see him in all his naked glory, but my nerves kept me from taking a peek. I felt foolish for worrying. I knew there was nothing to be scared of, but I'd heard other women talk about sex, and some of their stories had been awful.

There was talk about size, of course, but there had also been stories from the girls in high school about how disappointing sex had been. The women at the strip club, surprisingly, didn't talk about sex much at all. I had wondered if they had become desensitized to the whole act.

Curiosity finally got the better of me after I heard his heavy boots thump to the floor, and I finally lifted my head to look down my naked body to see Valen bent over, shoving his jeans down his thighs. After he lifted each foot, removing the denim completely, he straightened back up and placed a knee on the bed. The angle didn't allow me to catch more than a quick glimpse as he stroked himself.

The look in his eyes is what had me mesmerized, though. The green was fighting with the blackness that seemed to want to take over. It was fascinating to watch both halves of him fighting for dominance.

"Show me," I whispered as I fell into his gaze. I wasn't talking about his nakedness anymore. I needed to see the darkness that lay coiled inside of him, wanting to be set free. I wasn't scared of the dark anymore. As much as my parents tried to force me, as much as I had grown to hate the dark, I craved it from him. He was my light in the dark, the one that I had searched for.

He seemed to intuitively know what I meant because, even though he did remove his hand from his cock, revealing a size that had me swallowing in equal parts anticipation and trepidation, he allowed his demon complete control.

Dark wings swirling with shadows exploded from his back, and horns that curled up and back from the sides of his head appeared. Wisps of shadows danced around his body, and as he lowered himself over me, they seemed to lick playfully at my skin.

I felt movement, then a firm grasp on my thigh as his tail wrapped around my leg and lifted it, pulling my thigh back and widening my legs to allow him to settle his hips firmly against mine. I glanced down my body to see his heavy length settled on top of my mound and swallowed convulsively at the sheer size of him. The magnitude of what we were about to do had another shiver of anticipation racing up my spine.

I opened my thighs wider, welcoming him closer, and wrapped my arms around his back. I traced my fingertips over his wings and watched as he closed those black eyes, relishing my touch.

"Please, Valen. Make me yours."

At my whispered encouragement, Valen growled and shifted, aligning himself with my opening. We both held our breaths as his beautiful cock breached my entrance and slowly sank inside. I was more than ready for him, my wetness allowing him an easy glide forward, though he seemed to be struggling with himself.

"So tight. So hot." His words were guttural, spoken between clenched teeth. With a snarl, he pushed the last few inches fast and hard until our pelvises were flush together, and he threw his head back with a roar. "Mine!"

After a brief pause, he stilled, attempting to gain control. He lowered his head and stared at me, his black gaze fixated on my face. "My mate."

"Yours," I agreed, feeling him pulsing inside me, aching but needing more. So much more.

His lip lifted in another snarl as he withdrew before thrusting forward again, making my entire body jolt with the movement. He hit something inside of me that made liquid fire dance across my nerve endings.

"More," I breathed, desperately clawing at his back. "I need more."

"I'll give you everything and more, Mate."

There were no more slow withdrawals. Instead, Valen thrust hard and deep, jolting me each time until he wrapped an arm under my back, gripping onto my shoulder to hold me in place with one arm. His other hand was fisted next to my head, bracing his body as he knelt above me, giving himself full access to drive into me with each powerful thrust of his hips.

I watched his magnificent physique, each muscle rippling with his movements until I couldn't see anymore, my eyesight going hazy and my ears ringing with the pounding of my heartbeat. It took several moments before I realized the ringing in my ears was from my own screams as I called out his name over and over, sobbing from the unimaginable pleasure.

"Mine. My mate. Mine." Valen's growls filled the room, mingling with my cries. When my body began to stiffen, and that electric tingling feeling began dancing across my nerve endings again, I knew I was about to break apart. I was scared at the overwhelming sensations, not knowing if I would ever be the same again.

I threw back my head, my fingernails scrabbling at his back, needing to anchor myself before I flew apart into a million pieces. At my final scream, I vaguely heard Valen roar, and his hips stuttered in a final thrust before he pressed deep. A warmth unlike anything else filled me to overflowing as I lay there breathless and sobbing.

Warm lips pressed to my face, kissing away my tears and soothing me with softly spoken promises. It took several long moments until I was able to open my eyes again. Valen's handsome face loomed over me with a concerned expression. I gave him a tired, tremulous smile.

"Hi," I whispered huskily, my throat scratchy from overuse.

Valen leaned down and ran his nose along mine, then pressed a gentle kiss on my lips. The kiss turned into a lazy tangling of tongues, a new intimacy blooming between us that hadn't been there before. It was enough to make tears threaten again behind my eyelids. I willed them away, not wanting to appear like an emotional wreck, even though what we had just experienced seemed to destroy me and rebuild me in such a short span of time.

Valen pulled back, but not before dropping another soft kiss on my lips. "Stay right where you are, Mate." He slowly, carefully withdrew his semi-hard cock from my opening, and I did my best to hide my wince as he glided over newly awakened nerve endings.

He quickly climbed off the bed, and I heard him pad into the bathroom. The water turned on in the shower, and then he returned to walk back over to me. In one swift move, he scooped me into his arms and held me firmly against his broad chest.

His wings and horns were gone, and I ran my fingers over his naked back where they had been just a moment before. I was sorry to see them go, but I knew he would show me again whenever I asked. I snuggled my face into his neck and breathed him in. He smelled like leather and spice, with a hint of smoke. I decided it was my new favorite scent.

He carried me into the small shower stall. When I tried to loosen my grip on him so I could slide to my feet, he tightened his hold and tsked at me.

"It's my privilege to care for my mate," he said in his low, gravelly voice, making me melt back into his embrace. I didn't know how he would accomplish his task, but I was here for it. Any time he wanted to take care of me, I was more than willing to let him.

He held me under the hot shower spray, letting the heat soothe my raw nerves. Then, using his 3-in-1 shampoo and body wash, he cleaned away the evidence of our joining. It took several minutes before I noticed his wrist.

At the sight of the changed brand on his wrist, I lifted my own, pulling my arm from where I'd held his back, nearly making him drop me at my sudden movements. He grunted, then readjusted his hold, allowing me to get a good look at my arm.

What was once a dark red brand was now pitch black, the symbol there clearly displaying beautiful swirls and lines. Without me asking, he brought his own wrist to rest next to mine. I ran my gaze back and forth between our brands, marveling at how they were a perfectly matched pair.

"I wonder if it means anything? Like, is it a word? It almost looks ancient." My tone was full of wonder as I studied the markings, unable to get enough of them. I was fascinated by them, especially knowing how deep the meaning was. It was magical, being marked by Fate.

"I don't know," he admitted. "I feel like a fool for keeping myself away from my own kind all this time. If I hadn't, I would have known what it meant when I was marked the first time. I could have looked for you."

I couldn't help but laugh softly at his words. "I was a baby. I'm not sure that you would have wanted to find me back then."

He was silent for a long time. When he spoke again, it was with a serious expression. "I think it's time we get to know each other better. I need to know what your life was like."

I stiffened in his arms before I could control my reaction. He was right; we did need to learn more about each other, but I wasn't sure if I wanted to tell him about my parents. It wasn't a pretty story, and I didn't know how he would react to it.

He ran a soothing hand over my body, attempting to calm me. "I understand if you would rather not tell me about it. But it's probably best if you do. We can wait awhile, though."

I appreciated his words and turned to place a kiss on his jaw. "Thank you," I sighed gratefully. "But you should know. Just in case..." I let my words trail off and shuddered. He should know that I am not safe, and being with me meant he wasn't safe either. Not that I doubted he could take care of himself, but we could be so easily torn apart. Just the thought of it had a heavy weight settling into the pit of my stomach.

Valen reached out and turned the shower off, then grabbed the towel slung over the glass door. He patted me dry as best as he could without setting me down, then draped the towel over me. He carried me out of the bathroom and back over to the bed before tucking me in under the blankets. I watched as he quickly ran the towel over his body, and then I frowned as he tossed the towel to the floor. He slid under the covers, pulling my body snugly against his.

"Don't worry," he chuckled, seeing my disapproving look. "I'll pick it up later. Right now, I need to hold you."

I sighed and rested my head against his shoulder. I didn't know where to begin my story, so I thought of how I used to stare into my closet, knowing that there was nothing to be afraid of—not until later.

Then I started speaking.

Chapter 16

Kallista

"I'm not really sure where to start..." I trailed off as I thought back to the beginnings of my life. There were so many memories, ones I had wanted to forget forever.

"You don't have to tell me everything." He breathed in deeply, taking my scent into his lungs, then kissed the top of my head. "Just the most important things that will help me protect you."

I sighed and forced my limbs to relax, one at a time, not realizing how stiff they had become.

"I didn't know I was adopted. Not until I was close to around eight years old. It was pointed out to me by one of my teachers if you can believe it. Once that seed was planted in my mind, it was fairly easy to tell. My mother, she's blonde and blue eyed. Not that it mattered when I was a kid, but now that I am fully grown, our height difference is obvious, too. She's tall, nearly as tall as my father. He's dark haired like me, but he also has blue eyes. And then there's me—the only one with a darker skin tone and dark eyes. I imagine, based on my features and skin tone, that I am probably full of Native American blood. I thought about having a DNA test done, you know, one of those that you do through the mail? But I was afraid that somehow they would be able to find out."

I was rambling from nervousness, putting off explaining the real issue with my upbringing. I sighed again, then shrugged awkwardly against his side. "I guess I was... odd. I would get upset if my closet door was closed at night. I would lie awake as long as I could and stare into the darkness, hoping that whatever was there, hiding in the dark, would come out." I closed my eyes and thought back to those days before shuddering.

"My mother hated it," I said flatly. "She finally got tired of the way I would beg to have my door closed and have the nightlight off. I could hear my parents argue sometimes. She thought there was something wrong with me. She would blame it on my blood. I didn't know what she meant until later, realizing she thought it had something to do with my birth parents.

"Then, when I was about twelve, I had a bit of a temper tantrum. I can't even remember what I was so upset about, but my eyes changed for the first time. When my mother saw my eyes shift to black, she freaked out and called the priest from our church. She was convinced I was possessed by a demon."

Valen's arms tightened around me, and it was then I realized my whole body was trembling and my breaths were coming out in pants. "Shhh. I've got you, Mate. I'm right here, and nothing is going to hurt you." I let his soothing words wash over me, letting them calm my racing heart.

"The priest seemed eager to do the ceremony." My mouth twisted in a grimace. "Knowing what I know now, there is no way the church had approved what he was planning. I had been so scared. There were candles lit all over the place, and he was wearing these big, dark robes, waving around his hand, and speaking these strange words. I had been forced to lie on my bed and then tied down so I couldn't move. While the priest performed his exorcism, my mother stood back, watching. She didn't do anything to help me; just stared at me as I begged her. It was all too much for my mind. I guess I freaked out."

I squeezed my eyes shut as the terror of the first experience of being tied to my bed filled my gut, making me nauseous. I swallowed back the bile as my fingers clung tightly to Valen, using him as an anchor to keep me from falling deeper into the pit of fear-induced trauma.

"It happened several times throughout the years. The exorcisms were never successful, obviously," I smiled wryly. The smile dropped when I thought about the damage I'd caused. "During the first exorcism, the room started shaking as I lay there screaming. I didn't even know I was doing it; I was too freaked out by the ropes and the yelling."

I remembered the look on my mother's face, the sheer terror that had overtaken her usual expression of hatred as she stood next to the priest, staring down at my body as I thrashed on the bed. I had been struggling to get free, begging her to let me go.

"The walls cracked," I whispered. "Then the ceiling started to break apart. I watched a chunk of the ceiling hit the priest. Then, a piece hit my mother. I remember laying there, scared, as I watched a trail of blood slide down her forehead."

I let out a shuttering breath. "She was convinced I was evil. For years, she had been punishing me. She was convinced that my obsession with the dark was unhealthy. She had been locking me in a closet when my father wasn't home. He was hardly ever there, too busy with work. When he started campaigning, he was gone for days or weeks at a time. That was when she would have me stay in the closet the most. There were times I couldn't tell how many days I had been in there."

Valen had stiffened under me as he listened to my story. I wasn't sure if I was making much sense as the words flowed from me. It was the first time I had spoken them out loud to anyone. His chest rumbled with a growl, and somehow, it felt soothing to hear. It made me believe he cared about young me from the past.

"That was how I became scared of the shadows and darkness." My words came out strangled as they slipped past the lump in my throat.

"What happened after the ceiling collapsed? Not that I give a shit about those monsters, but you were tied to the bed. Did you get hurt?" He sounded as if he wanted to go back in time and save me from that awful day. I ran my hand over his chest, my turn to try to soothe him.

"I wasn't hurt, but the room was a mess. My mother had to confess to my father what she had been up to. He'd been livid. But not at what she was doing, just that she had done it at *home*. It was the day I lost trust in the only other person I thought cared about me. I learned then that the whole reason I was adopted was because my mother couldn't have children, and a politician needed to have a family to appeal to voters. A family man who cared enough to adopt a poor little orphan girl who was left on the doorstep of a firehouse? He would get votes for sure."

I wiped away a tear at the remembered feeling of loss and rejection. I think maybe he did love me in his own way at the beginning, but he became so obsessed with his career. Then, the way his wife would complain about me soured whatever paternal feelings he'd once had. I became a burden, one that had the potential to hurt his image more than help it.

"After that, I did my best to be the perfect daughter. I tried to control my emotions so I wouldn't give them a reason to punish me or worse, call in the priest again. For years, I did everything they wanted, studied what they wanted, and dressed how they wanted. It was awful. I felt like a part of me was dead inside.

"I left home about a year ago. I had been going to the local college, studying political science because that was what they wanted me to study. I was supposed to help my father's career. It was the whole reason I existed in their lives. Things had settled into a pattern of school, campaigns, and standing dutifully at his back next to my mother during speeches. Then, one night, I was attending one of their usual social dinner parties with people who could help him reach his ultimate goal. Between the first and second courses, it was announced that I would be getting married."

Valen's string of vile curses almost made me want to laugh, even though there was nothing funny about it. I had sat there in shocked disbelief as the man sitting next to me casually reached over and took my hand. When I glanced over at him, barely able to keep the incredulity out of my expression, he wasn't even paying attention to me. Instead, he was soaking up all the attention from the other dinner guests with a huge smile on his face, showing off his blindingly white teeth.

"I didn't even know him. I was sure I had seen him at one function or another, but hadn't spoken a word to him until that night when I'd asked him to pass me the rolls. When I confronted my father later that night in his study, he made it clear that it was my duty as his adopted daughter. There was no discussion, no other explanation. I looked my fiance up on my computer later that night and found out he was the son of another politician. Together, they believed that it would forge strong ties between our families, something that would elevate us into American royalty, like the Kennedys.

"I hated every second of it, but I felt I didn't have a choice. My parents paid for everything. My education, my car, my phone. I didn't have a job because my job was to be the future president's daughter. That meant when I wasn't at school, I was by his side at events or at my mother's side doing charity work. When the night before the wedding came... I panicked."

"So you ran."

I laughed bitterly. "I ran. I hadn't spent more than a few hours with the groom since the announcement. We went on a couple of dates for the sole purpose of being seen together in public. We had never so much as held hands, let alone kiss. Suddenly, I was supposed to marry him? Move in together and be intimate? I couldn't do it," I finished in a ragged whisper.

My mother had laid out my life for me that night. She made it clear that nothing was to change. I was to continue to support my father, and once I completed my schooling, I was to start working for him full-time. My job as a wife was to appear with my husband, who was just starting out in his own political career.

"But, Mother, I don't want to do this!" I had cried as I stared at the hideous white dress she had chosen for me to wear. It was a poufy monstrosity that probably weighed twenty pounds and had a train at least ten feet long. "I don't even know him. Please, don't make me do this."

"Shut up, you ungrateful little brat! After everything we've done for you. After everything you put us through." She reached up absently to touch her forehead where the scar had been before my father had paid thousands to have it removed. She straightened back her shoulders and glared at me with all the hatred I knew she felt. "You will do what you're told. Just lay there on your back and take it like a dutiful wife is supposed to. If you're lucky, he will have a mistress or two and only bother you once a month until you produce an heir."

I shook off the memory. After she had left me alone that night, I escaped with a small backpack of clothing and the engagement ring. I pawned the ring in the first shop I came across and used the money to get as far away as I could. It never seemed far enough. Frankly, I was surprised I hadn't been discovered yet. I knew they had to have been searching. I doubted it looked good on my family to have the bride run away while the groom was practically standing at the altar. With their money and connections, I understood how important it was to stay away from cities or places where I might be recognized.

The strip club had seemed like the perfect solution. And it had worked well until vampires came along.

"So, that's what I'm running from. Not only am I scared to face them for running away from my wedding, but I'm terrified of the punishment I will get if they find me. I don't think they'd be satisfied with locking me in a dark closet for a few days this time."

Chapter 17

After spilling my ugly past to Valen, I ended up falling into a fitful sleep. More than once, I was woken up by Valen rubbing my back, trying to soothe me. Though it worked, I would eventually start dreaming about the closet again once I drifted back to sleep. Or the priest standing over my bed, splashing me with holy water while chanting in Latin. Sometime in the early hours of the morning, I finally managed to fall into a deep, dreamless rest.

I woke with a moan on my lips, and my body already on the verge of a satisfying orgasm. All thoughts of my disturbing dreams were forgotten as my back bowed with the pleasure that was centered between my legs. "Valen," I rasped out in a sleep roughened voice. I reached down and grabbed onto his hair, holding him to my pussy. I was probably pulling his hair out by the roots with how hard I tugged, but all he did was groan, making the vibrations send me into orbit.

As I was still shaking, Valen climbed up my body. He had a

wicked gleam in his eyes as he licked his glistening lips. "Are you sore?"

I blinked up at him in a daze. "What?"

Valen moved one of his hands to his shaft, which was thick and shining with fluid at the tip. The head was almost purple as his thumb swept over it, smearing the fluid around. "Are you sore, Mate? I want to fuck you into the mattress until you forget your name. But if you're sore, I will have to mark your pussy from the outside."

I glanced down at myself as if I could see the effects of our mating from the outside, then wiggled my hips a bit. Surprisingly, I felt fine, great even. "I'm not sore," I whispered, a blush creeping over my cheeks and down my neck.

"Good," he grunted. "It's probably a benefit of our mating." He positioned himself at my entrance, his gaze watching his movements with a starved expression as he swiped the head of his cock over my clit. I jolted at the contact, still sensitive from my wake up call.

"What do you mean?" I asked breathlessly, then gasped as he let go of himself and pressed forward slowly. I didn't know if I would ever get used to his size.

He closed his eyes as he slid inside until his hips met mine. Then he opened them and stared down at me with a heated intensity that set my blood to a slow simmer. "I would have to ask someone to be certain, but I believe our mating has many benefits for the both of us." He withdrew slowly as I bit my lip to keep my sounds of satisfaction in. He then slammed forward hard enough to send an electric jolt of pleasure through me. "Increased healing. Matched longevity. Stronger control over our abilities. Stop holding back, Mate."

Then he was pounding into me at such a fast pace it took my breath away. There was no chance I could have held back. My cries were strangled, caught in my throat, but it was impossible to try to keep them in. Soon, I didn't care to try as I became lost in the pleasure.

My broken chant of *"More. More. More."* was met by the slapping of our skin and the grunts and low growls that escaped his chest. With a final snarl of "Mine!" he thrust one last time and held still. The pulsing inside of me and the feel of his hot release filling me had me tipping over into oblivion for the second time that morning.

I must have dozed off again for a minute, because I came to with the feeling of a warm, wet washcloth being gently swiped over my center.

"Good morning," I croaked out as Valen nuzzled the side of my neck. His low chuckle had goosebumps breaking out over my exposed skin, and a delighted shiver ran down my spine. I felt... wonderful. Better than I ever had in my life. A wave of contentment washed over me, and I raised my tired arms to wrap around him as he tossed the washcloth to the floor with a splat. "Thank you," I whispered into his neck.

I had to loosen my grip as he pulled back to stare down at me with warm green eyes. "For what, baby?"

I swallowed as I looked up at him. Feelings I wasn't ready to examine swirled in my chest. "For wanting me." I thought of how he could have rejected me, of how he almost did at the beginning before we got to know each other a little better.

Valen frowned, a crease forming between his brows as he studied me. I wanted to reach up and smooth the line away but held still instead of giving in to my impulse. "It was never a matter of not wanting you. From the moment I sensed your presence in the club, I was drawn to you. I was just scared."

He looked so vulnerable at that moment that I couldn't hold myself back any longer. I lifted my head and placed a kiss on his jaw. "But not anymore?" I asked quietly.

He shook his head and ran his gaze over me again. "No, Kallista. I'm not scared of being close to someone anymore. To you. You are the only one I want to be close to."

I blinked back the sudden moisture that filled my eyes. "That's the nicest thing anyone has ever said to me." My throat felt tight with emotion as that feeling in my chest warmed and grew.

He pulled back from me and sat up on his knees. "Good. Then get up so we can make plans and get something to eat." He smacked the side of my ass as he slid from the bed, making heat coil in my belly and a blush creep along my cheeks again.

I rolled to my side and watched as he pulled on a pair of jeans with no underwear underneath. I watched, fascinated, as he tucked his cock carefully away before sliding the zipper into place. "What do we need to make plans for?" I asked as he dug around in the pile of clothes he bought me. He tossed another pretty sundress onto the bed with a wink. The dress was red this time, with trailing white vines around the hem. It was gorgeous.

"Get dressed, and I'll tell you. If you keep laying there naked, looking like a goddess ready to fuck, I'll take what you're offering, and then we'll never go anywhere."

I seriously contemplated his words for a minute as his hungry gaze swept over me, but when he shook his head and turned away, heading to the kitchen. I sighed and sat up. I held the dress up before deciding that if I was going to be leaving the warehouse loft, I should probably wear undergarments. While he made coffee, I searched through the piles until I found what I needed and slipped them on.

I had the dress over my head and in place when he walked back over to me, holding out a steaming cup of fragrant coffee. I took it gratefully and then presented my back to him. "Do you mind helping me out with the zipper?"

"I'd rather help you out of it."

I grinned into my cup at the words he spoke in his deep tone. I would never get enough of his voice. Once the zipper was in place, I walked over to the small couch and sat down on one end, tucking a leg underneath me. Valen joined me a minute later with his own cup and sat, taking up the rest of the space. One of his large hands rested on my exposed knee, and I almost felt like squealing in delight that this big, gorgeous man—*demon*—chose me.

He took a minute to sip from his cup before meeting my eyes. "We have to decide if we are going to stay and help take care of the vampire issue in this town, or if we are going to let the local vampire leader do his job. Frankly, I vote to leave. It's not our problem. The vampires have Kings and Regionals for a reason. If they can't handle their own business, then the Council is supposed to step in and do it for them."

I nodded my head, not completely understanding everything he was saying but getting the general idea. Vampires had a hierarchy and took care of their own matters. The only thing that bothered me was that they didn't seem to be doing a good job of it. Humans were suffering the consequences.

"What about the girls at the club? They need help now. I'm not sure they can wait for the vampires to figure their shit out."

Valen was silent for a moment, considering my words, which I appreciated. No one had ever listened to me before or took my concerns seriously. "I might know someone I can call to get information about who we can contact. If I can get ahold of the local King or even the Council, then the whole problem will be out of our hands for good."

"And what about me?" I thought about how the vampires were after me specifically. "How do we leave without being stopped by them, or worse, hunted down?"

Valen growled, and the hand he was holding my leg with tightened its grip. "No one who tries to come for you will live to see the dawn."

That was actually a good point I hadn't thought of. If we left during the daylight, then they couldn't stop us. It wouldn't keep them from following after the sun set, but at least we would have a good head start.

I nodded my head slowly. "Okay. I'm good with that plan. As

long as you are able to get the right people involved first to make sure the girls won't be harmed if I leave."

"The only one I care about is you, but I'll make the call," he said with a grunt. He tilted back his head and finished the remains of his coffee before leaning over for a quick kiss on the lips. Then he stood and strode back to the sink and rinsed his cup before setting it aside.

He walked back over to the bed and sat down. I watched as he began to pull on a pair of socks and his boots. He shrugged a clean T-shirt over his head and picked up his leather jacket.

"Why don't you pack your clothes into my bag? Try to fold or roll them as tight as you can. We'll do our best to fit everything in my saddlebags when I get back." He looked over at the piles of colorful women's clothes he bought for me and shook his head. "I wasn't thinking about taking you with me when I bought them. I was only concerned about getting you things you needed."

I set my cup on the floor next to the couch and walked over to him. He was already taller than me by a great deal, but with me barefoot and him in his motorcycle boots, he was even taller. There was no way I'd be able to reach his face, even on my tiptoes.

I placed my hands on his chest and craned my neck back to look up at him. "Be safe while you're gone," I whispered. I wanted to tell him so much more but held my tongue, choosing instead to let him read my emotions through my expression. His eyes softened as he looked down at me. Then he bent down so we were almost at eye level.

"Stay safe, little Mate," he said, then took my mouth with a savage kiss that left me breathless and my mind spinning. Before I could come back to my senses, he was already typing the code into the panel and pressing the button to open the lift. "In case you need it, the code is 9-2-5-1. But don't use it unless it's an emergency, got it?"

"Got it," I replied, still breathless.

He stared at me for another long minute before hitting the

button to close the doors. A second later, the motor for the lift began to vibrate the floor, and he was gone. I glanced around the room at all the clothes and sighed. I wasn't sure if it was possible to get all of these clothes onto his bike. But they were too beautiful to leave behind, so I was going to do my very best to make it happen.

Chapter 18

VALEN

I rode out into the morning sunshine that did little to bring any warmth to the day. The ride was chilly, and I cursed under my breath as I thought of Kallista having to ride on my bike in the cold weather. At least it wasn't the dead of winter. We would have had to find a place to hole up in for the season much closer than I would have been comfortable with.

I drove to a small cafe that wasn't too far away and backed my bike into a parking space near the door. After I turned off the engine, I swung my leg over the side to head inside. I had been eyeing the buildings as I had passed, trying to tell if I was being watched or followed, but hadn't sensed anything. I was still uneasy leaving my mate behind, though. I wanted to order the food so I could get back to her as quickly as possible. Vampires weren't the only threat out there. If Syn showed herself again, I would be tempted to rip her pretty head off her shoulders. I wasn't sure if she would regenerate the way I would, and didn't give a shit. I had warned her. Repeatedly. If she continued to cause trouble, it would mean her end.

I pushed open the door, the bells above it jingling, announcing my arrival. As I strode to the counter, a waitress in a T-shirt with the cafe logo printed on it walked past with her arms loaded with plates. The food looked and smelled delicious, and I felt my stomach rumble angrily. It reminded me that all I had fed my mate yesterday were a couple of tacos, and I wanted to curse. I would have to do better about looking out for her welfare.

"I'll be right with you, sweetie. Take a seat anywhere." It was on the tip of my tongue to correct her. I was mated, and no one should be calling me by a pet name, but I held my words back. She meant no harm. Besides, if I were a human, she looked old enough to be my grandmother.

I slid onto a barstool and snatched a menu out of the holder in front of me. I thought about what Kallista might want to eat and decided to get a little of everything. We would need to fuel up. Especially if I ended up fucking her again before we left. I grinned to myself as I thought the odds were pretty fucking good that I wouldn't be able to keep my hands and cock off of her.

"Alright, young man, what can I get for you?" The woman appeared in front of me with a smile, and her pen was poised against her pad, which had several small grease stains on it. I rattled off my order, figuring I had probably gone overboard, when her eyes widened, and she had to flip the page to continue writing.

"Will that be for here or to go?" She asked as she peered up at me with wide eyes.

"To go, ma'am. Thank you."

"You got it, sweetie. It's, uh, going to be a few minutes. Would you like a cup of coffee while you wait? It's on the house."

I nodded and gave her my thanks. Once she handed me the steaming cup of black coffee I stood up. "I'm going to step outside to make a phone call. I'll be back in before the food is done."

"You got it, hun." She waved me off with a smile, then glanced down at her pad as she walked to the kitchen window.

I carried the cup outside with me and leaned against my bike as I pulled the phone out of my jacket pocket with one hand. I had very few contacts, but one I did have would be able to get me the information I needed.

The phone rang several times before a gruff voice answered angrily. "What the fuck do you want, asshole?"

"Now, Cyprian, is that any way to speak to your oldest friend?" I growled down the line.

His snort of amusement had my lips tipping up. "Ain't that fucking right? Oldest. Ha. The boy's got jokes. So what can I do for you? You only call when you need something." His tone was full of accusation, which was well warranted because he was right. I sighed.

"I need to get in touch with the local vampire King in the northeast region of the United States. There seems to be an infestation problem around these parts that needs exterminating."

"Oh damn. Why doesn't that surprise me? That fucker has been in charge for, what, five years, maybe a few more? And shit's been falling apart ever since. I hear that the Council is looking into finding a replacement." He sighed long and deep. "If shit's going down out there long enough to cause big problems, then he's not going to be able to help you. You're better off going straight to the Council. The previous King from that region would probably be very interested in hearing what you have to say. I'll get a message to him and have him call you."

Before I could say anything else, the call cut off, and I was left with nothing but silence. It was typical of the Wendigo demon. He probably kept to himself more than even I did. But he was one of the few I trusted after we met a few hundred years ago in a forest where he'd been practically starving. Wendigo demons didn't have to eat human flesh the way modern human stories portrayed, but they did have to ingest the occasional heart to keep from starving. Though they would never die from starvation, they would wither until they were little more than husks.

When I found him as I was passing through Europe, I couldn't help but feel sorry for the state he was in. I promised to help him, and as he looked up at me, full of doubt but still willing to trust me, I knew that I couldn't let him down. It didn't take long before I came across a group of highwaymen who had just slaughtered a young family of farmers. They were tying up the stolen horses and laughing at each other. A young child lay in the cold dirt not ten feet away, its life taken callously for what was probably only a few coins. It was one of the few times I wasn't sorry to use my ability to make a man deathly ill.

I knew diseases wouldn't hurt the Wendigo, so I was unconcerned when I dropped their still-breathing bodies in the dirt under the barren tree where the demon lay curled on his side. He jerked, bringing his frail body to sit upright with his back to the tree. He looked up at me, his demon eyes peering at me through the bleached bone of his skull.

"You came back," he breathed raggedly.

I crouched down in front of him with my dagger in my hand. I dragged the nearest man closer and struck the man through the chest, between his ribcage. "I promised I would, friend." He watched hungrily, licking his skull with his long tongue, as I reached into the still breathing human male's chest and ripped his heart out. I handed the warm heart over to the Wendigo. "My name is Valen."

After that day, we had stayed in touch. Cyprian had never forgotten what I had done for him that day, and I never forgave myself for not allowing him to come with me as I bade him farewell. But Cyprian was very good at tracking, and he made sure that he kept in touch throughout the years.

He was right, though, I thought with a grimace. I was shit at calling at any other time than when I needed information from him. Maybe that was something I could change now that I could feel the strength in the control I held over my power. Perhaps I could build friendships that were stronger than the occasional phone call. I grinned as I thought about my mate's reaction to seeing a Wendigo demon as I walked back inside the cafe.

The waitress was in the process of bagging up my food order, and I grimaced at the sheer amount of it. My saddlebags were going to be stuffed to the brim. I just hoped it all made it back to the warehouse without being too smashed from the way I'd have to pack the styrofoam boxes.

I set the empty coffee cup down and pulled the wallet from my back pocket. I withdrew some folded bills, checking to ensure there was plenty to cover the tab, along with a hefty tip. I set the bills on the counter in front of me just as the silver-haired waitress turned to face me with a broad smile on her gently lined face.

"Here you go, sweetie. Is there anything else I can get for you?"

"No, ma'am, this is perfect. Thank you," I replied, reaching out to take the bags from her.

"You got it. Drive safely, and come back to see us."

I nodded but didn't respond, knowing the chance of me returning to this area within her lifetime was slim at best. I turned, walking away from the counter and out through the front door. I had grown numb to the fact that nearly every being I came in contact with would die and wither to nothing but dust as I continued to roam this realm. Some much sooner than others. There were times, though, after meeting a human who stood out for their genuine kindness that I was reminded of my loneliness. Immortality was more of a curse than a gift, and I couldn't help but wonder over the years what I had done to deserve it. But then, there were several regrets I had that were worth being cursed for.

But now I had a mate who would share my longevity. I also suspected she held a power similar to mine for a reason. I would show her how to use it without fear, as well as how to use it to protect herself. With our mating came strength. We would both be immensely more powerful with better control. Though I hadn't been taught about any of those things, I could already sense it inside of me. The fact that we were connected so strongly suggested that the same would be true for her. Though, I did think that it was prudent to speak to someone sooner rather than later. We both had much to learn about our world and shouldn't wait to find someone to teach us.

As I finished packing away our food containers as well as I could, my phone began to ring inside my jacket where I had stashed it after my conversation with Cyprian. I withdrew it as I sat on my bike and frowned at the screen. The number wasn't one I recognized. I hit the answer button and brought it to my ear.

"Hello?"

The voice on the other end of the line was brisk and formal with a faint accent similar to the kind most long-lived supernatural beings held after living in so many different places through their long lives. It wasn't the voice that made me freeze, though.

"This is Councilman Crispin Decious. I received a message a few minutes ago that you might have information about an issue in one of our regions with rogue vampires."

My head was still spinning as I sat there numbly.

"Are you there?" His tone had turned from business serious to suspicious at my silence. I gripped the phone tighter.

"Crispin. As in the Crispin who singly-handedly defeated twenty skilled fighters carrying spears before finally allowing help from your teammates?"

It was his turn to become silent for a long beat. I heard what sounded like the creaking of a chair. "There are very few who might know me from that time."

I stared out across the parking lot as I got lost in a memory from nearly two thousand years ago. Crispin had been a human at that time; of that, I had no doubts. He'd been a volunteer gladiator, one who was fighting to earn money. Most who joined the ranks of the gladiators died in the Colosseum within the first year. Crispin had continued fighting for more than five that I could remember.

"I could imagine," I replied with a grunt.

"There is only one other man who survived that day." He wasn't wrong. It had been a brutal battle, and nearly all of our team had died. Crispin had felt he needed to prove something after his intended bride had shown up married to someone else. "I always knew there was something different about you."

I huffed out an amused breath. "Well, the human I knew back then definitely wasn't a high ranking vampire."

"How are you doing, Valen?"

"I'd be doing better if there weren't vermin threatening my mate."

It was his turn to grunt, disgust filling his tone. "That region has gone to shit since I left. I have been working with the other Council members to pick a new leader to take over for the worthless excuse of a King that's in place there now. Tell me everything you know, and I will be on the next plane out there." He paused. "Congratulations on your mate. We obviously need to catch up."

I shook my head at the turn of events. Never would I have suspected that the man I had fought with back then, and considered a friend for the short time I had stayed to fight in the Colosseum, would have become a vampire. I wondered how it had happened and if, perhaps, he wasn't one of the shitty ones.

Chapter 19

Kallista

I stood back and stared down at my handiwork. It had taken a lot of effort, but somehow, I managed to carefully roll each garment Valen had bought me into tight bundles for packing. It had worked, though my backpack and Valen's bag were bulging at the seams. My clothing would be a mess of wrinkles, but at least I would have them.

I wondered idly where we would go after we left here. I had never been to the West Coast. When I traveled with my father, it was usually to conventions. Then we headed straight back to the plane and on to our next campaign location. So even though I had traveled quite a bit, it had never been for vacation or to just have fun. I looked forward to all the places he could show me.

I paused in the process of hauling the bags toward the lift as the sound of an engine broke through the silence. I hadn't noticed until now how quiet it was in this area of town. I smiled as my heart made a little leap in my chest at the thought of Valen coming back. Then I realized that the sound I was hearing wasn't just one motorcycle engine.

I stood frozen as I listened to multiple engines approaching. I glanced over to the alarm panel, relieved to see it was blinking, indicating it was armed. As I continued to listen, the engines seemed to slow, making me tense up as fear began to crawl up my spine. As they roared past the warehouse, I let out a gust of air as my shoulders relaxed.

I took a step toward the lift so I could set the bags down when the group of bikes sounded as if they had turned the corner. Were they circling the warehouse? I held my breath, waiting to see if they would move on. Perhaps they were just on the wrong side of town and took a wrong turn. It wasn't until the sound of engines circled back around to the front of the warehouse that I began to panic.

"Shit, shit, shit! What do I do?" My gaze darted around the loft, bouncing over every surface as if searching for the answers that wouldn't come. I had no weapons and no experience with them, even if there was a gun or a knife. By the sound of what was outside, there were at least three motorcycles. There was no way for me to defend myself against that many men, even if I were trained to handle myself in a fight.

I looked at the window near the bed to see the sunlight streaming through. Vampires couldn't come out into the sun; that much I knew from what Valen had told me. So whoever it was wasn't a vampire. That was good, I supposed. But if it wasn't the vampires who were after me, then who the hell was outside?

The engines finally came to a stop and began to idle with a rough rumble that shook the floor beneath my bare feet. I listened intently for any sounds indicating what was happening below as my heart pounded so hard that it felt as if my ribs were going to bruise from the inside.

There was a muffled popping sound, and then suddenly, the window at the front of the building exploded inward. I screeched and ducked, dropping the bags I was carrying and throwing my arms up over my head. I stared, wide-eyed, as the small metal canister that had broken through the window rolled to a stop just a few feet from where I stood half-crouched. Before I could do anything more than blink, thick smoke began to pour from the canister.

"Oh, fuck!" I darted my gaze to the broken window and then to the bathroom. I didn't know if I should take my chances locked in the bathroom or...

I looked toward the window behind me. It was at the back of the building, and there was a fire escape for safety. Surely, the bad guys outside were waiting for me to escape the building, the way rats ran from sinking ships. If I even thought about climbing down the ladder, they would be waiting for me before I even reached the bottom.

I held my arm over my mouth as I began to cough nearly uncontrollably. I ran to the bed, yanked the blanket from the top of the mattress, and buried my face in it as I stumbled toward the bathroom door. The open door that had already allowed thick smoke to fill it. I was fucked.

It felt as if I were walking through thick sludge as I put one foot in front of the other, pushing myself to make it into the relative safety of the small room. The only thing I could allow myself to focus on was that maybe I could get the door shut, the blanket wedged under the door to stop any more gas from getting in, and the exhaust fan turned on to clear out the smoke. I couldn't think about *why* they were gassing me. If I thought too hard about what they hoped to accomplish, I was going to truly panic.

I slammed the door shut with my shoulder and leaned heavily against it as tears streamed down my cheeks. I started to stuff the blanket along the open bottom edge of the doorway to block any more smoke from making it inside, but my vision was wavering, and my chest was aching from the full body-wracking coughs that I was helpless to control. I became so weak I could barely force enough strength in my arms to push the thick blanket. With regret, I could see more of the noxious gas creeping under the door.

My last thoughts were of Valen as I was unable to keep my body from slumping into an ungraceful heap.

WAKING up was just as traumatic as passing out had been. It didn't take me long to figure out where I was, even if I didn't know the exact location. The sight of the blond vampire glaring at me from behind bars was enough of a dead giveaway.

I tore my eyes away from his and looked around me as I pushed myself to a sitting position with an embarrassing amount of effort and leaned my back against the wall. I was still wearing my pretty sundress. I intended to change into a pair of jeans and a long-sleeved shirt before we left. I hadn't done it yet in a secret hope that once Valen returned, I would be able to convince him to fuck me one last time before we got on the road. Now, I was sitting in what appeared to be a small six-foot by six-foot cell.

The floor was concrete, and the walls were cinder blocks, surrounding me on three sides. There was a row of evenly placed bars at the front of the tall cell, which conveniently allowed the pissed-off vampire to glare daggers at me. I did my best to ignore his presence as I took in the floor and walls. I took a second more thorough look around, and hugged myself, using my arms for the little warmth they provided.

It didn't take much time to see that there was literally nothing else to the cell other than a small bucket that sat in the far corner with a lid on it. I mean, at least there was a lid, right? I just hoped it was empty because if I had to use a shit bucket that already had someone else's shit in it, I would probably end up vomiting all over the floor.

I closed my eyes and dropped my head back against the cinder block wall. It took all the effort I possessed to stop myself from screaming and crying with all the despair I felt inside my heart.

Valen was going to lose his mind when he returned to the loft to find the place a mess and me missing. I could only imagine what my kidnappers had done to the place in order to get me out of it.

I heard footsteps moving somewhere out of sight, sounding as if they were descending stone steps. The footfalls grew closer the longer I tried to ignore them until they stopped right outside my new jail cell. I refused to open my tired and aching eyes to see who it was. Frankly, I didn't care. It was hard to care about anything without Valen here to comfort me.

"When did she wake up?"

The voice that spoke was not what I expected to hear, not that I had any specific expectations. But I certainly hadn't thought I'd hear a thick western drawl. I gave into temptation and cracked my eyes open to catch a glimpse of the man. I had to cut off my gasp of shock when I managed to understand what I was seeing.

The man's entire face looked as if it had been made of wax and was left outside on the hottest day of the year. His cheeks, jowls, and lower eyelids were so saggy that I was afraid the hanging flesh would fall right off and slip to the floor. A sour taste of bile filled the back of my throat, and I had to swallow hard to keep it from making an appearance all over the floor.

I tore my eyes away and instead stared at the branding on the inner portion of my wrist.

"The little bitch just came to a couple minutes ago, Master." Even if I hadn't recognized the blond vampire by sight, I would have remembered that voice as belonging to the man who had ripped the heart from Tiny's chest. A single tear managed to escape as my feelings became so overwhelmed by fear and grief that I couldn't hold it in any longer.

"Excellent. Go grab my chair so the lady and I may converse comfortably."

"Master."

I wanted to snort or curse at the suggestion of comfort. I was fucking freezing while sitting on the cold concrete floor in a goddamn sundress. There was the sound of heavy footsteps walking away, a pause, then a scraping sound.

"Pick the chair up, Claude." The words were exasperated, the way a parent might speak to a young child with whom they were attempting to be patient, but were becoming increasingly less so.

"Yes, Master." The scraping sound abruptly stopped, and the footsteps came close again quickly. The chair was placed down with a small thunk, and then there was a shuffling of feet as positions were shifted. Then, there was the unmistakable sound of someone sighing in relief as they sat down.

There was a long beat of silence, one so long that I began to tremble from more than the cold that was slowly seeping into my bones. I continued to keep my head down, refusing to give in to the man. That was until he spoke.

"Miss Hargrove, you sure have made a few people rather angry."

A gasp escaped my trembling lips, and my head whipped up at the use of my legal name. "H-how?"

A wicked smile curved his fleshy lips, revealing twin sets of sharp fangs that glinted in the dim lighting of the cell.

"I told you—you pissed off certain people bad enough that they decided to figure out what or who you were on the run from." He cocked his head to the side, the simple movement enough to set off a slight swinging of his loose skin. If I had to be any closer to him without the safety of solid iron bars between us, I would likely faint. "What do you think your rich senator father would have to say about the company you've been keeping?"

I swallowed hard and turned my head away to stare at the cold gray cinderblock a couple of feet to my side. At this close, I could see the imperfections in the concrete, the pits and pores that seemed to be steeped in icy cold. My father. It wasn't so much him that I was frightened of as it was my mother and her mental illness. I didn't know what her condition was exactly. I just knew that no sane person would go to the extremes that she did when she felt I was being evil.

What would my mother do if she knew that not only was I the mate to a demon hundreds or even thousands of years old, but that I was also literally part demon? That thought had a snort bursting out of me unbidden. For most of my life, she accused me of being possessed by a demon. Little did she know that I *was* the demon. *Can't exorcise my entire body, Mother.*

"Well," the vampire Master who sat in front of my cell murmured thoughtfully. "I have to say, that wasn't the reaction I was expecting. Care to share what is so humorous about the situation?"

I finally glanced back in his direction, bracing to keep myself from reacting to his appearance. "My mate is going to rip your fangs out of your face before he rips your heart from your chest."

His deep belly laugh had shivers skittering down my back as if hundreds of little spiders had scattered. He grinned at the reaction I couldn't hide from him. "Oh, lovely little girl. I want nothing more than to have your demon mate show up here. I have been hoping and planning on it for over two hundred years. He's been a little elusive. Then you show up and make all my dreams come true."

He shifted in his big cushioned chair, making the wooden frame creak from his bulk. "Tell me, Kallista, darlin', how well do you know the demon called Valen?"

My brows creased together in confusion. "I don't know? We were just getting to know each other." It seemed safe to admit. As well as this man already knew details about my life; it would be stupid to tell him otherwise.

"Ah. This is going to be fun then. Sit back, make yourself comfortable, and I will tell you all about the demon."

I glared up at him, pissed at his displaced humor. He damn well knew I was cold and miserable. To top off being cold and scared, I was fucking hungry. Valen had left to get us food probably hours ago now. Though there was no way to tell what time it was, my stomach told me that it was starved. Plus, these were vampires. I knew very little about how vampires lived, but I couldn't help but believe that they were nocturnal to the point they likely slept during the day. Which made me wonder, who the fuck attacked the warehouse loft?

"Did you know Valen has the ability to cause illness?"

I shook my head slowly. I didn't know what his power was other than to kill. I saw what he had done to the other vampire that had been holding me against my will the night we had met. The way the man's face had melted... Oh, shit. This vampire in front of me. The sagging skin. The way it appeared as if his face was melting...

"You've heard of the bubonic plague?"

I nodded hesitantly, horror starting to make my face go numb.

"They estimate 25 to 50 million people died." He smiled widely. "Small pox? More than 300 million people. Influenza? More than 50 million in 1918 alone. Imagine how many more have died before and after that tragic year?"

I was going to be sick. *Literally.* I scrambled over to the bucket a few feet away and ripped the lid off. I had the briefest of seconds to be thankful the bucket seemed to be brand new before what meager contents I held in my stomach were expelled viciously. I continued to dry heave as my stomach twisted as hard as my heart did in my chest.

"Ah, I see I don't have to explain that your precious mate is the one responsible for all those deaths. He is illness. He is a walking plague. Unfortunately, the demon can't die. I've done my research on him, too. There are stories about the man in black walking through dying villages. He would touch a person, and the next day, they would die. He has been hunted down, tortured, hung, and burned at the stake. I even found an accounting of him being drawn and quartered." Again, he cocked his head at me and studied me with his gleaming, scheming eyes. "You do know what being drawn and quartered means, yes?"

I was going to be sick again. I put my head back over the bucket, but when nothing but air came out of my body, I groaned weakly and placed the lid back on the bucket before scooting back to my spot against the wall. I wrapped my aching arms around my legs, hugging them tight to my chest. My entire body was trembling uncontrollably now.

"So, yes. I have plans for your mate. He won't be able to harm another innocent soul again."

Chapter 20

Kallista

"What do you plan on doing to him?" My teeth were chattering so hard that I was having difficulty getting the words out without stuttering. My heart was breaking into a million pieces in my chest, and I gripped my wrist tightly, the brand under my palm feeling like it was throbbing. I couldn't tell if it was my imagination or actually happening.

He chuckled darkly. I laid my cheek on my knees and stared at the wall again, refusing to look back up at the vampire who wanted to destroy my whole world. "Besides use you as bait?" I squeezed my eyes shut tightly against the wave of pain that washed over me. "I have had a long time to think about this. Ever since he did this to me," he paused before raising his voice. "Look at me!"

Slowly, I dragged my head off my knees and looked up at the man who was leaning forward in his chair, glaring down at me with hatred in his eyes. "I see you," I whispered hoarsely, my throat raw from the vomiting. "And it's disgusting."

For a moment, he looked as if he wanted to yank the door of my cell off its hinges and rip the arms from my body. I held my breath, waiting to see what he would do. Finally, he chuckled and sat back in his chair.

"I see what you are trying to do, little girl. Do you think I am going to throw away my revenge in a fit of rage? You think if you no longer live, that your mate will simply move on without giving me my chance to destroy him the way he did me?"

"Well," I mumbled into my knees. "You look dumb enough to fall for it." I shrugged one trembling shoulder as nonchalantly as I could manage.

It appeared as if he were trying to tighten his mouth in an angry line the way my father would when he was displeased, but the fleshy lumps did little more than wobble. I couldn't help a snort from escaping.

"You know, I am going to enjoy draining your body dry after he's entombed. It will add to his suffering, don't you think? To know his lovely little mate was killed while he was unable to do a fucking thing about it?" He glared at me with a triumphant smile. "You should hate him after all the innocent lives he took. He has murdered more people in a thousand years than any other human in history."

A tear tracked down my frozen cheek as I thought of all those lives. "You don't know Valen."

A meaty fist landed on the arm of the chair with a loud crack. A piece of the wood broke off and fell to the concrete floor. "I know him better than you will ever have a chance to!" he roared.

"Valen has probably suffered for every soul lost. If history says he walked through dying villages, it was probably so he could mourn their losses. Valen would never purposely kill an innocent person. There is a reason he has kept himself isolated, away from as many people as possible, without friends or loved ones. He has a good heart, and he has been suffering terribly."

He stood and glared down at me, his hands fisted on the bars, seconds away from breaking the door down. I closed my eyes and cried. This horrible man wanted to entomb Valen. Visions of my mate being locked away in a stone or metal coffin for the rest of eternity to wither away but never die, to know I was dead. It broke my heart into a million jagged pieces.

I didn't know how I could help him, whether or not it was even possible. We had just begun to get to know each other. I thought we'd have forever, instead, we'd had mere moments. What could I do to stop the inevitable?

The man let out a gusty sigh as if the whole situation were tedious for him. I peeked up at him from over my arm to see him retake his seat, relaxed and sprawled out in the chair. His pretend formality seemed to be gone as he let one knee spread wide while stretching the other leg far out in front of him.

"I'm not going to kill you," he began in a calmer tone, almost sounding bored. "I made a promise to someone in exchange for helping me. I understand your family is very eager to have you back. Something about obligations?" He left the question hanging as if he expected me to fulfill his curiosity. He could go to hell.

I dug my fingers into my legs hard enough to leave fingernail marks on my skin at the thought of being back under my parent's roof. I didn't know if the wedding would still take place, but it didn't matter. They would just find another man to take me as long as it could somehow help my father's career and look good for the public image he had created of a devoted family man. I tried to slow my breathing, not wanting this vampire to know how much his words affected me.

I lifted my head and glared at the vampire with all the hatred I had for him in my soul. He simply chuckled at my expression. "What did you do?" I asked him, pointedly staring at his melted face. I almost wanted to return his mocking laughter as the expression of mirth fell, and a glower took over. "Valen wouldn't have done that to you without a good reason. So," I tilted my head to study him closely. "What did you do to piss him off?"

I thought he was going to lie, to say something along the lines of him being innocent. Instead, he surprised me.

"I got rough with a whore." He threw his head back and laughed as if it were the funniest thing in the world. "A fucking whore. As if there weren't plenty more where that one came from. The demon heard her scream as he was passing through and decided to play white knight. He did this to me," he said with a snarl. "Then he carried me away, half-dead, on the back of his horse before tossing me in a ravine. I was left to die, to have my bones picked clean by the buzzards and my bones to be gnawed on by the wolves. Lucky me, a vampire came by and gave me a gift."

He spread his arms wide as he grinned maliciously. "I'll live forever. And now I am the Master of my own nest. I answer to no one, not even the one who changed me. I tore off his head and took over. No one can stop me, little girl. I became a fucking god."

"You are a comic book villain." I spit. "Valen is more powerful than you could ever dream of becoming. How do you plan to capture him?"

"You don't know much about vampires, do you?" he sneered at me. I gave a hesitant shake of my head. "Vampires are gifted special abilities when they are changed. There is no telling what it will be before it happens. There are all kinds of abilities, from mind reading to strength. Some can even shapeshift." He smirked at me, a gleam of triumph in his eyes. "Some can even take away someone else's abilities. Tell me, little girl, once Valen's ability to make someone sick is gone, what else will he have to fight with? If he were restrained and unable to fight, how would he be able to stop me from locking him away and tossing his tomb into the deepest part of the ocean?"

My mind was whirling. I had no idea about this world I was now immersed in, and every hour seemed to reveal more secrets. Humans would be scared every moment of their lives if they knew all of this existed around them. I tried not to think too hard about what he said awaited Valen. If I did, I would never be able to function again, and I had to stay strong. Somehow, I would do what I could to stop what was happening.

A sound came from somewhere down the hall. I jerked my head up, my heart beginning to pound behind my ribcage, hoping that it was and was not Valen in equal measures. I needed to see him. At the same time, I was terrified that he would show up and be captured by this evil man.

"Ah, it looks like our little conversation is over. It's been fun, but it's time for you to head on home!" The vampire stood from his seat and clapped his hands together in glee. I didn't think my hatred for him could get any stronger, but apparently, there was definitely room in my head for that emotion. I glared daggers at him as his fleshy lips expanded into a gruesome grin.

I stubbornly sat where I was as he pulled a heavy keyring from his pocket. The keys jingled obnoxiously in the quiet. He seemed to try to fit every single key into the hole before one finally made a scraping noise as it slid home and turned.

"Well, then. Come on, little girl, let's not make Daddy wait." I continued to refuse until his look of glee soured, and he made a move to step toward me. I scooted into the corner before bracing my hands on the rough walls behind me and stumbled to my feet. Everything ached from sitting on the cold floor for as long as I had.

Footsteps moved closer, and before I could see him, a loud booming voice I remembered clearly called out to my captor.

"Where is my daughter? What is this place? Why is she down here?" I wanted desperately to believe he cared about my whereabouts, but I knew he was only upset about the inconvenience my leaving had caused him. The fact that he had to pause his precious work to retrieve his wayward daughter was only going to make him even angrier. I wasn't worried about him hurting me physically; that had never been his thing. No, he was more neglectful and demanding of my time to suit his needs than being physically abusive. That was my mother's thing. At least I knew she would never come with him on this retrieval trip.

I stood there on my bare feet, shivering with anxiousness and regret. I wanted to do something to stop what was about to happen, but I was too upset to think clearly. I couldn't fight; I was too weak against the vampires that were filling the house. I briefly considered trying to use the abilities I had, but I was back to being terrified. What if I did try to use them down here? The whole house could collapse on top of us all.

I closed my eyes and cried out inside for Valen, wishing he could hear me. There was so much that we should have said to each other. It had only been a few days, but in that short amount of time, he had shown me more kindness and acceptance than anyone ever had in my entire life. I needed more. I needed a lifetime and then some.

As my father stepped up to the cell, I watched through teary eyes as his head snapped in my direction. He took me in from head to toe, and the disgust at the sight of me was blatant. The fact that he was more disgusted by my attire than the monster keeping me captive and holding the keys to my cell filled me with anguish. The little girl inside me, who always hoped for her daddy's love and acceptance, cried as her heart broke.

"Kallista! Get over here so we can leave this place." He looked around with distaste, actively avoiding glancing in the direction of the hideous vampire. "Mr. Hanover, thank you for holding my daughter. I'll be taking her with me now." He pulled a wad of cash from his pocket, and the men exchanged a brief handshake. The vampire grinned while my father avoided making eye contact and wiped his hand on his pants leg. He was probably going to throw all of his clothing in the trash the second we made it home.

"Oh, make sure you tell that woman I appreciate her phone call.

Come along Kallista." He turned and began walking back toward the stairs as one of his men took me roughly by the elbow and began pulling me along. I wondered what woman he was talking about. Who had called him? Then it hit me right before the vampire said his parting words with a chuckle.

"I'll be sure to pass your thanks onto Miss Syn."

CHAPTER 21

I sensed that something was wrong before I even turned the corner. As soon as the warehouse came into view, my entire body locked up, rage beginning to fill every cell of my body.

Glass was on the ground, and the second-story window over-looking the street was broken out. The elevator door meant for people to use was destroyed, as if someone had used a giant pry bar to peel back the metal. I pushed the button on my keyfob for the larger lift to open but got off my bike instead of pulling inside.

Once the elevator had risen to the second level, I braced myself for what I would see. As soon as the doors opened, the rage that boiled inside me caused my wings to explode from my back as my demon took control. I threw my head back and roared as I stormed forward to see the glass on the floor. There was a metal canister that had likely been filled with some kind of gas to make it easier to capture my mate lying in the middle of the floor. What was left of my control vanished at the sight of the bathroom door hanging on its hinges. There was a blanket on the floor that Kallista had probably used while trying to protect herself from the fumes.

My fist went through the wall, leaving plaster dust to scatter on the floor. Another rage-filled roar shook the entire building. As I glanced around the room, looking for something to destroy, I caught sight of our bags sitting by the service elevator. My mate had packed, and by the look of the bulging sides of the bags, she had done her best to ensure everything she owned, everything I had purchased for her, was inside them.

My tail whipped around me as I dropped to the floor beside her things. With a trembling hand, I reached out to brush lightly over the material before withdrawing and clenching it into a tight fist. Blood droplets hit the floor from the wounds my nails made in my palms as my mind searched for what to do. I needed to find her, to help her.

With renewed determination, I stumbled to my feet and wiped my bloodied hand on my leg. I was going to go straight to the vampire's lair. From there, not a soul would survive. I would tear each of them apart with my bare hands if I had to. I would get my mate back. Until she was safely in my arms again, I would rain hell on the earth.

I bent down to pick up our bags with one hand and stalked back to the lift. There was nothing left for me in the loft. I would never be back, not to the building and never to this town.

Somehow, I wasn't surprised to see Syn standing next to my motorcycle as I strode forward. I ignored her presence as I opened the saddlebags and began to toss the food to the ground. Once I had Kallista back, I would take her anywhere she wanted to eat. As long as it was far away from here.

"Val, please. I need to talk to you," Syn pleaded as I continued to ignore her. I pushed Kallista's backpack deep into the saddlebag, ensuring it was protected. "Val!" she snapped.

With a growl, I whipped my head up. I met her glare with a snarl until her face dropped. "I told you," she pleaded, "I needed to talk to you. You were supposed to meet me for lunch, remember?"

"I don't have time for your games, Syn!" I yelled as I turned back to latch the leather flap closed. "You need to leave. Go back to your club. Forget you ever knew me."

Her shocked gasp sounded from behind me, but I didn't care to look at her hurt expression. I had learned a lot about Syn over the last few days, and what I had learned told me I never knew the real her.

I swung my leg over the seat and started the engine, ready to head straight to the vampire nest I had scoped out the other day. I had zero doubts that it was them who had her. It was already heading towards noon. If they had human henchmen grab her, I still had a few hours left to get there, retrieve her, and set fire to the whole place with the vamps still in their beds.

"I murdered my mate for you." Syn's whispered words had me freezing. I slowly turned my head to face her, my blood turning to ice in my veins at her confession. I saw her looking down at her wrist, the same one she previously had covered with a wide bracelet. When I thought about it, I realized she'd had something on her arm the last few times I'd seen her.

The brand that was on her wrist, similar to the ones Kallista and I shared, was a faded brown. If a brand could look sickly, that one did. She stroked a finger over the blurred lines. "He wasn't what my heart wanted. Fate failed me." She looked up at me then, a tortured expression on her face. "From the moment I saw you, I knew no one else would do. I tried, Valen. I tried to get you to see me. When that girl was being attacked, and you stormed into my bordello to rescue a total stranger," she sighed dramatically. "I gave you my heart. I never thought I was capable of doing that." She laughed softly and shook her head.

I looked back on that day. I had been riding through a town, needing supplies for my horse and myself. When I heard the screams, I couldn't have stopped myself from intervening. As I remembered it, though, I began to see things in my mind that I hadn't noticed then. The way Syn had been sitting primly in a settee in the lobby, sipping tea, instead of going to her employee's rescue. She had followed me up the stairs, surprised at my appearance but saying nothing to stop me.

When I had entered the small room with nothing but a bed in the corner, I immediately spotted the man striking the naked young woman repeatedly in the face as he took what he wanted from her. My vision had turned red. I had never been able to withstand the abuse of innocents, so I acted quickly, yanking him off her and punching him in the face. It wasn't enough, though, as I listened to the young woman whimpering from the bed. I glanced back at her to see she had covered herself with a thin sheet as she wiped tears and blood from her face.

Syn had simply stood in the doorway, watching everything with a critical eye. My fury had been overwhelming as the man had screamed profanities at me and attempted to fight back. I'd used my ability to cause physical illness then without even thinking about it. It showed on his face as it began to sag, giving the appearance of melting candle wax, as his insides did the same. I could sense the damage I was causing but was unable to make myself feel sorry for what I was doing.

At the sound of the two women in the room screaming in terror at my actions, I pulled back before I had fully killed him. The illness I had inflected couldn't be undone, though. Knowing the man would die soon, I pulled him with me out of the house. Syn had followed me, asking my name. I gave it to her, and with a nod, I'd thrown the bastard on the back of my horse and rode out to the nearest ravine before tossing him over the edge. It wasn't a steep one, and I thought if the fall didn't kill him, the local wildlife would finish what I'd started. It was no more than what he'd deserved. I left without a backward glance, moving back towards town and to the feed store, which had been my original destination.

Syn had found me before I'd managed to leave town. From there, she seemed to pop back up in my life occasionally. I hadn't minded, or at least, I hadn't stopped her from doing so. I had sensed there was more to her, the same as there was more to me. I had seen her as nothing more than a friend and the occasional fount of information for demonkind. Since I had held myself isolated for most of my existence, it was a reluctant welcome change. If she was attempting to be more than friends, I had never noticed and wouldn't have been interested if she was.

"I never asked you to do that, Syn," I rasped out, horrified at what she had done. I couldn't imagine killing my mate now that I had found her. She completed me in a way I hadn't considered possible. I could only imagine how much better my existence would be in another hundred years with her by my side. I shook my head. "I should have realized when you began pushing me to murder Kallista. You knew what would happen with the bond because you had experienced it yourself."

Syn looked at me sadly. "I did. And I knew if you would just give me a chance, we could be perfect together."

"Syn," I said with a tone filled with every ounce of determination I had for her to understand my words. "I will never care for you in that way. Kallista is the only person I have ever come close to caring for. She's my mate, and I couldn't be prouder of that. You and I were never meant to be."

Her shoulders drooped at my words, then stiffened as her expression changed from one of heartbreak to fierce anger. "Just so you know, that man who you left for dead in the ravine? He's the same one who I agreed to let feed on my girls. We have been working together for the last two hundred years. I owed him for what happened in my bordello that day. We'd had an agreement then that he could do whatever he wanted to my girls as long as he paid well. You destroyed our agreement that day. He's the one who has your precious mate." She spit the last word out as if it were poison on her tongue.

I gritted my teeth as the implications washed over me. My mate was in the hands of a monster who'd somehow managed to survive that day. "He was made into a vampire?"

She nodded, a smile spreading over her face. "It hurts knowing the person you care for will never be in your life again, doesn't it? Now, maybe you understand how I feel."

I revved my engine, preparing to take off to rescue my mate before it was too late. I had no more time to waste on Syn and her vindictiveness. "If he hurts her, I am going to wrap my hands around your pretty little neck and squeeze until your head falls from your body. I can survive a beheading, can you?"

I turned my back on her and lifted my foot to leave when the unmistakable sound of a cocking gun had the hair on the back of my neck rising. "I can't let you do that, Valen."

I heard the loud report of a bullet leaving the chamber. It was several seconds before I registered the searing pain that consumed me as the bullet moved through bone and muscle. It tore a path straight into my heart. I knew I would survive the bullet. But before I collapsed off my motorcycle to fall face first onto the asphalt, I worried that I wouldn't make it to my mate in time before I lost her completely.

Chapter 22

Valen

Darkness greeted me as I came to. I was in a bare room with no windows or furniture. My arms were in thick iron shackles that were attached to the wall behind me. The chains sat beside me on the floor where I was lying. I sat up slowly, only a twinge of pain radiating from my chest as I moved. There was a ping of metal as the bullet Syn had shot me with fell to the floor, my body having worked it out as it healed.

Being injured wasn't a death sentence for me, but that didn't mean getting shot, stabbed, or lit on fire didn't hurt. My nerves felt every ounce of pain when it happened. My only saving grace was that I healed quickly, and as soon as my shredded flesh mended, the pain disappeared completely.

Experimentally, I tugged on the chains. They were only about four feet long, just enough to allow me to stand, sit, or lie down against the wall. The fact that they were here at all and that the manacles fit snugly against my skin as if made for me told me she had planned this.

With nothing else in the dark, dank room with me, I couldn't help but wonder what Syn's endgame was. She couldn't keep me prisoner for long, and she had to know that the second I got my hands on her, I was going to kill her without an ounce of regret or hesitation.

I gripped one of the chains in my hands, wrapping the inch thick iron around my fist for a good grip and pulled until cement began to crack around the bolt in the wall. Small bits began to crumble, falling to the floor. I pulled with all my strength, my muscles straining until they screamed from the effort. I paused, allowing my body time to regroup, then began again, pulling as more of the wall crumbled to the floor.

I continued on for what seemed like hours but was mere minutes while my mind begged me to get free. I needed to save Kallista. She was in the hands of a monster. I needed to be able to see her beautiful face again and hold her close. I would never let her out of my sight once I had her in my arms. I had the feeling I wouldn't be able to get past the terror of not knowing if she was okay or not for a very long time.

Finally, the bolt broke free from the wall, and I panted for breath as my muscles trembled. I was covered in sweat from the effort of pulling for so long. My eyes trailed over to the second bolt, and I gritted my teeth in determination. Every minute I was locked up in this room, which I guessed was in the basement of the strip club, due to the faint, heavy bass that seeped into the walls, my mate was in untold danger. I couldn't allow my mind to conjure visions of what that man was doing to her, or I would lose my fucking mind.

The second chain seemed to be even harder to pull out than the first. I had to stop several times to let my body heal as I shook from the exertion. Every time I felt my muscles tearing, I had to pause to give them a chance to recover.

The time it was taking was increasing my anxiety, and I had to take deep, calming breaths to stop my panic from rising out of control. My only thoughts were of Kallista. It was killing me slowly, not knowing if she was okay. The only thing that kept me going was knowing she was alive. After seeing Syn's mating brand, I knew what it would look like if I lost her. More than that, though, I could feel that she was still alive.

Her heart beat under my skin like it was my own pulse. I could feel her down to my soul. I felt pain, anger, and fear, but I couldn't tell if it was my own emotions being amplified, circling through me.

When the bolt was hanging by just a few threads, and there was a pile of rubble at the base of the wall, I took a deep breath and prepared myself for one final struggle with the chain. I readjusted my grip, making sure the chain was wrapped tightly around my fists and forearms, and then I pulled with every bit of strength I could muster, and let out a primal yell from the depths of my soul.

When the bolt broke free from the wall, I was thrown across the room. I landed on my back, the chains covering my neck and chest. The bolt must have hit my forehead because I felt a brief pain and sting before it faded. With a relieved laugh, I detangled myself from the chains I was still holding and reached up to swipe away the bit of blood that had managed to gather there before it healed.

I rolled over onto my side, cursing as I fought with the heavy iron that seemed to want to keep me trapped. I looked down as I got to my feet, staring at the length of heavy chains, and cursed again that I was still trapped by the manacles. There was nothing I could do about them short of breaking off my own hands to free myself. I healed quickly, but not quick enough to regrow my hands in time to reach my mate once I left this place.

With frustration, I picked up one chain and then the other, wrapping them around my forearms. It was bulky and would hinder me, but there was no other choice. I could probably use them as weapons, though. Flashbacks of my time in the gladiator ring reminded me that anything could be used as a weapon. It wouldn't be the first time I'd hate to fight to the death while wrapped in chains. Certainly not my own death, though.

I eyed the stairs and the darkness where they led. There was a possibility that the door was guarded, though I hadn't been quiet at the end, so it was doubtful anyone was lurking, or they would have come running already. Unless they never considered the possibility that I could escape. Syn was just arrogant enough to think she'd had me beat.

At the thought of Syn, I hardened my jaw, nearly grinding my molars into dust. The she-demon was going to pay for her part in this. I had no doubts that she had led the vampires straight to my door, delusional enough to hope that if my mate was gone, she might still have a chance. I hoped I made it abundantly clear that I would rather shove my cock in a hive full of angry bees than to ever touch her deranged pussy.

I stalked to the steps and stomped up them to the door. At the top, I eyed the heavy wooden panel that was locked securely with a deadbolt. I glanced down at my fists and the chains that were wrapped there and grinned. I drew back my fist and slammed it into the door. The reverberation made my arm ache, and the iron dug into my knuckles. I pulled back and hit it again, then again, ignoring the sting and the blood dripping down to fall onto the wooden steps.

After a few more strikes, a large crack appeared, along with the sound of breaking wood. I could see dim lighting on the other side, and the sound of heavy bass became louder as the 80s rock song became recognizable. I rammed my fist into the door several more times to the tune of Pour Some Sugar On Me and I knew I'd never be able to hear that song again without wanting to put my fist through the radio.

As soon as there was a large enough hole, I kicked out the remaining wood that was barring my way to my mate. I ignored the scraping of the jagged pieces of wood that dug into my skin and tore through my shirt. Syn was going to pay for taking my leather jacket as well. I liked that fucking thing.

There must have been guards, after all; they had just been too busy gawking at the dancers. I could tell immediately that they were vampires, and cursed, realizing night had already fallen during my time in the basement. I wondered how long Syn had been working with the assholes, but then, she'd told me already, hadn't she. Two hundred years, she'd let them use and abuse the women who worked for her.

The first one came at me with his teeth bared and pulled a large hunting knife from behind his back. I let the chain drop from around my right arm and swung it with all my strength. It flew in an arc through the air and then struck him across the face hard enough to rip open his flesh. He fell to the floor with a groan, the knife flying from his hand and skidding away to hit the wall.

The second vampire approached more cautiously, eyeing the bloody chain dragging the floor. He must have thought I couldn't get it back into position for another strike in time because he suddenly darted straight at me, fangs extended and eyes flashing.

I knew some vampires had abilities when they were changed, I also knew there was virtually no way to tell what they could be until they appeared. This one suddenly became a wolf mid-leap, his jaw opened wide and aiming straight for my throat.

I raised my left arm to block the attack just in time for the massive wolf to clamp down on the chains that were still wrapped around my forearm. If only Syn knew that she had provided me the tools to protect myself from her vampire thugs, she'd likely throw a fucking fit.

With the wolf still attached to my arm, I chuckled and watched as his eyes widened, finally catching on that he was in a world of trouble. With my free hand, I quickly tossed the loose chain around his thick neck, then reached around to grab the end. I yanked it tight until he gasped for breath and began to struggle in earnest to get free from my hold.

He let go of my forearm to snap his jaws at my face. The hot breath of the wolf bathed me in hot, moist air, making me want to gag at the fetid smell.

"You should really brush your teeth. Maybe eat a dental chew while in doggy form. Your breath stinks." I grinned at his answering snarl, then used my now freed hand to pull the chain around his neck even tighter. He whined pitifully before his eyes rolled to the back of his head and he went still. As I held him a moment longer, watching as his body changed back to that of a man, then I finally dropped his dead corpse to the ground.

The first vampire who attacked was making a poor effort to crawl away as he slipped in his own blood as it poured steadily down his face. I walked over to the knife that had slid to the wall and picked it up. My chains dragged behind me as I slowly stalked closer to the man. I placed a foot on his back, making his hands slip out from beneath him. I winced as his face hit the floor with a crack. He howled in pain as even more blood flowed to the floor from his broken nose.

I reached down and grabbed the long greasy hair on the back of his head and yanked it up, making his head bend backwards at what had to be an uncomfortable angle.

"You never should have taken my girl." With a quick swipe of my new blade, I slit his throat and then dropped his head back to the floor. I was done playing with these fuckers. It was time to get my mate back.

Chapter 23

Kallista

I sat huddled in a chair next to my father the entire plane ride back home. I'd sobbed until I had no tears left. By the time we had landed, my face was swollen from the amount of crying I'd done, and my father was enraged at having to listen to me. No matter how many times he'd snapped at me to shut up or threatened me if I didn't quit, I'd just sob harder.

The ride to the house from the airstrip was quiet as I sat in the passenger seat, staring out the window with my heart breaking into a million pieces. Each mile that took me away from Valen seemed to rip another hole in my soul. If I thought there was any way that I could escape, I would do it. I considered opening the door as we drove down the freeway and throwing myself out of the car. There was little traffic since it was so late at night, so the chances of being run over were slim. But the idea of the fall itself at such a high speed kept me from making the move.

I could feel my father's eyes on me during the entire ride and had a feeling he knew what I was thinking of doing. When he broke the silence, it was to warn me.

"If you do anything stupid, I promise your punishment will be worse than you can imagine." His tone was so calm, so matter of fact, I think it hurt worse than if he'd screamed at me. Instead, it showed me that I meant nothing to him. His concern wasn't for my safety or out of love. His only concern was making sure I didn't cause him any more trouble that would keep him from his campaign trail longer than he'd already been delayed.

"Why are you doing this?" I hated how weak I sounded, how broken. These people had already taken so much from me, and I didn't want to give them the satisfaction of seeing me so low. "I'll never be the daughter you want. I don't want this life! Please, if you ever loved me at all, just let me go!"

I turned my head so I could see his face, and so he could see the despair in my eyes. I don't know what I expected him to say or do, but hearing him scoff and look away from me in disgust was enough to have fresh tears fill my tired eyes. I guess I still had some left to shed after all.

"I've asked very little of you, Kallista. You just needed to be there for show. All you had to do was look happy for the cameras and marry into a rich family. You would have had all the comforts of being a rich politician's wife and daughter. This defiance changes nothing. I can't have the voters thinking I can't control my own child. What would they think? That I can't do my job, either? I took you in from the gutters and gave you a home. You would have been an orphan with no prospects other than to live on the streets. This is how you chose to repay me?"

"How do you know I'd be on the streets?" I cried. "You don't know that!"

"I saved you!" he roared, turning back to me with fury. "You will do what you're told, or I will tell the world that you died from the illness you developed over this last year."

I swallowed hard at the realization of what they'd done to excuse my absence. I suppose as explanations went, it was a good one. Not only would it let the public know why I had suddenly disappeared, but it would garner sympathy from both political parties. Who hasn't experienced the heartache of seeing a loved one suffer? If I died now, it would only help him. Either way, he wins. I give in and do what he wants, or he kills me, and they have a huge, elaborate funeral that is televised and brings in sympathy votes.

"I hate you," I whispered brokenly. There was only one hope left for me. I had to believe that Valen would come. He had to come. Only, I hadn't told him my full name, where I was from, or who my parents were. He had no way of finding me. I turned back to stare at the road as we exited the freeway and began taking the turns to reach my parent's estate.

"If you think I care, you really haven't known me very well, Kallie-bean." I ignored his mocking words and the hated nickname, choosing instead to plead with the universe that my mate would be okay without me.

The car turned, then slowed to a crawl as it approached the large gate that sat in front of the huge house at the end of the half-mile driveway. The driver rolled his window down and spoke a few quiet words to the gate guard before being waved forward. Before I was ready, the car came to a stop in front of the double doors with the leaded glass. I think I dreaded walking back into that house even more than when I woke up in the cold cell.

I waited until my door was opened for me. Before I could step out, a guard appeared next to the driver and took my arm, roughly pulling me to my feet. My father must have told them to treat me like a prisoner because before I'd left, everyone had treated me with kindness and respect. Now, I was nothing but the wayward daughter who couldn't be trusted. It was easy to see that my life would be drastically changed from here on out.

The guard kept a tight hold on me as he ushered me up the steps and waited until my father entered first before following him inside. When the heavy door closed with an echoing thud, my heart jolted along with my entire body.

My mother was standing in the foyer with her hands folded in front of her looking like a proper lady even though it was probably the middle of the night. Her makeup was immaculate and her hair was styled in its carefully wrapped chignon. The only time I'd ever seen her rumpled and with her hair a mess was the time I'd caused the ceiling to partially collapse.

She looked me up and down, a look of pure disgust making her stern but pretty face twist into an ugly grimace. "Take her upstairs and lock her in her room. Let Martha in when she arrives." She stared me down. "You will not fight Martha when she bathes you. Everything you're wearing will be removed and discarded. I will see you in the morning to discuss your future."

She turned on her heels, clacking away in the direction my father had disappeared to as soon as he walked through the door. I was sure they would have a brief discussion about where he'd found me and the events that happened during our trip home. Then they would go to bed and roll over in opposite directions to fall asleep, virtual strangers in their marital bed. My heart ached as I thought of Valen for the millionth time since I'd woken up in that cell. The way he'd held me as I slept, the way he'd gently taken care of me in the shower after we'd had sex for the first time.

I let the tears fall freely as I was pulled up the stairs and to my room at the end of the hall. The guard shoved me inside the room, making me stumble and have to catch myself with a hand on the desk against the wall before I landed on my face. I turned back to glare at the guard I didn't recognize. He just sneered at me then shut the door in my face, the lock snicking loudly in the silence of my empty room.

I looked around to see not much had changed, while at the same time, the changes were glaringly obvious. My bed was still there against the middle of the wall, but the cheerful bedding that I preferred with the pretty violet flowers was gone. In its place was a plain white comforter. The curtains had been changed out as well for the same bright white.

My bookshelf was still there against the far wall next to the bathroom door, but instead of the classic books that had been there since I was young, there were what appeared to be books on politics. I looked down at my desk where I still rested my trembling fingers to see all of my pretty supplies were replaced. The matching pen and paper holders were boring, plain white. I didn't bother to open any drawers, I already knew what I'd find.

I slowly walked toward my open bathroom door and flipped on the light. All my department store products had been replaced with items that could be purchased at any grocery store. My life of luxury was gone. My parents were showing me that I had clearly ruined whatever chances I'd once had of living a pampered life. If only they knew I couldn't care less. What I truly cared about was hundreds of miles away.

I stepped up to the sink so I could splash cold water on my face and stilled when I saw my reflection in the large mirror. I looked terrible, with dark circles under my eyes and dirt smudged on my face. I had a bruise I hadn't known was there on my forehead, likely from when I'd been hiding in the bathroom before I passed out at the warehouse loft. I gingerly touched it, surprised to see it was already yellowing as if it were days old instead of several hours. It didn't hurt, but there was a small bit of tenderness as I pressed on it.

My eyes froze on the brand on my wrist that was reflected in the mirror. I knew my parents would be outraged, thinking I had tattooed myself. They would probably try to have it removed as soon as they could make the appointment. I covered the mark with my other hand, as if I could protect it but laughed quietly to myself. I doubted there was anything on earth that could remove a mating brand other than to cut it off.

The sound of the lock turning on my bedroom door had me closing my eyes. Martha was a new maid who had been hired shortly before I had run away. When it came to the way all the staff treated me with kindness and respect, she was the one exception to the rule.

Ever since Martha had arrived to work at the estate, she'd acted as if we were enemies. She'd never been outright rude, but she'd never been polite, choosing instead to narrow her eyes at me when I passed. If she cleaned my room, I found that my sheets were still dirty or that small items would go missing. There was never anything that I would feel the need to report, and I'd ignored the stares, but it was evident that she didn't like me.

Martha strolled into the bathroom, looking like she'd been roused from sleep. She was wearing a robe and a smirk on her face. She was young and pretty, with shiny black hair pulled back in a ponytail. I had always wondered if we could be friends if she weren't so hellbent on hating me for reasons I couldn't understand.

"Oh, how the mighty have fallen, huh?" she said as she walked straight up to me without hesitation. She reached out and gripped the collar of my dress and yanked hard. I heard a ripping sound as the seams tore. With a gasp, I used both hands to hold the bodice up over my breasts. "Get over yourself, princess. I have a job I was woken up to do, and I'm going to do it. I don't care about your ugly tits."

With both hands, she pulled until I couldn't hold on to the fabric any longer. I lost the tug-of-war on the dress, and it fell to my waist. I crossed my arms over my bare breasts, uncomfortable at being naked with her, regardless of what she'd said.

"I dare you to fight me. I have instructions to call the guard in if you give me a hard time." She grinned at me but it was anything but playful. She seemed almost hopeful that I would put up a fight.

With one arm still over my chest, I reluctantly shimmied the destroyed dress Valen had bought for me down over my hips and thighs, letting it pool on the floor. I looked down at the once pretty fabric and mourned the loss of his gift. He hadn't needed to do something so nice for me. It was the only thing I had left from my time with him, and I wanted to scream and cry at the injustice of it all. Instead, I stepped out of the fabric and walked on wooden legs to the shower.

I heard Martha snort with laughter as I turned away from her. "No undergarments? My, my, what a little slut you are. Did you run away to be with a man? Tell me, slut, are you still the virtuous little princess you always pretended to be?"

I refused to answer, choosing to turn on the shower and step under the spray before it even warmed up. If I had to endure her presence, I could do it the way I was raised, with poise and grace.

My lack of response must have angered her even more because, by the time I was finished showering, my hair had been pulled and tangled so horribly that it would take me forever to get it straight again. She'd also managed to scratch me several times and tripped me as I stepped out of the shower. My towel had somehow ended up falling into the water, so it was cold and damp.

By the time I fell onto my bed after Martha was let out of my room with a parting satisfied smirk, I just wanted the whole night to be over with. I didn't know what dawn would bring, but it couldn't be much worse.

Chapter 24

I stepped over the bodies of the dead vampires and had to be grateful that Syn had left my boots on. However, I was definitely going to retrieve my leather jacket after I finished with this bullshit.

I stepped to the end of the hallway where all the private dance rooms were and, apparently, the door to the basement. I cautiously looked around the corner, expecting to see naked dancers gyrating on the stage. Instead, the stage was empty, and though the sound system loudly played another 80s song, Cherry Pie seemed inappropriate for what was happening in the main entertainment room.

Bodies were lying everywhere. Men were lying across tables, on the floor, and slumped back in the plush seating. I looked closely, studying the bodies without seeing any signs of life from any of them. I could only guess how Syn had accomplished it, but she somehow managed to murder her entire clientele. The sound of singing that could be heard just over the thumping music was my first clue.

I had never seen Syn in her demon form before. I shivered in revulsion as I watched the demoness half covering the body of a dead man. Her tail was long, probably a good six feet. The tailfins had long ribbon-like protrusions from the end that narrowed into sharp, thin points. The scales were iridescent, with blue, green, and purple glowing from within as if they were part bioluminescent.

Her naked torso was spotted with the same iridescent scales that covered her tail, and a large dorsal fin was situated along her spine. There were smaller fins along her forearms and the back of her upper arms. Her fingernails were dark purple and long, shaped into sharp points, easily able to puncture a victim and hold it to her. There was no need to use them at that moment, though, considering the man she was face to face with was dead as a doornail.

A body stepped up beside me as I watched Syn feeding from the poor soul. "I wasn't expecting to encounter a Siren when I decided to see to your complaint personally."

I turned to Crispin with a snort. "Does anybody really expect to see a Siren?" I grinned at him, and we grabbed each other's forearms in the way of the brotherhood. "Fight hard."

He responded to the greeting the way we always had nearly a thousand years ago. "Die well." He pulled me toward him, and we slapped each other's backs. "It's good to see you, Valen."

"Vampire, huh? How did that happen?" I asked as I turned back to watch Syn slide her body from her current victim and over to another, starting her process all over again. I noticed that the body she'd left behind looked like a chalky pale gray, as if he never had any life in him at all.

"It's a long story, but I'll make it short," he said as he caught one of his men by the back of his collar and pulled him back to where he'd been standing. He stuffed his finger in the man's ear, pushing the earplug in deeper. If I had to guess, I was sure I'd find similar earplugs in the vampires I'd left to bleed out in the hallway. "I was stabbed in the stomach with a sword. Kane said he admired my spirit and strength. Since the woman I'd thought I loved married another man, I had no reason to say no to his offer of eternal life."

"I remember the hatred you'd held to fuel you in the ring." I eyed him up and down, noting his crisp suit and the formal posture. If I didn't know any better, I'd say he was some kind of foreign royalty with his faint European accent that I could detect as I listened closely to his speech. "You've come a long way from the leather and chain-mail days. How is it you are able to withstand the singing?"

"I suppose it's because I am mated?" He eyed me with speculation. "Same as you, I would guess. How long have you been mated?"

I held up my wrist so he could see the black symbol forever branded on my flesh. "Just a day ago, actually." I jerked my chin in Syn's direction. "She's the one responsible for my mate being kidnapped by those rogue vampires you are here to deal with. But that Siren? She's mine."

He clapped me on the back again. "Understood. I'm surprised you haven't already ripped her heart out."

I frowned as I considered it. "How does one go about killing a Siren demon?" I asked as I turned to look at the man who'd once been human and who I had considered a friend and teammate. "I'm afraid to say I don't have a lot of knowledge when it comes to demonkind."

"There are a lot of myths out there about Sirens, just like all the other supernatural creatures. Most of them are made up stories by humans, though. Just like most creatures, losing the head, heart, or both should do the trick." I grunted. If he were to cut out my heart, I would simply regenerate a new one while my body shut down in suspended animation to allow time to heal. When I'd lost my head, I grew a new one. I am glad that there were no cell phones or cameras back then to document the event.

"Alrright, let me take care of this so I can show you where the vampire nest is." I strode forward until I stood in the middle of the room. The music was finally turned off in the middle of a Poison song, making the room eerily silent other than the sounds of Syn's deep breathing as she continued to suck the remaining life force out of the bodies. "Syn!" She jerked her head around when she heard her name.

Double rows of razor sharp pointed teeth snarled at me. They appeared to be serrated, and just the sight of them made me want to back away in revulsion. She hissed, her Siren song cutting off abruptly. Her expression swiftly changed from fury to embarrassment and finally to shock. "You escaped." Her voice was different in her Siren form. Her words made a hissing sound the way I would expect a talking snake to sound. She blinked as she stared at me in contemplation, her vertical pupils briefly disappearing behind vertical eyelids.

The rest of her face was just as strange. Her nose was a small bump with tiny slits for nostrils. I figured if she were a fish, she likely had gills on the side of her neck or behind her ears. Her stringy hair was falling forward, so I was unable to see them. Her mouth was lipless, and when she closed it, there was just a wide slash that concealed her jagged shark-like teeth.

"Of course I escaped. I'm insulted you thought some chains and manacles would be enough to keep me captive." I stalked closer to where she was lying still over the man she'd been inhaling. "I want my leather jacket back." I tilted my head as she moved to slither off the dead body of her victim. It was strange to witness a giant fish move around awkwardly on dry land. "What did you do with it?"

She leaned on one elbow as she waved her hand nonchalantly. "I think I put it in my office," she pouted, the slit of her mouth pulling down into a frown.

"Good," I nodded as I showed her the knife I had been holding down by my leg. "Do you want to do this in that form, or..." I trailed off as I considered the possible attack points. I knew she'd have weaknesses in either form, but though she was incapable of standing as a

Siren, I couldn't discount the strength of a demon in its true form. Plus, she had those sharp claws and nasty teeth.

She opened her mouth, and as she spoke, what she said came out melodic. "You don't want to hurt me, Valen. I'm your best friend and want to be so much more. You want to be more, too."

I could feel her words burrow into my skull and try to dig their way into my brain. It somehow hurt like a piercing dagger and felt soothing, like a caress at the same time. I chuckled.

"Did you forget I have a mate, Syn? Though, even if I didn't, I doubt you would have any effect on me anyway. Nice try, though." I held up my free hand and waved my fingers toward her in a come hither motion. "Let's get this over with. I have a mate to rescue and the rest of eternity to spend with her in my arms."

Her face twisted in a vicious snarl that I could see being the cause of nightmares for hundreds of sailors. I expected an attack, but I hadn't anticipated how quickly she could move out of the water. She lunged forward with her claws extended, aiming for my throat. I sidestepped with plenty of time. She may be fast and have built-in weapons, but I had experience on my side.

I spun around, slicing the dagger through the air. At the heavy thud of her body falling to the ground, her scream of pain and outrage had the unexpected effect of making me want to claw out my own eardrums. Perhaps it was another weapon in the Siren's arsenal. I shook my head to rid myself of the lingering effects.

While Syn lay there clutching at her bleeding belly, I took the chance to look back at Crispin and his vampires. They were watching in fascination while Crispin had his arms crossed, watching with a critical eye.

"Are you critiquing me?" I asked in disbelief.

He merely shrugged. "I wanted to see if you've lost your touch." He waved a hand toward the bleeding Siren. "You're doing well so far, though you've barely gotten started. Carry on."

"Arrogant bastard," I huffed out, then turned to walk back to Syn. She looked up at me with tears in her strangely shaped eyes. I had a moment of pity for the woman I had actually liked once upon a time, before I learned about the monster inside her that she had hidden so well. Or maybe I hadn't wanted to see it back then.

A large part of me regretted what I was about to do. Instead of allowing that useless emotion to keep me from following through, I focused all my attention on the fight in front of me. I reached down to haul Syn up, her heavy weight making it more of an effort than expected. I tightened my grasp on her dark hair, exposing her neck.

Just as I was about to plunge the knife into her neck, her demeanor changed from the one of hurt, weak prey to a vicious monster. Her claws swiped out, catching my side. I sucked in a breath at the instant pain that flared hotly from the wound. I didn't bother to look down at it; it was deep, and I could feel the way my blood was already running freely down my side. Knowing that regardless of how such a wound would have killed a mortal, I pressed on. I would heal quickly enough to finish this fight.

She wriggled then with so much effort I couldn't maintain a grip on her hair. Her body twisted and writhed, truly giving the appearance of a fish on a hook. As the hair I was holding tangled in my grasp, I could feel strands of it breaking at the root. If she continued her actions, she was going to have quite a large bald spot.

I bared my teeth at her, showing who was the biggest predator in the room, but she chose to ignore me, her only focus being her attempts to get away. Unfortunately, with her wild twisting, I was having trouble trying to aim properly with the knife. I arced the blade down, aiming for her chest. She seemed to sense my intention because she focused back on stopping me from stabbing her, forgetting her fight to get loose for a brief moment.

This time, when she swiped her claws at me, it was with the intention of severing my arm from my body. I dropped her hair at the final second and jumped back out of reach, but she'd still managed to leave deep groves in my forearm. I bent to grab her again. Perhaps I would just slice her through the way she seemed determined to do to me. Before I could follow through, she lunged as fast as a cobra.

Those razor sharp serrated teeth dug deep as Syn sank them into my thigh. I ground my jaw against the pain and used her distraction to my advantage. With her mouth firmly attached to my thigh, doing her best to take a chunk from my flesh, I gripped the knife tightly and, without hesitation, plunged it to the hilt straight into her heart. At least, I hoped it was where her heart was. There is no telling with demons in their natural forms. Her heart could have been in her tail for all I knew.

With a pained gasp, Syn finally released me. She dropped back to the floor, lying on her side, and panted. I watched her carefully, not trusting her to fake another injury. As I watched her face, her slitted pupils wide with pain and disbelief, I twisted the knife, intending to cause as much damage to her organ as I could.

She jolted as I withdrew the knife covered in dark purple blood. I shifted my gaze from the knife back to her face and watched as that same dark purple began to pour from her mouth. Her body spasmed, and she coughed, causing the blood to spray over the floor and her own body. She moved her lips, attempting to speak. I doubted there was anything that she could say that I wanted to hear. She's already said enough.

"L-love," she paused to cough again before continuing to struggle to get her final words out. "You."

I shook my head, sadness filling me. "Love isn't like this, Syn. Love is accepting the person for what and who they are and wanting them to be happy."

Knowing I needed to finish her death and ensure it was one she couldn't recover from, I slid the knife across her neck. I kept slicing, digging the blade in until finally, her head rolled away from her body.

I stood to my feet and limped toward the door separating her office from the rest of the club.

"I'm going to get my jacket. I hope someone grabbed my motorcycle."

Chapter 25

Kallista

I sat on the end of the bed, my hands folded primly in my lap as I stared down at the beige carpet. At any moment, somebody would be arriving to escort me to the dinner my parents were having for a few of their friends. It was a common occurrence, one I should have expected. I guess I hadn't thought they'd have a dinner party the day after they forced me back home.

I'd slept horribly, tossing and turning in the starched white sheets. Every time I closed my eyes, I saw visions of Valen the way he'd been when he smiled down at me or imagined the way his wings had felt under my fingertips. I clench my hand into a tight fist as if I could hold onto that sensation and never let it go.

I glanced at the window, considering, again, if I could escape through it. Unfortunately, I was on the second story. There was a concrete pad under my window, and guards had been posted nearby, easily spotted. Each time I'd wandered over to the window, I could see at least one, sometimes two, making a pass. There was always one holding the leash of a large dog. I wasn't stupid enough to think it was possible to outrun a trained guard dog.

I closed my eyes as hopelessness swamped my heart. If I were to escape on my own, my one and only chance would be to use the ability that had terrified me ever since I was a young girl when I'd lost control and nearly brought the house down. It frightened me. The thought of what could happen, the people I could kill. I could even hurt myself. It wasn't as if I could control the damage done.

My eyes opened, and I stared blankly at the wall as I remembered something Valen had said. After we'd sealed our bond, he'd told me that he could feel a difference in his abilities. He was no longer afraid that they would get out of control. He'd said he was stronger and implied that I was, too. Could it be true? Could I really control the damage I caused?

The sound of the key turning in the lock jarred me from my musings, and I jerked my head in the direction of the bedroom door. As soon as the door had swung open and I saw my mother standing there, I stood to my feet, nervously smoothing the pantsuit, hoping I hadn't caused it to wrinkle. The very last thing I wanted at that moment was to enrage my mother by not being perfect.

She walked over the carpet soundlessly on her high heels and came to a stop in front of me. She glared down into my face, and I couldn't help but fidget as she inspected my makeup. Martha had insisted that it was her duty to apply it for me. At first, I'd been worried that she would purposely apply it in a way that would get me into trouble. But as I'd looked myself over, I was surprised to see she'd done a fabulous job. It was light and without color, but it looked natural. I couldn't find fault in her work as she walked out the door with all the supplies with her. Even if I wanted to change anything, I wouldn't have been able to.

"You have bags under your eyes," she snapped at me once she was done with her inspection. Honestly, I'd thought Martha had done an outstanding job covering the tired bruises. I made a mental note to thank her later. Maybe it would help thaw her frosty attitude toward me.

This was the first time I had seen my mother since I'd arrived last night. She'd never had me brought to her for that talk she'd warned me about. I knew they'd get around to it eventually and I was torn over wanting to get it over with and putting it off until never.

I dropped my gaze to the floor, waiting for the verdict if I was suitable for their company, but caught the moment when her already stiff demeanor hardened into granite. I gasped as her hand shot out and snatched my wrist. Her nails dug cruelly into my skin as she held up my arm.

She sucked in a breath as she studied the mating brand. I had been worrying myself sick over what their reactions would be once they saw it. Frankly, I am surprised that my father never seemed to notice it yesterday on the trip. But that was him. Nothing mattered to him except for his own goal of reaching the White House.

"You got a tattoo," she hissed as she tightened her grip painfully. She dropped my arm in the next second as if I had burned her. Or at the thought that tattoos were contagious and she would suddenly sprout a tacky rose on her hip. "We will have it lasered off as soon as possible. In the meantime," she walked over to my dresser where the jewelry box sat. I hadn't bothered to open it, figuring everything inside had likely been removed.

She withdrew a cuff bracelet in hammered gold. I hated the thing when I'd received it as a birthday gift a couple of years ago. It wasn't my style, and I knew when I saw it that I would never wear it. I had murmured my thanks regardless and placed it in the jewelry box to gather dust along with the other bits and pieces of items I had been disappointed to receive over the years. It wasn't that I was ungrateful; it was that my parents had never bothered to really get to know me and, after 22 years, still didn't care to.

She snapped the cuff into place and then turned my arm this way and that, trying to determine if any part of the brand would show.

Instead of letting go of my arm, she pulled me in close with a hard yank. She spoke right into my face, invading my personal space. Her warm breath poured over my skin and it took everything within me to not grimace.

"You have so much to pay for. The money your father will have to shell out to get rid of that abomination on your skin will be paid back. Do you understand me? You're going to work off every penny. Maybe that will teach you not to go against my rules again." She ran her eyes over my face. "Did you whore around while you were gone, too?" she hissed.

My face flamed with heat, and she must have taken that for a yes because the next thing I knew, she was pulling back her arm and slapping me across the face. "You disgraceful little fool! We will make an appointment for that as well. Your future husband would have expected better from you."

I cupped my cheek, feeling the sting from her slap. She'd never really struck me before. Looking into her furious face, I came to the realization that she hated me. All my life, I have done everything I could to make my parents love me. I don't know if her love for me died the day I hurt her with my ability or if she'd never loved me at all. But I couldn't remember actually seeing the vile loathing she had for me until this moment.

"I'm not getting the br-tattoo removed. I'm also not going to the doctor. I am a grown woman, and what you are doing here to me is illegal and immoral." I glared right back at her. "What would father dearest's constituents think if they knew he had kidnapped me and you were holding me against my will?"

She lifted her hand to strike me again, but this time, I caught her wrist and held her hand away from me. I didn't resort to her level by digging my nails into her, but I did hold her firmly. "No, Mother. You will not touch me again." I could feel the moment my eyes bled to black. She gasped and tried to pull away from me, but I held her for another long second, just long enough to tell her without words that she was only free because I allowed it.

She all but ran to the door and pulled on the knob. She couldn't hide the way her hand shook as she failed to turn the knob the first time she pulled. Seeing that she was truly frightened of me caused a pang in my chest. I wish she knew that I could never purposely hurt her. She paused before opening the door to allow time to compose herself. The person who opened the door wasn't the same shaking, scared woman.

"Come along, Kallista. It's time to greet our guests for dinner." Without looking back at me, she began walking down the hall. I took a deep breath and stepped into the hallway. I started to follow her but was startled when my upper arm was gripped firmly. The guard walked me down the hall and to the sitting room, finally letting go before we came into sight of the guests. I resisted the urge to rub at the tenderness that his bruising grip had left behind. I turned to look at him, studying his features.

"Why the fuck are you looking at me?" he snarled.

"I want to remember who I need to tell my mate to kill when he comes to rescue me." Without waiting for a reaction to my words, I lifted my chin and walked into the sitting room where my parents and their guests were gathered for a drink before dinner. I forced a smile that I hoped looked genuine enough as I glanced around the room. There were faces I recognized from past dinner parties, but there were a couple that I hadn't seen yet.

I murmured a polite greeting, then walked over to a spare chair to sit on the edge of the seat. My feet were crossed and tucked to the side, my knees together. My hands were resting together in my lap and my back was straight as a board. I felt like a fraud. If I had learned anything from my time away, it was that I would wither and die if I had to live like this for the rest of my life.

"Kallista, dear, it's so nice to see you up and about. Your parents have told us that you have finally recovered from your illness. I was so sorry to hear that you had fallen ill. And you missed your wedding, too." The wife of the Mayor turned to a man who sat on a loveseat to my left. It took me a moment to finally recognize him as my groom. "Bradley, have you made new plans with our lovely Kallista yet? I do so love a beautiful wedding. I can't help but cry every time." She waved her hand at her face as if fanning away tears.

I kept my serene smile plastered to my face with the sheer force of will. I was grateful she had asked the question of someone else because I had plenty to say on the subject, but it wouldn't be pleasant.

"I believe since my lovely fiancée is doing better, we will have the wedding back up and running very soon," Bradley answered. I wasn't surprised at the response. I was sitting in a room full of politicians. They were nothing if not diplomatic and experts at side-stepping questions by answering without giving a full answer at all.

"That's wonderful to hear." The Mayor's wife thankfully turned to someone else to discuss plans for a charity event. I let my muscles relax the tiniest bit once the attention had been moved away from me. I glanced back at Bradley to see he was looking directly at me. There was a slight sneer on his face. Of course, he knew the real story. He had been jilted the night before his wedding, which had taken nearly a year to plan, so I understood his frustration with me. I would have pulled him aside a year ago to explain myself, but if he were anything like our fathers, he wouldn't understand, and nothing would have changed.

I lowered my head to stare at my folded hands, risking my mother's wrath for not engaging the guests in conversation, but I had already reached my limit. I wondered if there were any excuses I could make to politely leave the dinner party before the meal even got started, but I lost the chance a moment later when the cook entered the sitting room to announce to the room that dinner was ready.

I waited, hanging back as everyone stood and carried their glasses of wine to the dining room, as they chatted happily with each other.

Inside, I was dying slowly. I took the seat that my mother pointed to, making sure to keep my elbows off the table and that my posture was impeccable.

I hadn't noticed who was sitting next to me until a hand suddenly slid underneath the table and gripped my thigh hard enough to bruise. I held in my yelp of shock and pain at the last second; the only outward sign that Bradley was hurting me was the rigidness of my muscles.

"When you're my wife, I'm going to punish you severely for making me look like a fool. And if you spread your legs while you were gone, I'm going chain you to the bed and whip you until you bleed." The way he whispered the words into my ear sounded like a lover's promise of pleasure instead of the threats they were. I clenched my fists under the table to stop them from shaking, and I bit the inside of my cheek so hard I tasted blood.

I could feel the way the powerful emotions of fear, revulsion, and rage coursed through me. I was silently seething inside while doing my best to remain impassive. I could feel my demon side lurking just beneath the surface and knew at that moment Valen had been right. I was stronger and had better control. I wasn't going to allow these people to take from me any more than they already had.

With my new resolve in place, I lifted my head to look at my mother and saw that her eyes were already on me. I wondered if she knew what he was planning to do to me, but then it occurred to me that she wouldn't care as long as he didn't leave any marks that could be seen by the voters.

While maintaining eye contact with her, I allowed my demon to come forward. She immediately paled and jumped to her feet at the sight of my black eyes. I'd never seen her so flustered before, and seeing it, had a smile curving up the corner of my lips. I must have looked unhinged because my mother took a step back before glancing around the table to see everyone staring at her in confusion and concern. She raised her hand to literally grip her fucking pearls, making me laugh out loud.

"Kallista," she cleared her throat and changed her tone from panic to her usual calm, cultured tone, which she used for anyone who didn't live in our home. "Kallista, dear. You don't look well." She snapped a finger at the doorway, and my hateful guard appeared immediately. "Escort my daughter to her room, please." Then she smoothed her palms over the skirt of her dress and slid back into her seat without looking at me again.

I gripped the hand that was still bruising my thigh under the table and jerked it off of me. I turned to Bradley, not even attempting to hide my eyes from him or anyone else who chose to look. "If you ever lay your filthy hands on me again, I will cut out your heart and feed it to the guard dogs." With those parting words, I lifted my chin and walked from the room. I didn't fight when the guard grabbed my arm again and just gritted my teeth against the pain.

I wanted to use my ability to escape, but there were too many innocent people in the house. I would practice alone tonight, then, in the morning, I would do what I needed to.

Chapter 26

VALEN

No one had actually retrieved my motorcycle from the warehouse, so I was stuck riding inside the SUV that Crispin had rented for the trip. I gave directions as we headed to the other side of town toward the vampire nest. Knowing who the Master was shed a whole new light on the entire situation.

I took the drive to explain what I knew about the vampire. When I had described his face the way I last saw him Crispin cursed.

"I've had a run-in with him before."

"Is he someone we have to worry about?" I was thinking of the way vampires had abilities, not to mention their level of Power. If a vampire were strong in Power, they could literally force other vampires into submission without lifting a finger. It was why those who were higher up on the scale ended up in the vampire monarchy structure. Or even the Council, which was the governing body over all vampires.

Crispin snorted. "Not even remotely. His Power is mediocre at best. The reason why he has so many followers and has become a

Master is because he is charismatic, and he makes big promises to vampires who have been turned away from other nests or who just don't like falling in line with the law. He's a wannabe gangster who is still stuck in the old west and believes laws are suggestions that he can ignore."

"How did you know to give your men earplugs?" It was something I had wondered about since they'd shown up already prepared.

"I didn't. But I always have supplies ready, just in case. You never know what kind of situation you're going to walk into when you are the vampire version of the police."

I grunted and drummed my fingers on my bloody jeans. I was a fucking mess. My shirt was torn, and my jeans had a Siren-sized bite taken out of them. I also still had the goddamn manacles attached to me. The chains were piled on the floorboard at my feet, and I wanted nothing more than to toss them out of the window.

The car slowed down and turned into a parking lot. One glance told me the driver had pulled up to a hardware store. "Fuck, I'm going to owe you for decades for all your help."

Crispin grinned. "I'd accept, but I think I owe you far more than I could ever repay. There were quite a few close calls in that ring. Without your help, I might be nothing but brittle bones in an unmarked grave."

I shook my head. "You know that isn't true. For a human, you did pretty damn well holding your own."

"Well, I'll call us even then."

I turned to look at him, to really take a close look at what he had become in the last almost thousand years since I'd seen him. The way he carried himself was someone full of confidence in his abilities, and he knew he was more than capable of following through on whatever threat he made to his enemies. I'd always hated vampires and thought of them as little more than rats in the dark, looking for a human to suck on. But looking at Crispin and the men he had brought with him showed me a different side to vampires that I hadn't seen before.

"So, you're a Councilman? Before that, you were the King of this region?"

Crispin grimaced but nodded his head. "I wish I could say I had a choice, but I had neglected my duty for long enough. Vampirekind needed me to step up into the Council role, so I finally did. It helped that my mate was pregnant at the time, so we would have had to move to the island anyway."

"The mythical vampire island," I mused. In all my wanderings, I had never come across the sanctuary.

He grinned. "I can take you if you want to see it. Do you think your mate would enjoy a tropical vacation after this is all over?"

I nodded thoughtfully. "She probably would. I am still getting to know her, but from what I had gathered so far, her parents kept her on a pretty tight leash."

The car door opened next to me, and the vampire Sentinel held up a shiny new pair of bolt cutters with a grin. "You ready to break your chains?"

"More than," I grunted and shoved my hands towards him. It didn't take but a minute and the manacles dropped to the pavement with loud clangs. I reached down to grab handfuls of the chains and tossed them out, too. The vampire frowned down at the pile of metal.

"You shouldn't litter." I knew he was right, but I had already left my mate in the hands of a monster for far too long.

"After I get my mate back, I promise to come pick them up and toss them in a recycling bin."

He inclined his head, took one last look at my mess, and then backed away, shutting the door. I heard the trunk open, then slam shut, and finally, we were back on the road. We were nearly there. I could feel my heart beating harder and faster at the prospect of the upcoming confrontation. I knew Crispin had a job to do, but if I had the chance to end that man for good, I wouldn't hesitate. I should have completed the job the first time, and then none of this would have happened. There was a lurch in my chest at the thought that I might not have met Kallista if the vampire and Syn weren't involved, but as much as it pained me to think that I would have missed out on meeting her, at least she would be alive and well.

I felt Crispin's stare as we turned the corner and onto the street where the nest was located. I glanced at him briefly before turning back to watch for the house. "What is it?"

"You remind me of someone. I noticed it right away, but the longer I look at you, the more I see it."

I looked back at him, noticing the look of contemplation as he studied my features. "Well, tell me about it later. We're here."

I jerked on the handle to open the door before the vehicle came to a complete stop and jumped out. I was ready to head to the door to kick it in when Crispin placed a hand on my arm.

"Why don't I get you a weapon?"

I didn't need a weapon, but I nodded anyway, not wanting to waste a single more minute arguing. When he placed a sword in my hand, I couldn't stop the grin from spreading. It had been far too long since I'd held one. Swords used to be a part of life before the world changed. Swords and horses. Now, it was guns and motorcycles. I wasn't sure which one I preferred.

Together, we strode up the front walk, past the overgrown weeds, and up to the wooden door. I raised a boot and kicked, causing the door to crash open in a spray of splintered wood.

"Knock, knock, motherfuckers," I growled as I stalked forward into the open concept living area. Immediately, vampires swarmed, teeth bared and hissing. With just a few swings of our swords, Crispin and I were surrounded by headless bodies.

I kicked the head of a dark haired vampire who looked like he'd been about twenty-five and a meth addict when he'd been Turned. "Where to now?" I mused as I walked past the carnage and peered into what turned out to be a coat closet. I slammed the door shut. "If

I were an asshole keeping human women, where would I store them?"

I looked back at Crispin, who shrugged. "Probably the basement." I nodded in agreement.

"Let's find it then."

Crispin pointed at his men. "You go check upstairs, just in case. You go that way. Valen and I will check for the basement door in the kitchen area." He turned to me. "Shall we go?"

"We shall," I growled and moved in that direction. We both opened the doors as we went, finding nothing of importance. When I came across a door next to the kitchen pantry, I opened it to reveal steps leading down into a well-lit basement. We descended the steps with me in the lead. I stopped at the bottom, seeing a large open space with another door leading to another room. There was nothing inside except what appeared to be a metal coffin sitting in the middle of the floor.

I called out to Crispin. "I didn't think you vamps actually slept in coffins."

He stepped around me and grunted. "We don't."

"Isn't it strange that one is here?"

"Maybe the asshole has a kink?"

A man suddenly appeared, stepping into the space from the door to the second room. He looked smug, grinning deviously, and I immediately grew suspicious.

Without saying a word, he lifted his hands, palms forward, facing them toward me. I raised an eyebrow. "What is this, a magic show? Are you going to whip a rabbit out of your ass hole next?"

Then, I felt a strange sensation that caused me to become light-headed. I swayed on my feet, feeling as if I could pass out at any moment. He was doing something to me, though I had no idea what it was. Crispin snarled from beside me.

"You idiot. I'd ask if you know who the hell I am, but I honestly don't give a fuck. You can't suppress abilities from more than one person at a time, can you?"

His words caused the man to falter as he looked toward Crispin as if he hadn't even noticed him standing there. His expression immediately turned to one of shock and then trepidation as he took a hasty step back while dropping his arms to his sides.

"S-sir. I'm sorry. I was just paid to do a job. I had no idea you would be here."

Crispin snorted as my head started clearing rapidly. I looked back at the coffin, and the situation began to make more sense. "You were going to weaken me by stealing my ability." I pointed at the coffin. "Was that supposed to be for me?"

The vampire swallowed loud enough to be heard across the room. "It wasn't my plan. I swear I had nothing to do with it!" He looked back at Crispin before sinking to his knees. "Please, don't kill me, Councilman, sir. I have a mate."

"Does your mate know that you are a mercenary for hire? How many others have you helped destroy?" It was then that I felt it. Crispin had unleashed his Power against the vampire, effortlessly forcing him to submit.

The man couldn't answer without implicating himself, which was all the answers needed. Crispin sighed as he stared at the vampire without pity.

"You've left me no choice but to send you to the Citadel for punishment." The vampire began to cry then as footsteps descended the stairs. "Cuff him. He has some crimes to answer for." Jared stepped around us and headed straight to the man while pulling a pair of iron cuffs from his pocket. The man continued to sob as he was dragged to his feet and up the stairs.

"What a pathetic piece of shit," Crispin growled and turned to me, studying my appearance from head to toe. "Are you alright?"

All the residual effects from having my abilities removed had already dissipated, so I grunted. "I'm guessing that was someone the

Master hired in order to capture me. I'm a little insulted. Even without my ability, I wouldn't have been that easy to take." I took another long look at the coffin, saw metal clamps along the base of the lid, and shuddered. I could protest all I wanted, but just the thought of what could have happened to me had ice flowing through my veins. Who knows how long I would have been trapped inside that metal box?

"I'm guessing the Master is behind that door." I indicated the door with my chin. I eyed Crispin with a glare. "I want him," I growled.

He just gave me a look of understanding. "I won't stand in your way." I gave a short nod and headed toward the door, the borrowed sword held tightly in my grasp. I had no plans of taking his head, though.

The sight wasn't altogether unexpected, though it still turned my stomach to see the multiple women huddled together for safety. They looked malnourished, and all of them looked as if they had been abused, with bruises and blood staining their rumpled clothing.

"Well, hello there, boys. Don't you know it isn't polite to visit one's home without an invitation?"

Standing there, like the coward I knew him to be, was the man who I should have killed almost three hundred years ago. My poor decision that day to leave him for dead instead had cost countless women their lives and dignity. I had a lot of things that haunted me on a daily basis, but allowing him to keep living was one I would rectify tonight.

"Raymond Hanover. You've been a very naughty boy." Crispin sounded bored as he stood next to me, looking completely relaxed. I could see the signs of anger radiating from him, though, as he looked around at the group of young women. I, on the other hand, was visibly seething with rage. Kallista wasn't in the room, which meant he'd hidden her somewhere else.

"Where's my mate?" I growled through clenched teeth. I made to move forward, ready to grab the man by his disgusting throat, but he grabbed the nearest girl, yanking her in front of him as he produced a knife. A drop of blood appeared on her neck as he dug in the blade.

"Ah, the lovely Kallista Hargrove." He made a show of looking around the room, then shrugged his shoulders. "I don't see her here. Oh! That's right!" He grinned, his sagging jowls wobbling with his movements. "She's gone."

"Where is she?" Ice had replaced the burning fury, and different reasons for her to be gone ran through my mind. I glanced down at my wrist, reassuring myself that she was still alive. "What did you do with her?" I demanded in a deadly tone that had several of the girls whimpering. I couldn't take the time to worry about them, though. Someone would come and take care of them later. I needed to find Kallista *now*.

"Well, I suppose that depends on what the man I sold her to does with her. But me? I did nothing but house her for a few hours."

I looked at Crispin, and he gave me a short nod. I returned his nod, then turned back to the monster. Without lifting my hand and without causing harm to anyone else in the room, I allowed my ability to seep out of me and into him.

It happened too quickly for my liking. He deserved to be tortured for hours, his pain drawn out as punishment for all the atrocities against women that he had committed over the centuries. Instead, I did what I was created to do. It may be quick, but it was going to be agonizing. It was the best I could do in the short amount of time that I had.

The woman screamed as she saw the boils growing on the arm that held her. It was her scream that had alerted him something wasn't right. He looked down at the woman to tell her to shut up, but his words cut off abruptly when he saw his arm. As he stood there in shock, his arm loosened around the girl. She immediately shoved away from him and ran to the group of women, flinging herself into their arms.

He looked up at me with fear and anger blazing from his blood-shot eyes as a boil popped on his fleshy neck. I grimaced at the sight of him. I had to admit, it was pretty disgusting. "What did you do to me?" His voice was hoarse, and he seemed to get weaker by the second. He staggered to the side and tried to catch himself on the back of a chair, but his hand slipped. Fluid from the erupting boils was dripping down his arms and onto his hands, making them too slick to catch himself. He groaned as he fell to the floor.

I heard one of Crispin's Sentinels enter the room right before he gagged. The vampire moaned on the floor as the boils began to form and pop at a much more rapid pace.

"Oh, man. That's the worst thing I've ever seen." The Sentinel gagged again.

Crispin stepped forward, walking toward the dying vampire. He turned his head to the women. "Look away." Some of them did immediately, but a couple of them stared down at the man with hatred burning from their eyes.

Crispin lifted his sword and brought it down swiftly, slicing cleanly through Raymond Hanover's neck and ending his reign of terror forever.

Valen

I slammed my fist into the wall repeatedly, feeling the skin tear and repair itself with each strike. I needed the pain to make me feel anything other than hopelessness.

Crispin was pacing back and forth with his phone to his ear, speaking to someone on his team who was supposedly a tech genius. He had promised that if anyone could figure out who Kallista was, it would be him. I had no choice but to stand there, not even trying to fight back the despair that my mate could be lost to me forever.

One of his Sentinels came rushing in, his hand around the back of the neck of another of Hanover's rejects. He looked terrified, his eyes darting around the room, looking for an escape. I snarled and stomped over towards him, ready to rip him apart with my bare hands, starting with his arms so I could make his torture last longer. The Sentinel raised his hand to stop me, making me turn my glare in his direction.

"Sorry, Valen, but you are going to want to hear what this guy has to say. I found him hiding in a closet upstairs. I didn't even have to make any threats before he was spilling every secret the nest had."

We all turned to look at the vampire, who was cowering pathetically. The Sentinel gave him a harsh shake, and the guy let out a whimper. "Tell him about the girl, now!"

"I-I wasn't involved. I swear it! I just wanted a place to live, you know? I didn't know it would be like this!" He turned to the Sentinel with tears and snot slipping down his face. "I just want to be human again."

Crispin let out a sigh and told his caller to hold on while he stepped over to the young vampire. "Look, you're a vampire now. There's no going back. If you want me to end your existence, I can do that for you. But, you see that demon right there who looks ready to shred your flesh and eat your bones?" The guy darted a glance my way and paled dramatically. He looked back to Crispin, pleading with his eyes. "We need information on where your Master sent his mate off to. Do you know who bought her?"

The vampire swallowed and then nodded his head reluctantly. "If I tell you, will you kill me?"

Crispin frowned as he studied him. "Do you want me to kill you?"

"Y-yes," he stuttered out.

"Fine, I will grant you that wish, but only if what you have to say is helpful. If it's not, I will lock you in my dungeon and make you live the rest of your existence with only rats for sustenance. Do we have an understanding?"

His crying picked up in earnest, but at least he began to speak, even if I had to strain to understand him through his sobs. "The M-master sold her to some politician. Everyone was talking about it because this politician runs a big campaign on family values." He swallowed, then chanced another glance my way as I took a step forward.

"Who was it?"

He cringed back at my threatening tone. "It was S-senator Hargrove. That's all I know, I swear it!" His sobs grew louder as he shook.

Crispin immediately turned away, speaking rapidly into his phone. I frowned as something occurred to me that I missed at the time. I had been too focused on hurting the man who had stolen my woman. "Isn't that the name the Master called Kallista earlier?"

I turned to Crispin as he glanced up and gave me a look I wasn't sure how to interpret. "Senator Hargrove has a daughter who disappeared from the public eye a year ago. The family claimed that she was very sick at the time. Since then, the Senator has been garnering sympathy votes."

He looked down at his phone and then held it up for me to see. On the screen was a younger Kallista standing demurely behind the Senator, who must have been her adoptive father. I wanted to grab his phone and study every feature of my mate. She smiled for the camera, but her eyes told the story of how miserable she was.

"That's her," I rasped out through a suddenly tight throat.

Crispin nodded, then exchanged a few more words before hanging up and looking at me. "Senator Hargrove chartered a plane early today. The flight plan indicated a round trip from Arkansas and back two hours later. It looks like he picked up your girl and took her back home."

I walked straight past the sniveling vampire, not even caring about his fate. That was Crispin's deal. I only had one thing on my mind. I passed the broken front door and stood on the sidewalk, suddenly at a loss for what to do. I needed to get to Arkansas, but I only had a motorcycle, and that was back at my warehouse. I tilted my head back to look up at the moon. The sky was an inky black dotted with tiny stars, and the moon was nearly full. But I saw none of it.

A hand clasped me on the shoulder. "I'll take you to her. The Council has its own plane that can be here in the morning. If I'd known I needed it sooner, I would have kept it here, but one of the other Council members needed it for business." He shook his head and sighed. "The amount of shit we have to deal with on a weekly basis is ridiculous. If I'd known most of my job on the Council was going to be mediating arguments between rich old vampires as if they were a set of kindergarteners, I would have thought twice about taking the job."

I snorted, appreciating his levity. I looked over at him and saw that he was also staring up at the sky. "I appreciate it. I'm not sure how this whole thing would have gone down if you hadn't been here. If I haven't said it yet, I'm glad you're still alive. Even if you are a bloodsucking leech."

He grinned. "That's Councilman Leech."

"I'd really like to meet the kind of woman who decided to put up with your haughty ass." We walked to the SUV and climbed inside, waiting for the Sentinels to finish up in the house while we caught each other up on our lives.

IT TURNED out that the plane Crispin had been waiting on ended up being delayed twice. The first time was because of a mechanical issue that was an easy fix, but it took an entire day before it could fly again. Then we had to wait for the other Council member to fly back to the vampire island since they were done with whatever had taken them out to begin with. I had to concede that since the plane was still there with them, it didn't make sense to fly in circles. It didn't mean that I wasn't growing more impatient and furious by the moment.

The only thing that made it bearable was knowing she was with her parents. From what she'd told me, they were shit parents, and I didn't trust them to keep her safe, let alone happy. But at least it wasn't with human traffickers like I'd feared when I'd heard she'd been sold.

By the time I stepped on the small jet, I was nearly out of my mind. I settled into the large leather seat but hardly noticed the wealth and comfort around me. It wasn't until the plane began taxiing down the airstrip that I remembered I'd never flown before and dug my hands into the armrests. I ignored the chatter around me as I hung on for dear life and wondered how much it would hurt if we crashed and if it was finally something my body couldn't come back from.

"First time flying?" Jared grinned at me. I grunted and flipped him off, then immediately regretted taking my hand off the armrest.

I felt the plane level out, and everything became much smoother. It no longer felt like the entire piece of metal was going to fall apart, and I was finally able to pry my eyes open.

"You know, you're lucky your first time was in this plane and not a commercial flight. Those are crowded, smelly, and shake so badly you can't help but wonder if it lost a bolt or two during takeoff. These planes are so much smoother." I wasn't ready to say what I thought about their idea of smooth. I let my heart rate slow back to a somewhat normal pace as I gratefully drank the glass of scotch the flight attendant offered with a sympathetic smile.

It seemed like we'd only been in the air for a few minutes when the announcement came over the intercom that it was time to prepare for landing, which was no better than the takeoff. But at least I knew what to expect that time. It was when the wheels touched down that I nearly ripped the arms off the chair.

As soon as the doors opened, I was out of my seat and making a beeline for the door. I was happy to be back on solid ground but even more grateful that I was a short drive away from my mate.

Chapter 28

Kallista

I woke up, immediately sensing that something wasn't right. The room smelled like wax and something burning, bringing back memories I did my best to keep buried. I tried to roll out of bed but was pulled to a stop before I could move even an inch. I frantically darted my eyes around, seeing my wrists tied to the headboard. Dozens of candles were lit, sitting on every available surface of my furniture.

My gaze stopped on my mother before continuing over to see the man who had haunted my nightmares for ten years. Father Butler stood at the foot of my bed, looking smug as he stared down at me. His robes hadn't changed. Nothing about him had.

I chose to ignore his presence, knowing that his only goal was to hurt me. There would be no pleading with the priest. Instead, I looked back over at my mother, who stood further away by the door. She had her arms crossed over her chest, and her chin was jutted out.

"Mother, please don't do this." It was the only plea she would hear from my lips. If she ignored me the way she'd done all those other times, she would kill the last thread of familial bond I'd held for her.

"I saw you last night." She swallowed, then shored up her confidence with the squaring of her shoulders. "There is a demon inside of you. I tried to help you... before. It didn't work." She looked over at the priest, who was still staring down at me with a maniacal gleam in his beady eyes. "Father Butler has assured me that he can rid you of the demon once and for all." She swallowed thickly. "It might hurt a bit."

I laughed bitterly. I didn't know what he had planned, but if it was worse than the lashings he'd given me as a child, I knew I should be afraid. "The only demon inside of me is *me*, Mother."

Her eyes widened, and she let her arms drop to her sides as she took a step back. Her hand waved behind her back as she searched blindly for the doorknob. Once she found it, she quickly opened the door.

"Just let me know once it's done, Father." And then she was gone, the door closing with a bang as she slammed it closed.

I took my disbelieving gaze from the door, actually surprised that she had taken the coward's way out. I wasn't sure if she was more scared of me or what the priest had planned. I looked back at Father Butler.

"You're no priest." My words were sure and steady as I eyed him from my vulnerable position.

"We are what we believe we are." He grinned, looking as if he won the lottery as he took me in. "You believe that you are a demon?" He tilted his head. "That's interesting."

I gritted my teeth. "Why is that interesting?"

He walked around the bed to stand at my side. He loomed over me and caused the fear I had been trying so hard to hold back to rush in like a tsunami. "Because I *know* that I am."

I stared in disbelief. He looked human, but then, so did Valen until he changed forms. Something told me I did not want to see this man's demon. "Are you serious?" I whispered while trying to inch away as he leaned in even closer. There was something disturbing about his eyes that made my skin crawl.

He chuckled. "Oh, sweet child. I don't lie about that. I am, after all, a man of the cloth."

"A priest wouldn't be a demon."

He pouted as if I were ruining his fun. "Well, I suppose you're right." His expression brightened again. "But there's no rules against demons being priests!"

"I'm pretty sure there is somewhere," I muttered, trying to turn away but finding it difficult to look away from his eyes for long. Then it finally hit me. "My reflection is upside down!" I gasped.

"Oh, yes. It's one of the only things I can't hide from humans, even when I am in this form. Have you ever heard of an Aswang?" He seemed to be eager to share with me, and I got the feeling he didn't often get to speak with his victims before he killed them. And there was no doubt in my mind that was where we were headed if I didn't get myself together and get on with saving the day.

I glanced around the room, trying to figure out how my ability to make the floors and walls break would get me untied from this bed. "Umm, it sounds vaguely familiar?"

He let out a throaty hum and stepped back. I watched as he walked around the room blowing out candles. "We don't want to cause a house fire, do we?" When he started walking back toward the bed as smoke rose from the extinguished candles, he reached down. With horror, I realized that he was removing his robe.

"That's really disappointing. The lore doesn't have it completely right, of course, but to know that my favorite victim doesn't even know what I am capable of?" He tsked at me as he folded the robe carefully and placed it in the chair by the window. "Do you want to know?" He paused with an eager expression.

If he were talking, then he wouldn't be killing me, right? I should be able to figure out what to do. "Um, sure. I'd love to know all about your Assgang." *Why can't I break the headboard if I can break walls?*

"Aswang," he snapped, "It doesn't even sound anything like… you know what? Forget it." He sounded seriously irritated as he spoke between clenched teeth and pinched the bridge of his nose. He dropped his hand and stepped close to the bed again. He leaned over until his angry face was an inch away from mine. He gripped my chin, his fingernails digging deep enough into my cheeks to sting. "Listen closely." He pulled his hand away roughly, scoring those fingernails across my face.

"My kind smell our victims," he began speaking as his hands moved to his white dress shirt, undoing the buttons slowly and methodically. "When we get the scent in our minds, it's almost impossible to ignore. I scented you at church. You probably don't remember that day. We shook hands." He paused to get my reaction. I shook my head helplessly. I honestly didn't remember meeting him until the day he showed up at my house to perform the first of many exorcisms.

"Yes, well, I figured you wouldn't. You were a very quiet child, barely speaking and rarely looking up from your lap. Always polite, though." I was incredibly disturbed by how much he seemed to have watched me. "Anyway, I have an incredible sense of smell, and I knew when I caught your scent that there was more to you than it appeared."

He shrugged the shirt off and placed it in the chair on top of the robe. "My nose brought me to your house later that night, and I had full intentions of eating you then and there, but I saw you sitting in the middle of the bed, staring at your closet door. There was something about your expression that intrigued me. It was as if you longed to be in there yet were terrified of opening the door at the same time. After that, I had to get closer to you. The phone call from your mother gave me the perfect opportunity."

I kept my eyes away from him as he removed his pants, not caring to see anything that he would reveal. Honestly, the whole stripping thing was weird and couldn't mean anything good. Instead, I focused my eyes on the footboard and concentrated on getting the wood to crack or split enough to pull my legs free. As I focused, I felt the bed underneath me tremble the tiniest bit.

"You played with your food," I pointed out dryly, glancing at him from the corner of my eye to see he had folded his slacks and was placing them on the stack of clothing. I needed to move a whole lot quicker because I was sure the main event was about to begin.

He paused, then barked out a laugh. "I suppose I did. I was curious how you would react, plus it gave me time to get to know you better. I had never done that before. It was... refreshing."

I was so shocked by what he'd said I forgot that I didn't want to see his junk and jerked my head in his direction. Luckily, he was covered by a pair of tighty-whities. "Get to know me better? You beat me with a rope for hours!"

He rolled his eyes and huffed. "It was a silk rope we used to tie back the curtains for the baptism pool. It was soft and hardly left a mark."

I looked up at the ceiling. "I can't believe I'm arguing with a demon over getting the hell beat out of me."

"It's funny you say that. I actually used those words when I explained what I planned on doing to you."

"Beat the hell out of me? Because you're a punny guy, right?"

"I do try. Just so you know, she didn't hesitate for even a minute at my intended methods. You should really find a new mother, the one you have is pretty shitty."

"Thanks, I hadn't noticed," I responded dryly and had to hold back a smile of triumph when the footboard split with hardly a sound. It still needed a way to go before I'd be able to free my feet, but it was working.

"You became my favorite toy, and I enjoyed playing with you.

But, I am sad to say it must come to an end. Thank you for returning so I can say my goodbyes properly."

His words pissed me off. "I didn't come back for—" I choked on my words when I turned my head to glare at Father Butler to see he had changed his appearance. It was so unexpectedly horrifying that my tight hold over my ability slipped, and the room began to shake. With great effort, I managed to reign it in before any damage could be done. I needed to escape from this monster, not end up buried under ten feet of rubble.

His demon was truly terrifying as he dropped to all fours. His arms and legs grew to twice their original length, growing into thin, bony limbs that bent backward, closely resembling spider legs. His fingers and toenails lengthened into long, sharp claws that made me swallow back my bile when I saw them. But it was his tongue that made me start to yank frantically on my bindings.

I suddenly remembered what little I knew about the Aswang from our short lesson about mythical creatures back in tenth grade. It was said to be a creature from the Philippines that hunted children and pregnant women so they could eat the unborn baby. That long tongue with the pointy, razor-sharp forked end, the one that just whipped around the room as if he were tasting the air, is what they use to eat their victims.

"Holy shit. This can't be happening right now." I kept rambling to myself as I pulled on the ropes until my arms began to burn from the friction. The pain was enough to center me and helped to bring my focus back to escaping. I took a deep breath and concentrated hard on the footboard, knowing I didn't have time to be slow and stealthy. The time for stealth was long over. It was time to get the hell out of here.

Chapter 29

Kallista

The Aswang was playing with me; I just knew it. I would yell for help, but I knew that my mother had sent the guard away so he wouldn't hear the "exorcism" she assumed would be performed once she left. They probably wouldn't come anyway since my mother believed that he had planned to beat me again since she'd witnessed it many times in the past. She just hadn't known that the first time she'd actually left me alone with who she thought was a priest was actually a monster intent on eating me.

The Aswang was climbing the fucking wall, literally. He dug his sharp claws into the plaster and scaled the wall like he was fucking Spiderman. I had my feet free, so I scooted back until I was able to sit up on the bed to give my arms more slack. It seemed to amuse the demon since he made strange chuffing noises that sounded suspiciously like laughter.

I tried to calm myself, taking deep breaths so I could concentrate on the headboard, all while I tracked every movement the Aswang made as he gouged deep grooves into the plaster.

"My mother is going to kill you for damaging her walls," I muttered, then sighed with relief when I felt the first crack in the headboard. When he got to the top of the wall, my mouth dropped open as he simply held on and began to crawl across the ceiling. "What in the hell..."

His long tongue swept through the air again, this time much closer to my body, nearly making contact with the end of the bed where my feet had been just moments ago. With my heart racing frantically, I had to close my eyes to find my concentration again. When I felt the wood crack, my eyes popped back open, only to see the Aswang had moved across the ceiling to hang directly above me.

My breaths were coming out in rapid pants as I did my best to hold back the terror that made me want to curl into a ball and cry. I wasn't going to die this way. No way in hell would I let myself be eaten alive by a demon who looked like a hellhound and a bat had a baby.

I pulled hard while using my ability to break the wood. There was a loud cracking sound, and suddenly, my hands were free. He cocked his head and watched me, and I could swear that my actions only amused him. He was that confident, believing nothing I did would stop him from getting what he wanted.

He lashed his tongue out again, and with a yelp, I quickly rolled to the side, landing with a grunt on the floor. The Aswang dropped from the ceiling and landed on my bed with more grace than I would have thought possible. I tried to scoot away, my hands still tangled behind my back, with a large piece of the wooden headboard still stuck in the ropes.

I pulled frantically to free my wrists, knowing my chances were dimming with each second. I could tell he'd let me play enough. The way he was watching me now was no longer with amusement. His expression changed to one of hunger as he stalked closer until he was on the edge of the bed.

His tongue whipped out then, and with nowhere to run or hide, it struck me in the leg. The forked tongue was wicked sharp, slicing into me like a scalpel, burrowing in until it found a vein, and somehow I could feel the pull as he fed from my blood as if his tongue were a straw and I was a fucking milkshake.

The pain was excruciating, and I could no longer hold back my scream. He pulled back his tongue, and I grabbed my thigh, where the throbbing continued. He bunched his muscles in preparation to pounce on me, and I knew my time was over. I glanced down at my leg, just then realizing that my hand was free. Sometime during my struggles, I had slipped my wrist through the knot.

I pulled my other hand from behind my back, seeing the large, jagged piece of wood caught in the ropes. I gripped it tightly and looked back up at the Aswang just as he launched himself at me.

VALEN

The sky was lightening into a grayish purple as the sun began to make its ascent in the sky, and I was eager to get going. It had been two full days since I'd last seen Kallista as I left the loft to go get her breakfast. So much had happened since then, and I couldn't imagine what she had gone through with the vampires and then being force-fully taken back home with the father she had run away from.

Only Crispin and I climbed into the SUV that was waiting to take us to the estate where her parents lived. The Sentinels weren't able to stay awake during the daylight the way Crispin was, so it would only be the two of us. It wasn't a long drive, but by the time we had gotten close, the sun was already breaking the horizon. We slowed down before we got to the long fence line that bordered the property. That's where the two of us got out and made the driver wait for us to return.

Together, we scaled the fence, aware thanks to Crispin's tech guy that there were armed guards surrounding the property as well as attack dogs. It was going to take stealth and probably some brute force to make it into the house without setting off any alarms.

"This would have been easier if it were still dark outside." I had to agree with Crispin. Trying to be stealthy when the sun was starting to light up the whole damn place was definitely not ideal.

Everything was fine until we came to the first patrol. Super fast vampire speed kept the man from reaching his com unit, though, and he was put out of commission and stripped of his gear and weapons before he could make a sound. The dog wasn't as easy to dispose of, though.

As soon as the German Shepherd caught sight of us, he began barking, alerting any guards left in the area that there was trouble. The men were easy enough to dispatch, but we were both loathe to hurt the dog for doing what he was trained to do. In the end, Crispin surprised me with his ability to shift. In one second, he was a man; in the next, he was a giant fucking wolf standing over the German Shepherd with bared teeth.

The dog took one look at him and laid down on the ground with a whine. Crispin backed off and once he shifted again, he pet the dog while whispering to him in a calm voice that had the dog licking his hand. It was the dog who escorted us the rest of the way to the house, straight to a side door where he sat wagging his tail.

"Such a good boy," Crispin crooned at the dog. "Do you want to come home with me? I have a little girl who would love a pretty boy like you." The dog let out a yip and licked his hand again. Crispin turned to look at me. "Alright, chances are, the place is already up with staff moving around. It's up to you how we make this play."

I'd thought it over in my mind since yesterday when we'd found out where she'd been taken. The possible scenarios all ended with us getting caught and having to fight our way through. I shook my head. "Let's just go in as quietly as possible and head straight for her bedroom. The last door in the right wing, right? Your man isn't wrong about this?"

"I'd place my life on it," Crispin promised.

I nodded. "Okay, that's the plan then."

Everything went well. We hadn't seen anyone on our way, though we heard plenty of activity come from the direction of the kitchen. We passed an open doorway with a maid inside making a bed, but she had headphones on and was humming to herself, so we were able to sneak past the open doorway without her being any the wiser. But the plan for stealth went right out the window once we made it up the stairs to see a long empty hallway and heard a blood-curdling scream come from the door at the end of the hall.

KALLISTA

I screamed again and turned my face to the side as I thrust the wood in front of me on instinct. The weight of the monster hitting me had my back falling flat on the floor. My head struck the plush carpet hard enough to have me seeing stars.

I waited to feel the pain of being devoured alive, but all I felt was suffocation. I couldn't breathe with the demon on top of me. All of his weight was crushing me to the floor, and I couldn't move. My hands were trapped between our bodies, so I couldn't even try to push him off. Every time I breathed out, it got harder to pull more oxygen into my lungs as they became more and more compressed with every second.

Black dots filled my vision, and I didn't know if I was going to die from being crushed or from suffocation first. As tears leaked from the corners of my eyes, I heard a crash and a roar coming from my bedroom door and whimpered, wondering if a second monster had come in.

Suddenly, the weight was lifted off me, and I heard a thud as I drew in deep lungfuls of oxygen. Hands began to run over my body, from my arms to my legs, as I shook violently. It took a long minute for the rushing in my head to subside before I could finally hear the words being said.

"Baby, are you hurt? Please tell me you're okay. I don't know if she's okay! She's covered in blood! Fuck! There's so much blood."

"I don't think it's hers, Valen. Look at the demon. She stabbed it through the heart."

"She's not speaking. Kallista, answer me, damn it! I need to know you're okay."

I cracked my eyes open to see a figure crouched above me, his long black hair falling over his face as he continued to check my body for injuries. "Valen." My whisper was quiet but filled with every bit of relief I felt at having him here with me. "Valen, I'm okay." At least, I thought I was okay. I was alive and not being digested in the belly of an Aswang, so it was a good day, right?

Hands cupped my face, and I leaned into them. "Fuck, baby. I was so worried. Seeing you like that…"

I tried to raise my hands to touch him, but I was so exhausted, and my body felt like it was bruised from head to toe. "Valen," I gasped, the pain finally making itself known. I glanced down at my chest, where most of the pain was centered, but couldn't see anything but my nightgown soaked in dark blood. But there was definitely something wrong. "Maybe I'm not okay…"

"Let me look, Valen. She probably has at least one broken rib."

Valen barely shifted as another man moved to my other side and gently prodded along my rib cage. When he hit a particular spot, I hissed in a breath as the pressure sent bolts of pain zinging through my system.

"She definitely has a broken rib. The way that wood was, it probably jammed into her ribcage when the demon fell on her. She's lucky it didn't go through her chest, too."

Valen let out a vicious snarl that cut off as soon as I let out a pathetic whimper. "Can we get her up off the floor?"

"Sure, just try not to jostle her too much and keep her torso from bending. It's a good thing you're already mated. The accelerated healing will have her fixed up in no time. Probably nothing, a small ache by tonight."

Multiple hands grabbed me gently, and together, they got me to my feet. My bed was broken from the Aswang dropping down onto it, so they walked me over to the chair, where someone knocked the neat pile of clothes to the floor.

"What is going on in here? Who are you people? How did you get in here? I'm calling the police! Patrick!" My mother started screaming for my father until the handsome man in a suit stepped up to her. Her mouth closed abruptly as she shrank back against the wall.

"Mrs. Hargrove, my name is Crispin Decious. We are here to make sure your daughter is okay. Are you aware she was being stalked by that priest?"

"St-stalked? What? No! He was here to—here to…" She looked over to where I was sitting in the chair, covered from my neck to my feet in blood, and paled. "Is she hurt?"

Well, it was good to see she cared enough about me to ask. "It's a little late to give a shit, Mother." Every second I sat there, the pain eased a tiny bit, and I found it easier to take a deep breath. "All my life, you accused me of being possessed," I laughed, then groaned as my ribs told me how much of a stupid idea that was. "Guess what? Not only am I half demon but I'm also mated to a full-blooded one."

I reached out to take Valen's hand in mine. He squeezed my fingers gently. "The only monsters here are you and that so-called priest who wanted to have me for breakfast." I sighed and looked up at Valen with pleading eyes. "Can we go now? Please?"

He bent down and kissed my lips softly. "Of course."

Chapter 30

Kallista

My father appeared in the doorway as Valen was helping me to my feet. The questions began all over again, and I rolled my eyes, choosing to ignore them and let someone else give the answers. We stepped around the body of the Aswang and headed toward the bathroom. I needed to shower off the blood that was coating my body first before I left the estate for good.

I could hear the man who'd come with Valen speak to my father in the same calm tones, explaining the situation. I doubted it would do any good. The day my father cares more about people than his career plans is the day I fall into a dead faint.

As soon as the door was closed behind us, Valen began to undress me with the gentleness one would show for a newborn baby. My plain white cotton nightgown was sticky and wet with dark blood, so he held it away from my face as he lifted it over my head, which I was eternally grateful for. It dropped to the floor, and I was left in just my panties. He knelt down and, while looking up at my face, tapped first one foot and then the other after sliding them down my legs. Once I was fully naked, Valen quickly stripped out of his own clothing.

We took a hot shower together where Valen did all the work and I let him. Exhaustion from the adrenaline crash was making me want to close my eyes and just lean on him. The gentle brushing of his hands against my skin felt so soothing and the way he kissed the dark bruise on my ribs where the wood had dug into me made tears spring to my eyes.

"Valen," I whispered hoarsely, but he just shushed me softly as he stood to his feet and gathered me in his warm embrace. In his arms, I'd never felt safer, and I never wanted to leave them again.

VALEN

I wasn't sure if Kallista was aware of how much her body was shaking throughout the shower. I was so proud of her for battling the demon and winning. I shudder to think of what would have happened if we hadn't arrived when we did. I had faith that she would have been able to find the strength to get out from under the Aswang demon, but there was no use dwelling on it. She was safe, and I could touch her again and feel how alive she was.

Once I turned the water off, I quickly dried her and wrapped a towel around her body. It didn't escape my notice that while she had a nice bedroom and attached bathroom, she had just the barest of essentials available. With as much money as the large, fancy house indicated her parents had, I would have expected more.

I peeked my head out of the bathroom door to see if anyone was around, only to find the bedroom empty except for a young woman who held a pile of folded clothing. When she heard me open the door, she jerked her gaze away from the bloody mess on the other side of the room. Her eyes widened in shock as she took in my appearance with just a towel wrapped around my waist.

"Are those for Kallista?" I asked in a gruff tone to get her attention back from my body.

"Um, yes." She walked over to me, scanning my chest again, her gaze turning predatory. "I am usually responsible for taking care of her. If you want, I can come in..."

I didn't like her eyes on me, and I didn't like the way her face had changed when she mentioned my mate. I grabbed the clothing from her. "No, thanks. You won't be needed any longer." I replied curtly and shut the door in her face, reaching for the lock only to realize there wasn't one. I shook my head and turned back to Kallista, who was leaning heavily on the counter.

"That was Martha. My mother put her in charge of bathing and dressing me to make sure I didn't do anything she would disapprove of. She has taken her job a little too seriously."

"I don't like her," I muttered as I took her panties and had her step into them.

She huffed out a laugh. "Neither do I."

I froze at the strained tone of her voice. "Did she hurt you? Who else in this house caused you harm?" I demanded, lifting her eyes to meet mine with a finger under her chin. "Tell me, Mate."

She blinked at me, then smiled brilliantly. "Are you going to avenge me?"

I growled, then bent to nip at her bottom lip. "You're damn right I am going to avenge my woman. No one is going to get away with hurting you. Ever." I had plans to make my mate's parents suffer as well, though it would be a much longer torture than what the others would get.

She was hesitant but told me what I needed to hear. "There is a guard that I may have threatened last night."

I cocked my head as I studied her. "Oh yeah?"

She looked sheepish as her face turned red, but didn't break eye contact. "I, um, may have said that my mate would kill him for laying his hands on me."

I carefully pulled her close with my hand against her lower back, mindful not to jerk her body as I did so. "He touched you?" I growled as my demon came close to the surface. She immediately began shaking her head.

"Not the way you are thinking. He was just rough when he grabbed me."

It was enough, in my mind, to deserve to die. The guard, as well as that woman. I kissed the top of her head as she rested her cheek on my chest. "Thank you for telling me." She said nothing in return, and I could sense her guilt. I would have tried to convince her that she had nothing to be guilty for; she wasn't the one who'd hurt another. But her soft heart would just have to get used to having a mate who wouldn't allow transgressions against her to go unpunished.

As soon as we were finished getting dressed, I found a brush and worked the wet tangles from her hair as carefully as I could, not wanting to cause her any more discomfort than she was already in. After I set the brush down, I looked her over. She was wearing a plain beige pantsuit that, while she looked good in anything, it just didn't suit her. I cursed myself for leaving behind her bag of clothing in the SUV.

"You ready to get out of here?" I held out my hand and she took it with a relieved expression.

"Yeah, pookie bear. Extremely."

I growled, but inside, I was secretly smiling.

When we exited the bathroom, the room was empty. Even the body of the dead demon had been removed. I opened the bedroom door but paused. "Is there anything here you would like to take with you?"

She looked around the room and shook her head sadly. "No, there's nothing here for me." She gave my hand a squeeze, and together, we exited the destroyed bedroom and headed toward the stairs. As we descended toward the main floor, voices could be heard nearby. We followed the sound to see Crispin standing in front of what looked to be the entire staff.

It only took a minute to figure out what was going on. I could feel Kallista relax into my side as if a weight had been lifted from her shoulders. She, too, had realized Crispin was using compulsion to manipulate their minds. He was erasing our presence and everything that had happened this morning.

"Kallista is free to go and will no longer be under your control. You won't have any contact with her in the future. If asked by anyone, you will explain that she is exploring the world and that you support her, wishing her a happy life."

Her parents nodded, agreeing with his commands readily. The rest of the staff, including the maid who had delivered the clothing, all murmured their agreements as well. Crispin turned to Kallista. "Is there anything you want to say or something you would like for me to include?"

She looked at her parents, the same sad expression she'd had while looking at her bedroom crossing her features briefly before turning away from them, her spine straight and her shoulders held back. "No, I think you've covered the important bits. Thank you."

Crispin inclined his head regally. Before we turned to leave, I stepped forward and eyed the guards with speculation. With his menacing glare even Crispin's compulsion couldn't tame, it easily became clear to me which one had placed his hands on my mate. I turned to Kallista and indicated the man with a jerk of my head and a raised brow. She sighed but made me proud when she squared back her shoulders and lifted her chin, giving me a jerky nod.

Without another word, I turned away from the assembled group of people and took Kallista's hand. Together, we walked toward the front door. Before we'd even reached the foyer, screams, both masculine and feminine, echoed around us. I gently squeezed my mate's hand as her steps faltered. Again, she had pride warming my chest as she determinedly strode toward the door without looking back.

The two victims of my wrath would be dead before we drove away from a sudden and mysterious illness. Her parents, on the other hand, would suffer much, much longer.

The SUV was waiting near the front door for us as we walked down the front steps and into the sunshine, leaving the horrors from the house behind. Crispin opened the back hatch of the vehicle and let out a shrill whistle. The sound of racing feet came from around the side of the house, and he held the door open wide as the German Shepherd didn't hesitate to leap into the back. After we all climbed inside and buckled our seatbelts, Kallista turned to me as she scratched the thick fur at the neck of the dog.

"What do we do now?" She looked a little lost and a lot hopeful. I noticed she hadn't bothered looking back as we drove down the long drive and out onto the street.

"That's entirely up to you," I told her as I put my arm around her and held her close to my side. "We can go anywhere you like. I have places just about everywhere."

She wrinkled her cute nose. "Are they all like the warehouse loft? I mean, it wasn't a bad place, but it had no... warmth." She looked up at me. "It was pretty plain," she said with a small smile.

"You can decorate any of my homes however you like. I have a feeling we will be staying in one place more often than I used to."

"If I may make a suggestion," Crispin called from the front seat, turning to look at me over the headrest. "There is someone who I think you should meet."

I studied his face, but he kept his expression neutral, not giving away any indication of who or why. I glanced down at Kallista, who gave a shrug. "I don't have anything on my agenda. Do you?"

There was plenty that I wanted to do, but none of it would be appropriate in front of our audience. After my mate was physically healed from her trauma this morning, I would be making her mine again in every way possible. The need to reestablish our bond was a growing compulsion I wouldn't be able to ignore for long.

"Okay," I told Crispin after reassuring myself that Kallista looked comfortable with his suggestion. "When would you like to go?"

He glanced at my mate, then back to me. "Why don't we give it a day? We'll get a hotel near the airstrip, and you can relax. I'm sure by tonight you'll be feeling much better," he said to Kallista. "Tomorrow will be early enough to go." Though I did like his suggestion to wait, considering what I planned to do with my woman once she could move without pain, his vagueness in regard to our destination was making me suspicious.

We pulled up to a nice hotel where Crispin got out and walked inside to the front desk. It only took him a few minutes before he returned holding two sets of room keycards.

"There is a restaurant inside that is currently serving lunch, with room service available 24 hours. I'm going straight to bed. I can withstand the sun for extended periods, but that doesn't mean I don't need to sleep. I think we could both use some rest." He snapped his fingers and the dog came to sit at his side while looking up at him adoringly.

I took the keycard gratefully. "I owe you."

"Stop saying that. You don't owe me shit. I am happy that I get to know you again, and I'm glad to help you with your mate. Ivy will want to get to know her as well, so plan to visit the island regularly."

"I think that would be nice," Kallista answered, giving him a smile as she leaned against my side.

As soon as we made it into our room, I set the two bags down on the floor and stripped her of the ugly pantsuit. "I'd burn these, but we would get kicked out of the hotel," I muttered as I dropped the clothing in the wastebasket."

I ushered her to the bed and pulled the covers back. "In you go."

"What about you?" she asked with a wide yawn.

"I haven't slept since you disappeared. I'm going to be right by your side."

She yawned again and gingerly laid down. I hadn't bothered to put new clothing on her so I could see every delectable inch of her body. My gaze stopped on the bruise along her ribs. It was already changing colors, yellow forming around the edges as her accelerated healing took over. Crispin was right; she should be back to normal by the time we wake up later. And then, I would show her exactly how much I missed my mate.

CHAPTER 31

Warm hands smoothed over my body, touching me everywhere and making my back arch at the delicious feelings they invoked. I reached down to grab the back of Valen's head as his tongue swiped over first one hard nipple and then the other. Before I could catch my breath, he was returning to the first one and sucking it deep into his mouth. Zings of electricity shot through my body as the sensations quickly overwhelmed me.

Valen began kissing down my stomach, briefly hovering over my ribs. I glanced down to see the bruise was entirely gone and realized that I didn't feel any pain. "I'm okay," I whispered as I ran my fingers through his hair.

"I never want to see you hurt again," he replied gruffly.

He continued on his journey down my body. "What are you doing, Valen?" I moaned as he took a long swipe up my center with his tongue.

"Reminding you."

I gasped as he plunged a finger inside me, then shivered at the sensation of him rubbing along my g-spot. I was already on the verge of an explosive orgasm. One good lick of my clit would probably send me over the edge. "Remind me of what?" I asked breathlessly once I was able to get my tongue to work again.

He climbed back up my body to hover over me. "Why I am the perfect mate for you." At his words, he plunged inside of me, his thick cock filling me up to just shy of painful. After several thrusts where I was already calling his name, not knowing if I wanted him to slow down or go even faster, he pulled out completely.

"No!" I wailed in denial.

He grabbed my hips and flipped me over onto my belly before I could blink. "Don't worry, Mate, I'm not stopping. Ever." At his words, he drove back in and began to pound into me ruthlessly. I put my head down into the pillow to muffle my screams, just then remembering that we were in a hotel and the people next to us could likely hear everything.

"Your body was made for me," he growled as he took a handful of my hair and pulled until my neck was bent back. "I'm going to spend the next thousand years proving it to you every single day." Then he slid a hand under my belly and lifted my hips. The new angle had me seeing stars as the sensation of having my hair pulled made me even wetter. "Mine!"

I began chanting his name like a prayer as he took me hard and fast. I cracked my eyes open to see his wings were out and caging me in. His shadows were dancing around the two of us, licking at my skin and making goosebumps erupt over my body. There was no holding back my scream as he dropped his hold on my hair and leaned over to bite into the place where my neck met my shoulder.

He released my flesh with a growl and a lick. "I will spend the rest of my existence showing you what you mean to me."

"Valen, please..." I couldn't finish my words as my orgasm started barreling towards me. And then I was there. All thought flew from my brain as I became nothing but sensation. My world narrowed until the only thing that existed in it was Valen and the pleasure he had wrung out of me.

I was vaguely aware of Valen's body stiffening over mine a second before his cock thickened and then began to pulse inside of me. The grunt he made as he released was guttural, making his chest vibrate against my back. I lay there panting while my body trembled with aftershocks.

"I fucking love you, Kallista."

I gasped so hard at his words that I began to cough as I inhaled my own saliva. I heard Valen hiss as my movements forced him from my body. He gently flipped me over and swept my hair out of my face as I stared wide-eyed up at him. The look in his eyes had my mouth snapping shut. There was a softness to his features as he smiled down at me in what I could only describe as adoration.

"From the moment I became aware that you existed, I was so scared of what you would do to me." He ran a finger over my cheek-bone as he took in every feature of my face. "You were going to change everything, and I wasn't ready to accept that my existence could be changed for the better. Then I met you, and you took my breath away with your beauty, even as you shook with fear. When I got to know you better, you showed me the beauty of your heart." He smiled down at me as a tear escaped and soaked into the hair at my temple. "I haven't witnessed much beauty in my very long existence.

"I should be surprised at how quickly I have come to crave your presence, but how could I not? When we cemented our bond, though, is when my heart knew yours. Losing you was enough to make me lose my mind. It made me accept what my heart had already known." He thumbed my tears away and bent to kiss my trembling lips softly. "It only took me a day to fall in love with you."

There was no way for me to speak. I was so overwhelmed as every word he said broke my chest wide open while healing me at the same time. I hadn't realized that there was a part of me that I was holding back from my mate until he said the words that I needed to hear. Valen telling me that he thought I was beautiful inside and out was healing all the jagged edges of my broken spirit. Each crack I'd suffered through the years of neglect and pain were being filled with his love.

"Valen," I choked out brokenly through my tears.

"Shh. I didn't say it for you to say it back. I can see what you feel for me in your eyes. If you need more time, I can wait, but I'll be waiting while still loving you. Thank you for being my mate. I know we didn't have a choice. But if I did, I would still choose you. Every time."

All I could do was blink up at him, wishing I had the words to say but trusting him to know. I would tell him when I could because I did love him. I knew it when we mated; I just didn't let my heart accept it then. But now? There was no barrier left between my heart and mind any longer. He had thoroughly torn down that wall. I just closed my eyes and let myself be filled with the warm glow that was all him.

After several long minutes, I opened my eyes to see him looking more content than I had ever seen him before, as if he felt as whole as I did.

"Valen? I-" I bit my lip, wanting to ask my question but worried that it would hurt him if I did.

"Ask me whatever it is on your mind, baby," he said softly.

"That man, that vampire that took me. He said some things. I was curious about them, but I don't want you to think I am judging you."

His expression grew wary but not guarded, as if he already knew what I wanted to ask. He didn't say a word; just nodded at me.

"The illnesses throughout history... the plagues and stuff... he said that you were responsible for them." It wasn't a question, really, but he knew what I was asking. It wouldn't change how I felt about him, regardless of his answer.

He sighed and rolled to his back and pulled me firmly into his side. I laid my head on his shoulder and drew circles on his chest with my fingertip, relishing the warm feel of his skin.

"I honestly don't know if I was directly responsible for them," he admitted. "It's something that I have struggled with since the first time I came upon a village that was suffering. I don't think I could have been, considering most of the time, they were already sick when I arrived. But it never left my mind that it was something I was capable of. It was the largest reason why, for most of my life, I chose to stay away from all humans. When I did spend any length of time around them, I did my best to control my ability from causing that kind of harm."

"He said you would walk through the villages that were dying."

The sound he made in his chest was one of anguish, and I placed my palm flat over his thudding heart in an effort to offer him comfort. "I did it as a reminder to myself, to remember why I needed to stay away. Seeing those innocent children suffer, all those families..." He cut himself off as if the memories were too hard for him to bear.

"I don't think you were responsible for them," I whispered, feeling it in my soul.

"We'll never know," he rasped out.

"Maybe not," I allowed, "but even if you had, it wouldn't have been your fault. But, Valen, the way you mourned over strangers, the way you still mourn their losses, you aren't the monster you think you are. And you said that you are in full control now. You'll never have to live with that kind of fear ever again."

"Thanks to you."

I shook my head, then pushed myself up on my elbow so I could peer down into his eyes. "No, Valen, not me. But I will agree that together, we are stronger." I swallowed then, and forced myself to continue past the last bit of my fear of rejection. "I'm glad you're my mate. And I need you to know that I love you, too. I guess my human half is telling me it's too soon, but the other half of me knows that it's fated and it's real."

Before I could say another word, Valen pushed up, rolling me onto my back again, and kissed me breathless. No more words needed to be said between us. We let our bodies and hearts do all the speaking that needed to be said. We moved together, our only sounds were the ones of passion.

When the knock on the door came, telling us it was time to head back to the airplane, we were dressed and holding onto each other, just relishing being in each other's arms.

Epilogue

VALEN

I held onto Kallista's hand as we were ushered into a large home that seemed to be built in the middle of nowhere. There was a large wall surrounding the place with guards watching over everything like sentries.

Crispin had been very vague from the moment we'd stepped on the plane in the middle of the night. The only thing he would say was that he was sure I would want to meet whoever owned the giant fortress.

We were led into a large room by an older woman who I was certain was another demon, though I couldn't place what kind. She had smiled warmly at Kallista but froze for a moment when she first saw me, swiftly moving her gaze to Crispin, who had merely nodded once at her. She shook her head after glancing back at me. I wanted to demand what was going on, but Crispin gestured for me to follow the woman as she walked further inside the home while muttering to herself too low for me to understand.

It wasn't until we stepped into the room filled with comfortable furniture and baby toys that I began to understand. It was Kallista's gasp of surprise that made me finally react to what was in front of me.

The man stood from his seat as I froze, my body going rigid. A low rumble spilled from my chest as I pulled my mate behind me protectively. When a young woman with long white-blonde hair holding a young infant let out a similar gasp to my mate's and reached out to grasp the man's hand, he reacted the same as I had. He had tugged her back gently before stepping in front of her and the child as if to shield her from me.

At Crispin's chuckle, we both turned in his direction to glare at him. "Varek, I'd like you to meet Valen. Valen, this is Varek." He gestured with his hand toward each of us in turn. "I thought it would be a good idea for you to meet since I'm fairly certain you are brothers."

At his words, everyone who wasn't already standing shot to their feet. It was the first time I noticed there were other people in the room. I sensed they were also demons, and my instinct to protect my mate became my only need at that moment. I wrapped my arms around her and turned, ready to rush out of the house, feeling my heart begin to race with an emotion I wasn't willing to name.

Crispin stopped my retreat, stepping in front of me. I growled at him, baring my teeth in warning. It was only Kallista's comforting touch on my chest as she turned to face me that stopped me from doing something I'd regret to my oldest friend.

"Valen," she whispered as she craned her neck back to stare at me with wide eyes. "Please wait. I think he's right."

I blinked down at her, the fog of anger clearing from my mind as I took in her beauty. I looked back at Crispin as he waited with a patient expression. Then I looked over my shoulder to see the small woman holding the baby, comforting the other man in much the same way. I met the man's eyes as he looked up from her to stare back at me.

We just took each other in for a long moment before I looked back down at my mate and gave her a nod. She smiled up at me, the warmth in her smile causing some of the tension in my body to melt. Together, we turned back to the couple and waited.

"I used to know Valen from back when I was a human," Crispin began as he walked forward, moving further into the room and taking a seat on one of the chairs. "It took me a minute after seeing him again, but the more I looked at him, the more it became obvious." He looked between us again, then sighed. "If you aren't brothers, I'd be astonished."

One of the demons who had jumped to his feet in shock snorted in amusement and sat back down, relaxing and spreading his arms over the back of the couch. I continued to stare at the other man as he watched me back, both of our expressions carefully blank.

"If that isn't the understatement of the century." The other one sat down as well, looking intrigued.

The blonde woman cleared her throat and prompted, "Varek?"

He glanced back down at her before sighing and squeezing her hand gently. He looked back at me then took a few steps forward until we were only a couple of paces apart. My mind tried to fight it, but there was no denying the resemblance between us. We had the same build, the same eyes, the same color hair.

I felt Kallista release my hand and take a step away. I wanted to pull her back into my side, realizing I needed the comfort and reassurance of her presence, but instead, I swallowed and then stepped forward. I lifted my hand and watched as he did the same. As we touched, a feeling of vertigo swept through me. I squeezed my eyes shut, and we grasped each other tightly.

Memories assailed my mind, rushing in like a flood, some clear, but many were seen as though through a dense fog. As scenes from the distant past continued to fill my mind, I could sense someone entering the room.

"Varek, I need to talk to you—" The words cut off abruptly and I opened my eyes, a slight sensation of dizziness causing me to sway. Varek and I stared, the expressions between us no longer guarded.

"Brother," I rasped out.

"Brother," he replied in the same strangled tone.

Gasps and murmurs could be heard around the room, though I couldn't have placed by whom. All I could focus on at the moment was the brother I had been forced to forget.

"I see you already know." Together, we turned toward the man who had entered the room. He was tall and had the same white-blond hair as my brother's mate. He crossed his arms as he studied the two of us standing side by side. "My memories started coming back a few days ago," he said grimly. "I could barely grasp them before they started to fade again. But they suddenly came rushing back, clearer than before. But I see you already know."

He looked at me from head to toe, taking in my boots and leather jacket. As I looked at him, there was a vague recognition, but it was as if I were looking through distorted glass, my memories still unclear. "Pestilence," he said. I nodded, my existence finally making sense. "You need to find your brothers," he said, glancing between us. Varek and I both nodded.

"Famine," I said, a hint of anger in my tone.

"Wrath," Varek replied through clenched teeth.

"Lucifer," the other man began as both my brother and I snarled as one.

"Must die," we responded together.

The man sighed and rubbed his forehead. "I had believed that there were only seven Kings of the Underworld all this time. He must have cast a powerful spell to be able to block everyone's memories the way he did. I don't know why I remembered Death, though." He looked at me in apology. "I'm sorry I didn't remember."

Varek growled, sounding much the same as I did when I was angry. "It's not your fault, Charon."

I shook my head, still unsure of who he was but knowing there was only one person at fault for what had been done to me and my brothers. "Lucifer is responsible, no one else." I turned to Death. "We need to find our brothers and return to the Underworld."

His expression was grim, and he glanced at his mate and child. "It's not going to be easy."

I looked down at my own mate to see her watching everyone with wide eyes. "No, it won't be." A new kind of fear began to fill me.

The demon, Charon, stepped toward my brother's mate and reached out to the baby, which the woman handed over without hesitation. He handled the infant carefully, with obvious experience. "I believe that each of you will need your mates at your sides. There is a reason that the spell he cast is starting to break. I believe it is because you have begun to find your mates."

Everything within me wanted to argue, knowing that there would be dangers that a half-demon may not be able to survive. The very thought of leading my mate into the Underworld willingly sent chills of apprehension down my spine. But as I looked down at her, I knew deep in my soul that he was right.

I glanced at Varek, and we shared a grim expression. "We need to train them so they can protect themselves," I said.

The blonde woman stepped beside her mate and crossed her arms. "I think I have already proven that I am capable of protecting myself."

My brother put his arm around her shoulders. "You are a fierce little mate, Juliette. But the Underworld is unlike anything you have ever imagined in your worst nightmares." She gave a little growl that sounded like an angry kitten, making me smile at my new sister.

I took Kallista's hand. "We don't know what kind of dangers we will face, but we can't let our guards down while we hunt for Lucifer."

Kallista shuddered and leaned into me. "I'm willing to learn if it will help." I nodded down at her with relief that she wouldn't fight me on this. Knowing that this world was new to her was likely frightening, but I also knew that she had a fierce strength inside of her. Starting now, I would spend every moment I could ensuring that she was ready when the time came to face the devil.

AFTERWORD

Do you want to know more about Crispin and Varek?

Read Crispin and Ivy's story in this complete vampire trilogy!
<u>Hunter's Blood</u>
Monsters exist.

They are all around us...
and I am the one they want the most.
They crave my blood.

The biggest secret of all?
I'm one of those monsters, too.

<u>Hunter's Promise</u>
I was strong, I was deadly, I was a Hunter
Until I became more.

There was an enemy with a plan to take over all vampirekind.

They were creating revenants that were smarter than they should be.

They listened, they followed directions, they killed.

They killed *me*.

Hunter's Forever

Someone from Crispin's human life reemerges

leaving us both reeling in shock.

If that wasn't enough-

My mate was dying,

and I was hiding a secret that would change our lives forever.

Suddenly,

the threat of someone dethroning all the leaders became very real.

We were in for the fight of our lives to save all vampirekind.

Read about Varek and Ivy in this standalone demon romance!

Lovely Darkness

The first time she knew real happiness was when she found out that the man who raised her wasn't her real father.

She knew that there couldn't be monsters in the world that were any worse than the monster she had called 'daddy' for most of her life.

Then she stumbled into the world of demons.

The Demon King knew the second his fated mate had been brought into the world.

After living years too numerous to count, it meant little to him other than to keep him from living as he had.

He now belonged to only one female - and he would have to wait years for her to mature enough to matter.

How stupid and vain he had been to think that his fated wouldn't matter.

The very moment she entered his club he knew he had been wrong to ignore fate.

She was his.

And he was going to destroy everyone that hurt her, even if he had to burn the Earth realm to the ground.

ACKNOWLEDGMENTS

To Dani- A shout out for choosing the name of our heroine in Craving Darkness! Thank you, Dani! I loved her name so much! (Kallista was chosen as the winner of my 'choose the heroine's name' contest in my FB group!)

To Rebecca - thank you for suffering through the writing of Craving. I know I didn't make it easy, but I want you to know that your feedback has been invaluable! I hope you'll be willing to Alpha read for me again, if I haven't scared you away from it! lol
Every single Beta reader- you don't realize how much you really help make my life easier with your feedback. Thank you from the bottom of my heart.

To Nicole- thank you for always being my personal cheerleader. I don't know what I would do without you! Love you!

About the Author

R. Sullins is a USA Today bestselling author, an International Bestseller, and a KDP All Star.

Family is number one in her life, followed by her menagerie of pets. Be patient with her, she's not very good at peopling.

She is a lover of fairies, tattoos, and coffee cups, has a vast collection of them all, and receives a glare from her teenager every time she brings home a new cup to squeeze into the cabinet.

When she's not writing, you will probably be able to find her reading a book. But, no matter what genre you find her immersed in, there is always one thing that her favorite stories have in common... you will never, ever find her reading any book with cheating. So rest assured! She will never write one, either.

A bit of drama, a dash of spice, a little bit of innocence, and a large dab of alpha is what makes up the recipe for her stories. Find more of her here: www.rsullins.com

Free Book

For a **free short story** that is only available through this link - Join my newsletter!

She wasn't sure what she was doing at the cabin.

It was run down and needed serious attention.

She should sell it and be done with it, but her grandmother left it to her.

It was all she had left in the world.

He hadn't shifted back into his human form for years.

He held the responsibility for his family's death in his heart.

The only thing that kept him moving one paw in front of the other

was the need to make sure the same fate didn't happen to anyone else in his pack.

Then everything changed when a new scent filled the forest.

How was the Alpha wolf supposed to stay away when her scent just kept drawing him in?

TEMPTING THE WOLF BY R SULLINS

ALSO BY R SULLINS

CONTEMPORARY ROMANCE

Cry For Me - All For You series Book 1

A high school romance

Light from the Dark - Protecting What's Theirs

An MMF serial killer romance

The Nightmare King - Book One in The Nightmare Duet

An MC romance

The Queen of Nightmares - Book Two in The Nightmare Duet

An MC romance

Planned releases:

Break For Me

An All For You novel

Fall For Me

An All For You novel

Running Home

A contemporary romance

PARANORMAL ROMANCE

The Hunter series

Hunter's Blood is book one in a <u>complete</u> vampire trilogy

Jared

A standalone in the Hunter series

Those Who Whisper

A standalone ghost romance

Planned releases:

<u>Crimson Fate</u>

A standalone in The Hunter series

<u>Ohhs, Ahhhs, and Orbs</u>

A witchy murder mystery romance

www.ingramcontent.com/pod-product-compliance
Lightning Source LLC
Chambersburg PA
CBHW071732150726
47998CB00005B/1607